THE ROAD HOME

Books by Michael Thomas Ford

LAST SUMMER

LOOKING FOR IT

TANGLED SHEETS

FULL CIRCLE

CHANGING TIDES

WHAT WE REMEMBER

THE ROAD HOME

THE PATH OF THE GREEN MAN

MASTERS OF MIDNIGHT
(with William J. Mann, Sean Wolfe, and Jeff Mann)

MIDNIGHT THIRSTS
(with Timothy Ridge, Greg Herren, and Sean Wolfe)

Published by Kensington Publishing Corporation

THE ROAD HOME

MICHAEL THOMAS FORD

KENSINGTON BOOKS
www.kensingtonbooks.com

KENSINGTON BOOKS are published by

Kensington Publishing Corp.
119 West 40th Street
New York, NY 10018

All Kensington titles, imprints and distributed lines are available at special quantity discounts for bulk purchases for sales promotion, premiums, fund-raising, educational or institutional use.

Special book excerpts or customized printings can also be created to fit specific needs. For details, write or phone the office of the Kensington Special Sales Manager: Kensington Publishing Corp., 119 West 40th Street, New York, NY, 10018. Attn. Special Sales Department. Phone: 1-800-221-2647.

Kensington and the K logo Reg. U.S. Pat. & TM Off.

Library of Congress Card Catalogue Number: 2010921529
ISBN-13: 978-0-7582-1853-7
ISBN-10: 0-7582-1853-2

First Printing: June 2010
10 9 8 7 6 5 4 3 2 1

Printed in the United States of America

For
Michael Joseph McGuire,
who sent it in a new direction

Author's Note

Although this is a work of fiction, several real-life locations and people appear in the story.

There is a real Radical Faerie sanctuary in Vermont called Faerie Camp Destiny. It is a wonderful place. In this novel I have used it in name only, to honor the many Faeries and kindred spirits who have devoted their energy to bringing Destiny to fruition. The details of the camp, the names and descriptions of participants, and the rituals as they appear in this book are of my own invention. For more information on the real Faerie Camp Destiny, you may visit www.faerie campdestiny.org.

Sarah Higdon, whose work hangs in the fictional Colton Beresford Gallery in the novel, is a real artist. You may visit her at www.sarah higdon.com.

The story "Midsummer," which is included in Sam Guffrey's fictional book *In the Wood of the Holly King,* first appeared in my own book *The Path of the Green Man* (Citadel Press, 2005) as "A Night in Maeve's Wood."

CHAPTER 1

And there were in the same country shepherds abiding in the field, keeping watch over their flock by night. And, lo, the angel of the Lord came upon them, and the glory of the Lord shone round about them; and they were sore afraid. And the angel said unto them, Fear not: for, behold, I bring you good tidings of great joy. . . .

Burke couldn't remember the rest. It was something about peace and singing. That much he knew. But the exact words escaped him. He closed his eyes and pictured himself standing at the front of the church, just as Mrs. Throckton had told him to do. He was wearing a long brown robe and holding a staff made from a mop handle. Two other shepherds stood near him, while a couple of little kids dressed as sheep wandered around looking lost.

The problem was his beard. Made of cotton balls glued to construction paper and attached to his face with pieces of string that hooked around his ears, it made it difficult for him to speak. He felt himself growing anxious as he cleared his throat and tried again. But the words seemed to be stuck. He couldn't get them to come out of his mouth. All he could do was look out at the pews filled with people waiting for him to deliver his speech—the most important part of the whole pageant.

He opened his eyes. His heart was beating fast in his chest, and for a moment he couldn't breathe. Then he looked around, saw that he was standing on top of the hill, and he began to calm down. *It's okay,* he reassured himself. *It's okay.*

He moved his feet, his boots crunching in the snow. It had gotten colder since he'd come out an hour ago. He looked up at the sky and saw that it was darkening. Night was coming. Soon he would have dinner with his parents, and then his father would drive them to church, where Burke would play his part in the Nativity pageant. If he could say his lines.

He tried not to think about it, concentrating instead on the hill, and specifically on the path he'd made for the toboggan. It was a good path. He'd planned it carefully, first tamping the snow down with his feet and then dragging the toboggan up and down the hill several times, until the path was exactly wide enough and deep enough to keep the sled on track. It had been a lot of work, and he was tired. But the anticipation of a spectacular ride energized him. As he looked down the hill, he could already feel the shaking of the toboggan as it slid over the hard-packed snow.

The best part, of course, was the jump. Admittedly, it wasn't exactly a jump, more of a very large bump. But it would do the trick. He'd chosen the route precisely because it took him over a mound that stuck out of the hill about halfway down. If he could get up enough speed, the toboggan would hit the bump and lift up enough to create the sensation of flying. This was assuming that he'd planned correctly. Toboggans were tricky things and didn't always do what one wanted them to.

He'd waxed the bottom of his, rubbing the paraffin into the wood until the boards were shiny and slick. So far it had performed admirably, sliding over the snow with a satisfying shushing sound. True, it had once or twice attempted to go sideways or break free from the path, but that was the nature of toboggans, and Burke admired its refusal to be entirely tamed.

It had begun to snow again. Thick flakes tumbled from the sky. Although he loved snow, he wished it would stop, at least until he was finished. New snow filled in the path and slowed the toboggan's pace. A clean, almost icy surface was preferable. Still, he had time before the new snow accumulated enough to affect things too badly.

Get going, he told himself. *This is what you've been waiting for.*

Still he held back, scanning the track for any imperfections, moving the toboggan back and forth across the snow to make sure its underside was still slippery. He knew that he was hesitating because now that the long-awaited moment had arrived, he was afraid of failure. His mind flashed suddenly to the image of himself standing onstage, unable to remember the words of the angel of the Lord.

He pulled the toboggan to the crest of the hill and the start of the track. Positioning it so that the front extended just over the hill's peak, he sat down and took hold of the guide rope. Tucking his feet into the hollow made by the upward curve of the wood, he used his hands to push the toboggan forward until he felt the front tip. Then, giving one final push, he leaned forward and let the weight of his body propel the toboggan into the fall.

Cold air buffeted his face, making his eyes tear up. He blinked, clearing them, and looked straight ahead. The toboggan was gathering speed, and the snow whispered excitedly as Burke sailed over it. Everything was working perfectly. *It's going to fly,* he told himself.

The mound was coming up. Only a few more yards. He pushed against the wind, trying to use as much of his weight as he could to help the toboggan accelerate. *Come on,* he urged. *You can do it.*

The front of the toboggan began to rise. Burke held his breath, praying that it wouldn't bog down in the snow. It didn't, and a moment later he was lifted into the air. He seemed to rise above the toboggan. Below him the snow spread out like a frozen sea, and he appeared to be flying over the tops of the pine trees that lined the edge of the field. Exultant, he threw his arms out wide and shouted with joy.

This spontaneous expression of happiness was his undoing. The toboggan, its balance upset, veered from its intended trajectory and lurched to the left as it descended. The prow struck the edge of the track at an angle, and the toboggan tipped sideways. Burke, clutching the guide rope, managed to remain seated, but the toboggan itself spun so that it was now moving backward down the hill. It was also picking up speed.

Disoriented and unable to control the toboggan, Burke could only hold on and wait for the ride to end. He had no idea where the toboggan was going, but eventually it had to stop. If he could just hang on, he would be fine.

And then there came another lurch. The toboggan, catching in a bit of frozen snow, upended. Burke once again rose into the air, but this time he could not hang on. His body was thrown from the sled. He somehow turned so that he was facing the sky, and for a moment he thought everything would be fine. Then he struck something with great force, and all went black.

When he next opened his eyes, it was dark and he was cold. Snow was falling on his face, and he lifted his hand to wipe it away. The fingers of his gloves were stiff and scratched his skin. When he breathed, a sharp pain exploded in his chest. He couldn't feel his legs.

He was lying beside a tree, but he couldn't recall how he had gotten there. His mind filled with jumbled images—snow, flying, a toboggan. It all began to come together. Then, all of a sudden, a blinding light filled the sky above him. He shielded his eyes with his hand. The light burned like fire and turned the world gold. Then a voice came from within it.

Fear not: for, behold, I bring you good tidings of great joy, which shall be to all people. For unto you is born this day in the city of David a Savior, which is Christ the Lord. And this shall be a sign unto you; Ye shall find the babe wrapped in swaddling clothes, lying in a manger.

The voice ceased, and Burke heard himself speak. "And suddenly there was with the angel a multitude of the heavenly host praising God, and saying, Glory to God in the highest, and on earth peace, good will toward men."

The air was filled with an unearthly sound—high-pitched cries that hurt his ears and shattered the tranquility. The light around him changed, becoming colder. He was racked with pain and heard himself cry out for help.

"Mr. Crenshaw," a voice said. "Mr. Crenshaw, can you hear me?"

He tried to answer, but his throat was filled with something. *Snow,* he thought vaguely. He was choking on snow. He coughed, trying to clear it.

"Just lie still, Mr. Crenshaw," the voice ordered. "You're going to be fine."

The light lessened, and he looked up into the face of a stranger. From somewhere to the side of him came flashes of red, like fireworks. The strange wailing sounds continued to fill his ears.

"I have to get to church," he told the man who was looking down at him. "I have to be in the pageant. I remember my lines now." He tried to sit up and found that he couldn't.

"Lie still," the man said again. "We're going to get you out of here."

"The toboggan," Burke said. "The snow. There's no snow now. Where did it go?"

A second face—a woman's—came into view above him. "How's he doing?" she said.

"He's pretty banged up," the man answered. "But he's alive."

"He's lucky," said the woman. "The way that car looks, he shouldn't be here."

Burke wondered who they were talking about. He started to ask, but then the light came again. This time it refused to be blotted out by the closing of his eyes. It filled his head, exploding as a chorus of voices rang out.

And once more the world went black.

CHAPTER 2

"I thought you said you were okay with turning forty."

Burke opened his eyes. He had been sleeping off and on for most of the morning. His head was still fuzzy from the pain medication the nurse had injected into his IV when, at dawn, he had woken up screaming. He was no longer convinced that he was dying, but his whole body ached, despite the numbing effects of the Demerol. He looked at the face hovering over him and blinked several times, trying to place it.

"Gregg?" he asked, fishing a name from the depths of his foggy memory. He coughed, clearing his throat, and a glass of water found its way into his hand.

"Here," said Gregg. "Drink up."

Burke drained most of the glass, then handed it back to his friend. "How did you know?" he asked Gregg.

"Apparently, I'm still listed as your emergency contact with your insurance company," Gregg replied.

Burke tried to laugh, but it hurt his chest, and he ended up coughing instead. He and Gregg had been broken up for almost three years, yet it had never occurred to him to change his insurance information. Now he was glad he hadn't.

"I always thought the three-in-the-morning phone call would be about my mother dropping dead," said Gregg as he pulled a chair up beside the bed and sat down. "Frankly, I was a little disappointed that it wasn't."

"Did they say what happened?" Burke asked. "All I remember is driving home after the party."

"Raccoon," said Gregg. "Or maybe a dog. You swerved to avoid hitting it and ran off the road. Lucky for you, the guy behind you saw the whole thing and stopped. You should send him a thank-you card."

"My leg's busted," said Burke.

"I noticed," Gregg replied. He nodded at the pulley system that elevated Burke's right leg—which was wrapped in a cast—above the bed. "Your arm doesn't look too good, either."

Burke glanced down and saw the cast that covered his left forearm. "Not the left one," he said. "Fuck me."

"What else did you manage to break?" Gregg asked.

Burke shook his head. "I'm not sure," he said. "I kind of just got here."

Gregg laughed. "Well, we'll find out," he said. He reached behind Burke. "Sit up if you can," he ordered.

Burke tried, wincing at the pain. Gregg adjusted the pillows behind Burke, and Burke lay back against them. "Thanks," he said.

"Yeah, well, I know what a baby you are when you're sick," said Gregg.

Burke nodded. It was true, he hated not feeling well. It made him feel out of control and, worse, dependent on someone else. He'd never been good at being taken care of.

Gregg went to the window and opened the curtains, letting in the bright morning light. Watching him, Burke was reminded of how much of a nester Gregg was. He loved taking care of things—houses, animals, people. Ironically, it had been the thing that had ended their relationship. Gregg had wanted them to move in together; Burke had been afraid the closeness would be smothering. After a year of waiting for Burke to change his mind, Gregg had moved on.

"That's better," Gregg said, looking around the room. "I hear hospital chic is in this year. Martha Stewart just did a segment on decorating with catheters and speculums."

"I understand they make great Christmas ornaments," said a voice from the doorway. A woman in a long white jacket walked in and extended her hand to Gregg. "I'm Dr. Liu," she said. "I assume you're the husband?"

"No," Gregg said. "The ex-husband."

"Oh, I'm sorry," the doctor said.

"Don't be," Gregg assured her. "He was a lousy husband."

Dr. Liu smiled and turned to Burke. "And how are you feeling today?"

"Not as good as I did yesterday," said Burke.

"I wouldn't think so," the doctor replied. "You knocked yourself around pretty thoroughly."

"My leg and my arm," Burke said vaguely.

"Among other things," Dr. Liu told him. "You also broke a couple of ribs and came this close to shattering your pelvis." She held her fingers an inch apart to emphasize how fortunate Burke was not to have done that. "But the leg is the big thing," she continued. "It took a lot to put it back together. Lucky for you, I'm good at puzzles."

"I like her," said Gregg, grinning at Burke.

Burke ignored him. "When can I get out of here?" he asked.

"Let's talk about that," said Dr. Liu. "I want you here for at least a week."

"A week!" Burke exclaimed. "But I've got work lined up. I'm supposed to shoot Angelina Jolie for *Boston* magazine on Tuesday."

"Not going to happen," said Dr. Liu. "You're not walking on that leg for a while."

"What's a while?" Burke demanded.

"Six weeks minimum," the doctor answered. "Maybe longer."

"No," said Burke, shaking his head. "I can't be laid up for six weeks. No way."

"What did I say?" Gregg said, wagging a finger at him. "You. Sick. Big baby."

Burke groaned. "I have to get out of here," he said.

"You're going to need help," said Dr. Liu. "Do you have someone who can stay with you?"

"I don't know," said Burke. He was irritated now and couldn't think. The pain was coming back, and he wanted more Demerol. "Maybe."

"Well, think about it," said the doctor. "As I said, I want you here for the next week. You can make arrangements for when you're released. But I won't let you out of here until you do."

Dr. Liu excused herself to see other patients and left Burke and Gregg alone again. Burke, thinking about what she'd said, stared at the ceiling. After a few minutes he realized that Gregg had grown oddly quiet. He looked over at his former lover, who was sitting in the chair, looking at his hands.

"Hey," said Burke, "could I . . ."

"No," Gregg said quickly.

"How do you know what I'm going to ask?" said Burke.

"You can't stay with me," said Gregg. "I'm sorry, but it's just a bad idea. Besides, Rick wouldn't go for it."

"How do you know?" Burke argued.

"He doesn't like you," said Gregg.

Burke, surprised, looked at him.

"I'm sorry, sweetie, but he doesn't. He thinks you're overbearing."

"I am not," Burke objected.

Gregg gave him a small smile. "You kind of are," he said. "Besides, I have to work. What about your insurance? Maybe they'll pay for an in-home nurse. You might even get a hot one," he added.

"My insurance doesn't pay for anything," said Burke. "I'll be lucky if they cough up anything for this little vacation."

"I can call them for you," Gregg said. "We'll find out."

"I don't want a nurse," Burke complained. "The last thing I need is a stranger helping me to the toilet and trying to talk to me about his life while he's giving me a sponge bath."

Gregg didn't come back with a smart response, which surprised Burke. It also worried him. Gregg's sharp sense of humor waned only when he was trying to avoid confrontation. The fact that he wasn't saying anything meant that he didn't want to discuss the situation.

"Fine," Burke said after a minute or two had gone by. "Call the insurance company. See what they'll do. I'll figure something out." He waited for Gregg to nod in agreement, then added, "I'm tired. I think I should sleep now."

Gregg got up. "I'll let you know what they say. And you're welcome."

Burke didn't look at him as he mumbled, "Thanks."

"I'll be back tonight," said Gregg.

When Gregg was gone, Burke tried to form a plan. He hoped his insurance would come through, although he really doubted it. Having never been really sick, he'd always managed to get by with the bare minimum, figuring he would up his coverage when he got older.

Yeah, well, you are *old now,* he told himself.

He ran through a list of his friends, thinking about who might be able either to take him in or, better, to come live with him for a month or two, if he needed help for that long. He didn't like the idea of having to move in with someone else. He liked being in his own place, even if he couldn't get around it very well.

Gregg apparently was out as a potential nursemaid. But he had other friends. Oscar, maybe, or Dane. But Oscar worked long hours, and Dane was too much of a cock hound. Burke didn't relish the idea of being in Dane's guest room and listening to his host getting it on with one of his numerous tricks.

What about Tony? he wondered. Tony lived alone, and as a writer, he worked out of his house. *But he has cats,* Burke reminded himself. Just the thought of Tony's three Himalayans—LaVerne, Maxine, and Patty—made his throat close up. No, his allergies would never survive an extended stay with the Andrews Sisters.

He continued mentally working his way through his address book. But for one reason or another, nobody fit the bill. Abe's apartment was too small. Jesse was a slob. Ellen was a vegan. One by one he crossed the names off his list until he had run out of options. Then he rang for the nurse, asked for another shot of Demerol, and drifted into sleep.

When he awoke again, it was dark outside and his room smelled like his elementary school cafeteria. Gregg was once again seated in the chair by Burke's bed. He indicated a tray on the table beside him.

"Salisbury steak," he said. "And Tater Tots. Who's a lucky boy?"

He picked the tray up and placed it on the movable tabletop that swung out from the wall beside Burke's bed. Positioning the tabletop in front of Burke, he laid out the napkin and silverware as if he were setting a table.

"And what will you be drinking this evening, sir?" he asked.

"Gin and tonic," said Burke. "Make it a double."

"Water it is," Gregg replied, pouring some from the plastic pitcher that sat on the table beside the bed.

Burke picked up the fork and poked at the meat on his plate. "When I was a kid, I always loved Wednesdays, because it was Salisbury steak day at school," he told Gregg. "I was in college before I realized that it was just a fancy name for hamburger."

"That explains your sophisticated palate," Gregg joked. It was another difference between them—Gregg loved fine dining (Burke called it snob food), and Burke's idea of cooking was opening a can of soup.

Burke was suddenly ravenous. He attacked his dinner with his good hand, managing despite the fact that he was a lefty and the utensils felt alien in his right hand. He wolfed down the Salisbury steak and Tater Tots. He even ate the green beans, which normally he would ignore. Only when he turned his attention to the small dish of chocolate pudding did he resume talking to Gregg.

"Did you talk to the insurance people?"

"I did," Gregg answered. He cleared away Burke's tray before continuing. "And you were right. They aren't going to be particularly helpful."

"Define 'particularly,'" said Burke.

Gregg sat down. "They'll pay only fifty dollars a day for in-home care," he said.

Burke swore.

"And that's after the five-thousand-dollar deductible," Gregg informed him.

Burke's response brought one of the nurses to his door. "Are you all right?" she asked, looking more than a little concerned.

"He's fine," Gregg assured her. "He's having sticker shock."

The nurse waited for Burke to confirm that he didn't need anything, then left the men alone.

Gregg sighed. "So where does that leave us?" he asked. "I mean you. Where does that leave you?"

"I don't know," Burke told him. "You don't want me, and I can't think of anyone else."

"It's not that I don't want you," said Gregg. "It's—"

"I know," Burke interrupted. "I'm overbearing."

"Just a tad," said Gregg. "And I work. Don't forget that. What about your other friends?"

"Sluts," said Burke, waving a hand around. "Cats. Smokers. Don't eat meat."

"I see," Gregg said. "Which brings us back to square one."

"I have to pee," said Burke.

"What?" Gregg asked.

"Pee," Burke repeated. "I have to pee. Help me up."

"Um, you're not getting up," Gregg said. "Remember?"

Burke glanced at his leg. "What am I supposed to do?" he said.

"This," Gregg said. He held up a plastic container that he'd taken from a shelf beneath the bedside table. It resembled a water bottle on its side, with one end slightly angled up and ending in a wide mouth.

"You've got to be kidding," Burke said.

"Come on," said Gregg. "It's not that hard." He pulled back the blanket on Burke's bed and started to lift Burke's gown.

"Hey!" Burke said.

"Relax," said Gregg. "It's not like I haven't seen it before."

Burke relented, and Gregg hiked up the hospital gown, exposing Burke's crotch. He placed the urine bottle between Burke's legs.

"Ow," Burke said. "Slow down."

He tried to spread his legs, but when pain shot through the right one, he gave up and balanced the bottle on his thighs. Taking his penis in his right hand, he positioned the head at the mouth of the bottle and tried to pee. At first nothing happened. Then, as if a valve had been opened, urine spurted from his dick. Startled, he let go, and the bottle toppled sideways as he continued to pee. He attempted to grab at the bottle and hold on to his penis at the same time, but his left arm was useless, and he could accomplish only one of his goals. He clamped down, forcing the flow of urine to stop, but not before the hair on his legs was covered in drops of piss.

Gregg, who had prevented the bottle from falling to the floor, repositioned it. "Hold it," he ordered Burke, who placed his right hand on the bottle. Gregg took Burke's cock in his hand and inserted it into the bottle's mouth.

"Don't watch," Burke said.

Rolling his eyes, Gregg looked away. After a moment Burke was able to pee freely. He tried to ignore the fact that Gregg's hand was holding his dick as he drained his bladder. He watched as the bottle filled up. For a moment he was afraid it might overflow, but then the stream slowed to a trickle. To his horror, Gregg milked the last few drops out before removing the bottle.

"Thanks," Burke said.

Gregg took the bottle into the bathroom and poured it into the toilet. When he returned, he had a washcloth in his hand, which he used to wipe the spilled piss from Burke's legs.

"I can do that," Burke protested.

"Shut up," said Gregg. "You don't always have to be the big top, you know."

Burke grunted. He wasn't going to get into that particular argument with Gregg.

"There," Gregg said as he put Burke's gown back into place and pulled the sheet and blanket up. "Feel better?"

"No," said Burke. He was already worrying about what he would do when he had to pee and Gregg wasn't there. He certainly wasn't going to ask any of the nurses for help.

"I had a thought," Gregg said.

"About what?" asked Burke.

"About where you could stay."

"Oh yeah?" Burke said hopefully. "Where?"

Gregg paused for a long moment. "With your father," he said.

Burke laughed. "Right," he said.

"I'm serious," Gregg told him. "He has the room. He's home all the time. It's perfect."

"Except that it's my father," said Burke.

Gregg looked him in the eyes. "You don't have a lot of choices, Burke," he said. "This is a good solution."

"I'm not staying with my father for six weeks," Burke said. "I'm not staying in *Vermont*."

"There's nothing wrong with Vermont," Gregg argued. "It's beautiful this time of year."

"No," Burke repeated. "End of discussion. I'd rather stay in this place than go there. I'll think of something."

"Okay," Gregg said. "Just keep your options open."

"Don't try that on me," said Burke.

"Try what?"

"That thing you do," Burke said. "Whenever you wanted me to do something and I said no, you would tell me to keep my options open. That always meant you thought I would come around and do what you had wanted to do in the first place."

"That's not true," Gregg said.

"No?" said Burke. "Have you forgotten about the vacation in Provincetown? The tile in my bathroom? The Volvo station wagon?"

"That Volvo saved your life," Gregg said. "And I didn't make you do any of those things. I just suggested."

"Well, stop suggesting," said Burke. "I'm not asking my father if I can stay with him."

Gregg nodded. "All right," he said. He looked at his watch. "I should go." He leaned down and kissed Burke on the forehead. "Just think about it."

"Get out," Burke said, only half feigning irritation.

"Good night," Gregg said as he left. "Don't stay up too late. It's a school night."

CHAPTER 3

"Why didn't you tell me there was only one road in Vermont?" Gregg asked as his Saab crested the top of a hill and descended into yet another green-grassed dell. On either side of the road black-and-white cows grazed lazily, only occasionally raising their heads to look at the passing car. "It really does look like a Ben & Jerry's ice cream carton here, doesn't it?" Gregg continued. "I keep expecting to see a Chubby Hubby tree."

"Very funny," Burke muttered. "Now you know why I never came back."

"Stop it," said Gregg. "It's beautiful. And it's just for the summer. Your mother and I will be back to pick you up in August."

"You're loving this, aren't you?" Burke said.

Gregg grinned. "Maybe a little," he admitted.

Burke shifted in his seat. His leg hurt like hell, and every time Gregg hit a rise or bump in the road, it sent another jolt of pain through the broken bone. "It would have been easier if the crash had just killed me," he complained, attempting to shift into a more comfortable position and failing.

"Think of it as going to a sanatorium," Gregg suggested. "Like one of those tragic tubercular women. Maybe you'll meet some handsome man who was poisoned by mustard gas at Ypres and has been sent here for a rest cure."

Burke stared at his friend. "You're really not helping," he said.

Gregg sighed deeply. "You're determined to make this as miserable an experience as possible, aren't you? I can tell. This is *exactly* how you were that time we took the house in Provincetown with Randy and Clifford."

Burke groaned. "Heckle and Jeckle?" he said. "Those two talked nonstop from the time we picked them up until we dropped them off in Back Bay seven days later. It was all 'When we saw Madonna at the White Party . . .' and 'Last season at the ballet . . .' and 'This cilantro is *so* good.' Also, I have a broken leg *and* a broken arm."

"Whatever," Gregg said. "Are we almost there?"

"What was the last town we went through?"

"I believe it was Grover's Corners," Gregg said teasingly. "Or maybe Fraser," he said truthfully when Burke gave him a vicious look.

"Then we're about twenty miles away from Wellston," Burke informed Gregg.

They rode the rest of the way mostly in silence. Burke looked out the window, dreading the moment when they would pull into the driveway of his father's house. This was exactly how he'd felt returning to Vermont after his freshman and sophomore years at college— like he was being sent back to prison after a too-brief time on the outside. By the summer of his junior year, he'd found a job that allowed him to stay in Boston, and he hadn't looked back. Apart from some Christmases during those first years following graduation and before he'd acquired his own circle of friends, he'd been back only a handful of times in twenty years.

"Wellston," Gregg said as they passed the sign marking the edge of town. "Population three hundred forty-nine. Why, that's practically a metropolis." He leaned toward Burke. "I bet there's even a Wal-Mart."

Burke ignored him. He was watching the familiar landmarks of his youth appear outside the car window like the ghosts of school-yard bullies, each one greeting him with its own particular taunt. The Ebenezer Baptist Church (GOD CAN'T SAY THANKS FOR COMING IF YOU DON'T STOP BY!). The Eezy-Freezy (GET A HOT DOG AND A COLD CONE!). The Farmers Co-op (BARRED ROCK CHICKS $13.99 A DOZEN!). They all looked exactly as they had for decades, as if the entire town had been trapped in amber like a Cenozoic Era mosquito.

"Once we're through town, turn left onto Crenshaw Road," Burke told Gregg.

"He's got his own *road?*" Gregg exclaimed.

Burke nodded. "When I was a kid, it was just RFD seventeen," he said. "About ten years ago the county decided it needed a real name. Since my father's place is the only one out here, they thought it would be funny to name it after him. It's that dry Yankee humor you've no doubt heard so much about."

They passed the Wellston General School (OUR GRADS ARE GREAT!), which marked the other side of town, and a quarter mile later turned onto Crenshaw Road. Narrow enough that the branches of the trees on either side created a kind of canopy overhead, and rutted enough that every few feet brought fresh curses from Burke's mouth as his body was jarred by yet another bump, it wound lazily through a patch of woods before emerging into a long meadow. A post-and-wire fence separated the meadow from the road, and two chestnut horses peered over it hopefully, as if someone might at any moment toss them an apple.

The road curved to the right and became a driveway that led to a large white farmhouse. Daylilies, their orange and yellow heads bouncing lightly in the breeze, were planted in front of the screened-in porch that ran along the front of the house. A beat-up red pickup truck was parked outside, and beside that stood a tall, somewhat heavy man with white hair, dressed in chinos and a red plaid flannel shirt. As the Saab approached, he lifted one hand to about chest level before returning it to his pocket.

"That means 'hello' in Vermontese," Burke said. "It also means 'You're probably right about that snowstorm,' 'Them politicians is a bunch of fools,' and 'Sure I'll have a piece of blueberry pie.'"

"He's a good-looking man," Gregg remarked as he pulled the car to a stop. "You don't look anything like him."

Burke rolled his window down. "Hi, Dad," he said.

His father leaned in. "How was the drive?" he asked. "You hit traffic around St. Albans?"

"It was fine," said Burke. "Could you help me out of here?"

His father opened the car door as Gregg got out and came around from the other side.

"Dad, this is Gregg," Burke said as he turned sideways in his seat and swung his leg out.

"It's a pleasure to meet you, Mr. Crenshaw," said Gregg.

"Ed," the man replied. When Gregg looked confused, he said, "Call me Ed. Everybody does." He then squatted down, put Burke's arm around his shoulder, and lifted his son up and out of the car.

"Do you want me to help you with that?" Gregg asked.

Ed shook his head. "He's no heavier than a foal," he said. "And he's only got the two legs to contend with."

As Ed helped Burke toward the house, Gregg opened the Saab's trunk and removed the two bags he had packed under Burke's exacting command. He followed the two men into the house, setting the bags down on the smooth, wide planks of the living room floor.

"Thought we'd put you in your old room," Ed told his son.

"Upstairs?" Burke objected. "I can't manage the stairs every time I need to come down here."

"What do you have to come down for?" asked his father. "It's not like you're going to be feeding the horses or working in the garden."

"What about meals?" said Burke.

"We got ourselves a Chinese restaurant in town now," his father said. "Where the Tar-N-Feather was before Sandy accidentally set it on fire during his divorce from that California woman. It's called Golden Pagoda, although as far as I can see, it's not gold and there's no pagoda. Run by a nice Japanese family. The father says he thought about sushi, but he didn't think it would go over well in this part of the state. I suspect he's right about that. Anyway, they deliver, so that takes care of that."

He paused a few moments as Burke and Gregg stared at him. "I see you've lost your sense of humor, living in Boston," he said. "Lucy and I can bring you anything you need." Apparently having settled the matter, he steered Burke to a flight of stairs. "Gregg, if you'd be so good as to get his other side," he said.

Gregg obliged, and together they got Burke up the stairs, but not before Burke had banged his cast against the wall half a dozen times and uttered a different curse each time.

When they reached the top, Ed looked at his son and remarked, "Excellent vocabulary you've developed over the years. But we're not so smart here, so maybe you can keep it simple. Nothing wrong with a plain old 'damn' every now and then if you really feel the need. So long as you put enough weight behind it, people will get your meaning."

"Sorry," said Burke.

"No need," his father replied as they moved down a long hallway with doors on either side. "How do you like the color of these walls? Lucy picked it out."

Burke looked around. "Weren't they always blue?" he said.

"You'd think so," said his father. "But apparently what we had before was plain old blue. This is Nantucket Cottage."

"Sort of like blue with a pedigree," Gregg suggested as they stopped before one of the doors and Mr. Crenshaw opened it.

"Name brand," Ed agreed.

They walked Burke to a large bed with an antique wrought-iron frame painted white. The mattress was covered by a colorful hand-pieced quilt that looked almost as old as the bed itself. Burke sank onto it with a groan. "Looks like you painted in here, too," he commented.

"Same color it always was, though," said his father. "I thought we might try something else, but Lucy said no to that. She said you'd be back someday, and she wanted it just the way you had it." He walked back into the hallway. "I've got a few things to attend to in the barn," he told them. "I'll leave you to get settled in."

When Ed was gone, Gregg took a long look around the room. "So this is where Burke Crenshaw became a man," he said.

"No, that happened in room 717 of Crone Hall after Shane Mc-Covey and I downed a six-pack and he dared me to suck his cock," Burke said, lying back against the pillows.

"Yes," Gregg agreed. "But this is where you began to explore the strange yearnings of your budding homosexual self," he elaborated dramatically. He looked seriously at Burke. "By which, of course, I mean you beat yourself off while thinking about being Harrison Ford's sex slave," he said, nodding at the *Raiders of the Lost Ark* one-sheet that hung on the wall across from the bed.

Burke glanced at the poster. He hadn't noticed it and hadn't even thought about it in fifteen or more years. "I can't believe she put it back up after they repainted," he said.

"She who?" Gregg asked.

"Lucy," said Burke. "My father's girlfriend."

Gregg raised an eyebrow. "Is she a Maleficent?" he asked. "A Mommie Dearest?"

"Hardly," Burke replied. "She's really nice."

"She must be to have kept this museum to your teenage years," said Gregg. He picked up a trophy that was on the white painted dresser beneath one of the room's two large windows. It was a gold cup topped by the figure of a horse. "What's this?"

"Four-H," Burke explained. "I raised a colt."

Gregg set the trophy down. "How agricultural," he said. He then began to examine the books in the small bookcase beside the desk. "I see you delved deeply into the oeuvre of Stephen King," he said. "Also Frank Herbert and Terry Brooks. Very eclectic."

"Put a pillow under my leg, Marian Librarian," Burke commanded.

Gregg did so, elevating Burke's foot. "Is that better?" he asked, sitting on the edge of the bed.

"It's as better as it's going to get," Burke replied.

Gregg looked out the window. "At least you have a nice view from here," he said. "Very pastoral."

"Are the horses out?" asked Burke.

"Not unless they've invented horses that are short, woolly, and have no tails," Gregg answered. "I'm making an uneducated guess here, but I *think* these might be sheep."

"Dad must be renting out pastureland," said Burke. "Are they Blackface?"

"Isn't that racist?" Gregg said. "And no, they have plain old white faces." He stood up. "Well, if there's nothing else I can do for you, Mr. Crenshaw, I have other patients who need attending to."

"What?" said Burke. "You're not leaving?"

Gregg nodded. "I'm afraid so, sweetie. I'm allergic to the country. If I go more than a hundred miles from a Starbucks, I go into anaphylactic shock. Besides, I have a client meeting tomorrow morning."

"But you can't," said Burke, his voice tightening. "I'll be all alone with"—he gestured around—"this."

"*This* seems perfectly lovely," Gregg told him. "I'd *love* to recuperate in a place like this."

"What about Starbucks?" said Burke, mimicking Gregg's voice. "And anaphylactic shock?"

"All right, I'm just trying to make you feel better," Gregg admitted. "The truth is, I'd probably down a bottle of cold medicine and throw myself down those stairs after twenty-four hours here. But we're not talking about me. For you, it's fine. Now bye." He leaned down and gave Burke a kiss on the forehead. "I'll call you."

Burke began to protest again as Gregg left the room, but he knew there was no point. Gregg was right about one thing—he wasn't the sort who could fit comfortably into country life. Burke put his head back and looked around the all too familiar room.

The question is, can you? he wondered.

CHAPTER 4

He awoke to the smell of roast chicken. When he opened his eyes, he saw a thin, red-haired woman standing beside the bed, looking down at him. Her bright blue eyes sparkled, and her head was cocked to the side, giving her the appearance of a curious banty hen regarding a beetle.

"Have a nice nap?" she asked.

Burke rubbed his eyes. "Lucy," he said. "Hi."

"Nice to have you home, sweetie," Lucy said, kissing him on the forehead as if he were a little boy. "We've missed you."

Burke tried to sit up, forgot about his leg, and yelped in pain. Immediately Lucy was there, helping him lean forward as she slipped a pillow behind his back. "There you go," she said as Burke sighed with relief.

Lucy turned to the dresser, on top of which sat a tray holding a plate of chicken, mashed potatoes, and green beans. She picked the tray up and brought it to the bed, where she set it across Burke's lap. He inhaled the delicious scents and felt his stomach rumble.

"Eat up," Lucy said. "You need it. I bet you've been living on take-out down there in the city."

Burke took up a fork and tried to cut a piece of chicken. Unused to using his right hand for such things, he succeeded mostly in hacking at the meat.

"Here," Lucy said, taking the fork from him and using a knife to cut the chicken into manageable pieces.

"Thanks," said Burke, embarrassed that he required her assistance for something so basic as eating. Stabbing one of the pieces with his fork, he put it in his mouth and chewed slowly. "This is fantastic," he said.

"Your father made it," Lucy answered. "But don't tell him you know. He's a little sensitive about it."

Burke shook his head. "You're joking," he said. "Mom could barely get him to open a can." He speared a green bean and popped it in his mouth. "And these are *fresh,*" he said, amazed.

"From his own garden," said Lucy.

"How'd you do it?" Burke asked.

Lucy laughed. "I told him either he could learn to cook or he could take me out to dinner every night. I cooked for Jerry for forty years, with only my birthday off. I'm through cooking. Unless there's a good reason," she said, patting Burke's leg.

Burke plowed into the mashed potatoes, rich with butter. After a week of hospital food, it was if he were eating for the first time. Lucy watched him, waiting until he slowed down before continuing the conversation.

"You put quite a scare into your father," she said when Burke paused for a moment in between bites of chicken.

"He seems fine," said Burke.

"*Now* he is," Lucy replied. "But when he got that phone call from your friend Gregg, it really shook him up."

"But I'm okay," Burke said. "Apart from this." He gestured at his leg with his fork. "And this," he added, lifting his arm.

Lucy nodded. "It's different when you've already lost someone," she said quietly.

"I lost Mom, too," Burke reminded her.

"I know," Lucy told him. "But it's different when it's your wife or husband or . . . whatever," she concluded. She seemed to drift away for a moment. Then she shook her head. "Anyway, as you say, he's fine now. I just thought you should know that he was worried."

Burke stabbed a green bean. He knew what Lucy was doing, and although part of him appreciated her kindness, another part resented her trying to play the role of his mother. He'd lived with his father longer than Lucy had. He didn't need to be reminded of their sometimes awkward relationship.

"Do you think your mother would have liked me?" Lucy asked suddenly.

Burke looked at her. She looked back, not blinking. It was Burke who turned away first. "I don't know," he said. "I guess so. Why?"

Lucy shrugged. "Oh, I don't know," she said. "It's just something I was thinking about the other day. I was at the cemetery—it was Jerry's birthday—and I was talking to him like I do, and it occurred to me that I think he and your father would have been good friends."

"I'm surprised they weren't," said Burke. "You live only one town over. I don't know how you all lived this close to one another and never met."

"Don't forget, Jerry and I had only been here five years when he died," said Lucy. "In Vermont terms we were just vacationing."

Burke grinned. "Does it still bother Dad that some of the old-timers call him a flatlander?"

Lucy suppressed a laugh. "It's his own fault for suggesting they change things and keep the library open one hour later on Saturdays."

"That was forty-five years ago!" Burke said in a perfect imitation of his father.

They both chuckled. Lucy wiped her eyes. "Jerry could be just as stubborn," she said. "Particularly after he got sick."

Burke didn't know much about Lucy's late husband other than that he was dead. His father had mentioned Jerry only once, and Burke had not asked for anything more. The whole topic of his father and Lucy's relationship was one he avoided, not because it upset him, but because discussing their personal lives was not something the Crenshaw men did. Particularly when one of them was having relationships with other men.

"I know when Mom was going through chemo, she got pretty testy," Burke told Lucy. "Sometimes it was like talking to a completely different person."

"It happens," said Lucy. "When Jerry was first diagnosed with Alzheimer's, I thought it would be a gradual process, a kind of long, slow descent into forgetfulness. I thought I would have time to get used to the person he was becoming before that person got there." She paused. "But it wasn't like that," she continued, her voice softer, more fragile. "One day he was forgetting the names of the flowers in the garden. A week later he wandered down the road and had to be brought back by the postman. After that it seemed like every day another piece of him vanished into thin air. Pretty soon he looked at me as if he'd never seen me before." She looked at Burke. "The funny thing is, I was thinking exactly the same thing."

Burke looked down at his plate. A few green beans lay among the chicken bones. A smear of mashed potatoes curved along one side of the plate. He cleared his throat, which suddenly felt blocked. "I didn't know," he said.

"That's because we've never talked about it," said Lucy. "There are lots of things we've never talked about. Lucky for you, we have all summer to get caught up. Now, do you want to pee?"

Burke looked up. "What?" he said.

"Pee," Lucy repeated. "You probably need to pee." She went to the dresser, opened the top drawer, and pulled out one of the hated plastic containers Burke remembered all too well from his time in the hospital. Lucy waved it at him. "I got this from my friend Alice. She works at the old folks' home over in Paullis Springs. All you have to do is put your—"

"I know how it works," Burke interrupted. He wished Lucy would stop talking about his need to pee, mostly because her talking about it was making him have to do it.

"Then you just dump it out in the toilet—or I suppose you could put it in the sink—and rinse it out. It's really pretty clever, when you think about it." She set the urine bottle down and picked up Burke's tray, setting it on the dresser top. "Let's just get those pants down," she said, coming back to the bed.

"No!" Burke said firmly. "I mean, it's okay. I can handle things. As it were."

Lucy rolled her eyes. "I *have* seen one before," she said. "It's not like they're all that different. And it's not like you had anything to do with how it looks, anyway. Honestly, it's like you men think your dicks are floral centerpieces you have arranged and are being judged on. You all want the blue ribbon."

Burke felt himself blushing at Lucy's use of such a crude term for his penis. Mom would never have said that, he found himself thinking.

"All right," Lucy said. She handed him the bottle. "Do it yourself. But if you need any help, just holler. And leave that on the bedside table. I'll pick it up later. Do you need anything else?"

"Um, my pills," Burke said. "I think Gregg put them all in a big plastic bag in the small suitcase."

"Already downstairs," said Lucy. "I unpacked while you were sleeping. Those are some fancy underpants you got there. I'll get the pills and some water. You take care of business while I'm gone."

She took up the tray and left the room, shutting the door behind her. Burke looked at the bottle on the table, then reluctantly picked it up and began the laborious process of using it. He hadn't finished when, a few minutes later, Lucy opened the door without knocking and came in.

"Here you go," she said brightly, shaking a bottle of pills and then placing it on the bedside table.

Burke quickly finished and pulled the covers up just in time for Lucy to take the still warm bottle of urine from him.

She placed a glass of water on the bedside table. "Now, take only *two* of those," she said, nodding at the pills. "I'm going to be counting."

Burke picked the bottle of pills up, then held it out to Lucy. "Childproof cap," he explained.

Lucy set down the urine bottle, opened the pills, and shook two of them into her hand. She gave them to Burke, who downed them with a swallow of water.

"We should get you into your pj's," Lucy said. "Can't have you sleeping in your clothes."

"Oh, I sleep in my boxers," Burke told her.

"Then let's get those shorts off," said Lucy.

Burke began to object but realized that he didn't really have a choice. He'd already experimented with trying to dress himself, an undertaking that had nearly earned him another few days in the hospital when he had gotten his arm cast stuck while trying to put on a sweatshirt and had nearly fallen off the bed, attempting to extricate himself.

Because of the cast on Burke's leg, he couldn't wear regular pants and had resorted to shorts. Lucy undid Burke's belt and began tugging his shorts down. He tried to help but couldn't do much more than lift his butt up a little. Lucy, struggling to get him undressed, managed to grab Burke's underwear along with the shorts. When she pulled the shorts down, the boxers came with them, leaving Burke bare assed.

"Sorry about that," said Lucy, helping him pull his boxers back up. "But don't worry. I had my eyes closed."

Burke, blushing, pulled the covers up. Lucy picked up the urine bottle and walked to the door. Holding the bottle up as if it were a gravy boat, she said, "There's a bell on the table. If you need anything, just ring. And don't go trying to walk around by yourself. I'll see you in the morning."

When the door was shut, Burke lay back and looked around the room. He had slept for quite some time and, as a result, was no longer tired. Outside the sky was the purple black of twilight, and although night was not far behind, it was still far too early to try and get back to sleep. He would just wake up in the middle of the night.

He'd forgotten what it was like in the country. The so-called quiet was actually far from silent. The noises of traffic and people were gone, but they were replaced by the sounds of birds and crickets. *And who knows what else,* Burke thought as he listened to the assorted chirping sounds coming through the open window. *Probably owls. Or bats.* He shuddered at the thought.

Also, it was too dark. When night fell here, it *really* fell. Apart from the moon and the stars, there was nothing to illuminate the world. No streetlamps or porch lights. No well-lit windows in buildings across the way. Not even a television in the room. How was he going to live without television? He'd brought his laptop, of course, but it occurred to him with rapidly growing horror that the likelihood of finding a wireless signal in this part of the world was about as great as finding a Kenneth Cole outlet.

You can always read, he reminded himself. He glanced over at the bookcase. He couldn't reach it without getting out of bed, and he wasn't about to ring for help. But when he looked back at the bedside table, he saw that there were three battered paperbacks already stacked there. He wondered if he'd left them there years ago or if Lucy had set them out for him.

He picked up the first one. It was *Watership Down.* He couldn't remember ever having read it, but maybe he had, although he couldn't imagine why he would want to read a novel about rabbits. The second was *Dune,* which he had read half a dozen times and was in no hurry to read again. This left the third book, which he hoped would be more appealing than the first two.

When he saw the cover, he just about dropped the book. The picture showed a handsome, dark-haired man in a bathing suit, sitting on a yacht. Behind him stood another man in a swimsuit, his hand on the first man's shoulder. A bottle of champagne sat in a bucket of ice in front of them. The title was *Now Let's Talk About Music.*

Burke hadn't seen the Gordon Merrick novel since he'd hidden it beneath the sweatshirts in his dresser drawer almost twenty-five years before. In fact, he could have sworn he'd thrown it away. But here it was, and it appeared to be the same well-used copy. He didn't want to know how it had ended up on the bedside table.

He opened the novel. Before long he was caught up in the erotic adventures of Gerry Kennicutt as he traveled to Bangkok in search of love. Merrick's sex scenes were frequent and detailed, and Burke found himself with an erection, which pressed painfully against his underwear. *Just like when you were fifteen and reading this,* he thought.

He still remembered finding the book at a Waldenbooks during a shopping trip to Burlington with his mother. Burke was about to start his sophomore year, and they were in search of school clothes. At some point he had escaped his mother and made his way to the bookstore, where he'd looked to see if there were any Douglas Adams books he hadn't read yet. The covers of the Merrick novels had caught his eye, and he'd picked one up. As soon as he'd figured out what it was about, he'd put it down and walked quickly to another section, sure that his burning cheeks were giving him away. But after fifteen minutes of pretending to look at Tom Clancy novels, he'd gone back to the Merrick novel and, before he could talk himself out of it, taken it to the checkout counter. There a male clerk had rung up the purchase and, with a knowing smile, tucked the paperback into a bag. "Enjoy it," he'd said to Burke.

And he *had* enjoyed it. Many times. It was the first time he'd ever read descriptions of two men having sex. The first time he'd read through the novel, it had taken a week, at the end of which his cock was rubbed raw, the floor beneath his bed was littered with crumpled-up tissues, and his head was filled with images that kept him awake at night.

Now he again found himself playing with his erect dick, stroking it as he imagined Gerry Kennicutt and the equally handsome Ernst von Hallers fucking on the floor of the yacht. He hadn't jacked off since being in the hospital, afraid that it might somehow exacerbate his injuries, but now he didn't care. He hiked his T-shirt up, exposing his belly and chest, and felt himself getting close.

Then, from downstairs, he heard the sound of squeaking. This was followed by a soft thud, and soon he distinguished a distinct rhythm. *Squeak-squeak-thud. Squeak-squeak-thud.* It took him a moment to realize what it was.

They're fucking, he thought. *Dad and Lucy are fucking in Mom and Dad's bed.*

Once he'd identified the sound, it was impossible to ignore. His parents' room was beneath his, and the sounds were coming up through the floor. *Squeak-squeak. That's the bedsprings. Thud. That's the headboard hitting the wall.* He had a sudden, and unwelcome, mental image.

Immediately he let go of his cock, which was rapidly deflating. His balls, confused by his having stopped so close to achieving their objective, urged him to continue for just a little longer. But the moment had been ruined, possibly forever. Burke closed the book and slapped it on the bedside table. Turning off the light, he picked up one of the pillows, placed it over his head to drown out the hideous squeaking and thudding, and prayed that it would all be over soon.

CHAPTER 5

Burke awoke to the sound of thumping. His first thought was that his father and Lucy were still going at it, and that he'd simply dozed off for a few minutes. But then he realized that the noise was coming through the window, not through the floor. It took another half a minute to determine the source of the noise—someone was hammering.

His second thought was that he very badly had to piss. Glancing at the bedside table, he saw that the plastic bottle had been returned sometime during the night. Lucy must have checked in on him. The idea that she'd been in the room and he hadn't woken up was slightly disturbing, but he was thankful.

As he reached for the urine bottle, however, he realized that he needed to do more than empty his bladder. He was going to have to get up. And that meant being helped by Lucy or his father. Not only did he not relish that idea, but the morning erection he was sporting made it even more of a problem. He knew from experience that it wouldn't go away until he'd peed.

Faced with this situation, his body reacted by stressing the necessity of getting to a toilet *quickly.* He started to reach for the summoning bell, then stopped. *You can get to the bathroom by yourself,* he told himself. *It's just out the door and down the hall. You're going to have to do it sometime.*

Encouraged by his anxious eliminatory systems, he threw back the sheet, blanket, and quilt. Using his one good hand, he carefully lifted his right leg and moved it to the side of the bed. *All you have to do is turn and sit up,* he told himself. *Then you can stand up.*

He tried, using his right arm to move his body sideways on the bed. But as soon as his leg slipped off the bed, pain shot through him and he bellowed. "Shit!" he yelled as his body tipped sideways and the weight of the cast on his injured leg pulled him farther off the bed. He gripped the quilt with his fingers, trying to hang on. His only consolation was that the unexpected pain had killed his erection.

Immediately he heard footsteps on the stairs. Then his door flew open, and Lucy ran to him. She started to lift him into bed, but he stopped her. "Bathroom," he gasped. "Need to get to the bathroom."

"Ah," Lucy said. "I see. All right. Let's go."

"Maybe you should get Dad," said Burke.

Lucy shook her head. "He's busy," she said. "The vet's here to look after Old Jack. Besides, I can manage you just fine."

"What's wrong with Old Jack?" Burke asked as Lucy helped him slide off the bed and stand, his arm around her shoulder.

"Just a little case of founder," said Lucy. "Nothing serious. Got out and ate too much grass too quickly. We caught it in time, and he's mostly better." She chuckled. "Come to think of it, you two have a little bit in common."

"Ha-ha," said Burke as he shuffle-hopped out of the room and into the hallway. "Maybe you should have the vet put me down. It would be easier."

They reached the bathroom and went inside. "Do you need help sitting?" Lucy asked.

Burke eyed the toilet. Fortunately, the sink was beside it, and he could use it for support. "No," he told Lucy. "I'll be fine."

"All right," she said. "I'll just wait outside."

"Why don't you just come back in ten minutes?" Burke suggested.

Lucy nodded in agreement. "You don't need me hovering," she said.

She left, shutting the door behind her. Burke turned, his hand on the edge of the sink for balance, and shucked his boxers down. Unable to bend his right leg, he lowered himself quickly. There was a brief moment of panic when he feared he might not hit the seat, but then it was beneath him. *I'm never going to get used to this,* he thought.

When Lucy returned ten minutes later, Burke had managed to stand up and wash his hands, and was leaning against the sink, waiting for her help. "Everything come out all right?" Lucy asked.

"Just fine," said Burke as he limped along next to her. "Thanks for asking."

When they reached the bedroom, Burke sat on the bed while Lucy plumped his pillows. "Do you want to get dressed?" Lucy asked.

"Actually, no," Burke answered. "I think I'll play the invalid for a little while."

"I don't blame you," said Lucy as she pulled the blanket and quilt over his lap. "You just sit here. I'll get your breakfast."

Burke watched her go. What was he going to do all day? He could read only for so long. He would have to ask Lucy about Internet service. Then he could at least see what was going on in the real world. And he had some movies saved on his laptop. He could watch those. Still, it felt like being in the hospital. He looked out the window. The hammering had stopped, and he could see his father standing in the paddock, next to Old Jack. The big brown horse was facing away from Burke. His black tail switched lazily back and forth, and one ear was bent to the side.

He's annoyed, Burke thought. *The vet must be checking his feet.*

A moment later a head appeared next to Old Jack's as a man stood up. He turned his face toward the window, and Burke felt his heart stop. "Mars," he whispered.

The man was ruggedly handsome, with a wide face and strong jaw. His dark hair, slightly too long, curled over his forehead and brushed the collar of his blue work shirt. He said something and smiled, one side of his mouth curling up in an expression Burke remembered all too well. He patted Old Jack's neck with one large hand and laughed. The sound slipped through the window, and Burke felt his skin dimple as a shiver of excitement rippled through him.

It was Mars Janks, all right. Burke would have known that face and voice anywhere. But something wasn't right. *He's your age,* Burke reminded himself. *He wouldn't look the same now as he did in high school.*

Lucy interrupted his thoughts, appearing with the same tray as the night before. Only this time it held a plate of eggs, bacon, and toast and a glass of milk. She brought it to the bed and set it down.

"Who's out there with Dad?" Burke asked.

Lucy looked out. "The Janks boy," she answered.

"Mars?" said Burke, his stomach tightening.

Lucy shook her head. "Will," she said. "Marshall's son."

"Will," Burke said. "Of course. He must be what, seventeen?"

"Twenty," said Lucy.

Burke looked out the window again. Will was gone, but Burke recalled his face clearly. "He looks just like Mars did at that age," he said.

"He's a real nice boy," said Lucy. "Just like his father."

"He's going to be a vet?" asked Burke.

Lucy smiled. "If his father has anything to say about it, he will," she answered. "Now, eat your breakfast before it gets cold."

Left alone, Burke sat staring out the window. The eggs, untouched, cooled as he became lost in thought. He couldn't get Will Janks's face out of his head. More accurately, he couldn't get *Mars* Janks's face out of his head. He hadn't thought of Mars in a long time. Now, seeing Will, it all came back to him.

They had become friends as children, making one another's acquaintance in Sunday school shortly after Mars and his family moved to Wellston. Mrs. Forth, sharing with the class the miracle of Christ's birth, had glossed over the particulars of Mary's pregnancy, leaving most of them with the impression that she had gotten with child when a dove flew up her dress. Mars, however, had announced with authority, "A woman gets pregnant when a man puts his penis in her vagina and ejaculates sperm. The sperm fertilize her egg, and that makes a baby." He had broken the silence that resulted by asking their gape-jawed teacher, "So who put his penis in Mary's vagina?"

He had received this information from his father, who was an obstetrician and firmly believed that children should not be lied to when it came to matters of scientific fact. Burke, impressed by the new boy's knowledge, had quickly introduced himself. A meeting between their mothers following church resulted in an invitation for Marshall to spend the following Friday night at the Crenshaw home, and from there their friendship had grown until they were almost constantly together.

Over the years they shared many things: birthdays, Little League, learning to drive. Practically brothers, they were easily mistaken as such by those who didn't know them. They weathered the occasional fight but rarely went more than a day or two before falling back into their easy relationship.

Then, their junior year in high school, Mars developed a crush on one of a pair of twins, Shana and Sherrie Youngblood. Burke couldn't tell the two girls apart, but Mars was insistent that Shana was the more beautiful of the two. Because Shana would do nothing without her sister, Mars begged Burke to ask Sherrie to the upcoming Halloween dance, to which Shana had conditionally accepted Mars's invitation. Burke reluctantly agreed, and the four spent an evening dancing to the songs of Prince, Journey, and Cyndi Lauper. During a slow dance to Wham!'s "Careless Whisper," Sherrie surprised Burke with a kiss, after which she informed him in a hoarse whisper that she would be amenable to giving him a blow job.

Mars, meanwhile, had been trying to convince Shana to grant him the same favor, and although she had yet to commit to anything, she had agreed to his suggestion that they all drive somewhere and enjoy some of the beer he had liberated from the grocery store at which he worked as a stock boy. And so the four of them rode in Mars's hand-me-down Volvo to the secluded parking area by the lake, where after two beers each, Mars began making out with Shana in the front seat, while in the back Burke endured Sherrie's sloppy kisses and fumbling attempts to unzip his pants.

Burke had for some time been aware of his sexual inclinations but had managed to keep them to himself. Now, faced with Sherrie's uncomfortably aggressive behavior, he found himself panicking. He could fake making out with her, but anything beyond that wasn't going to end well for either of them. As he once again guided her fingers away from his crotch, he prayed for some divine intervention that would rescue him from the predicament.

He got it a moment later, when Shana opened the passenger-side door and threw up her beer. Almost instantly Sherrie, too, was reaching for the door handle, joining her sister in sickness. As the twins vomited loudly and assured each other that everything would be okay, Mars looked back at Burke and with great irritation said, "I guess they really *do* do everything together."

Half an hour later the Youngblood twins had been deposited at their house, and Burke and Mars were back at the lake, Burke having replaced Shana in the front seat. Each boy had a beer in his hand. Mars's was already half empty.

"What a couple of teases those two were, huh?" Mars said.

Burke sipped his beer. "Well, they were pretty sick," he said.

Mars looked over at him. "So she was really going to give you a hummer?"

"That's what she said," Burke confirmed.

Mars laughed. "Your balls must be aching something fierce. I know mine are. Shit, I bet Shana faked puking just to get out of sucking my dick."

"If she was faking it, she did a pretty good job," said Burke.

Both of them laughed. Mars drained his beer and tossed the empty bottle out the window. "All I know is I'm fucking hard as a rock," he said. He leaned back in his seat and rubbed his crotch. "Damn, this sucks!"

"Yeah," Burke said, trying to sound annoyed. "I know what you mean." He took another swig of beer and swallowed it. "I guess we'll just have to jerk off later."

Mars opened another beer, drank deeply, and said, "What do you think it feels like?"

"Jerking off?" Burke answered. "You should know. You do it five times a day."

"Not jerking off," said Mars, hitting him lightly with his hand. "Getting a blow job."

Burke shrugged. "Wet, probably," he said. "Warm. I don't know."

Mars groaned. "We were *this* close to finding out," he said. "Damn it!"

A few seconds later Burke heard the sound of a zipper being pulled down. When he looked over, he saw that Mars had shucked his jeans down and was slowly stroking his erect cock. He still held the beer bottle in his left hand.

His breath caught in his throat. He had seen Mars's cock before, but never hard, and he'd never seen him playing with it. Mars's head was back and his eyes were closed. Burke could hear him breathing.

What happened next seemed to occur in slow motion. Before he could stop himself, Burke reached across and took Mars's dick in his hand. Mars stopped stroking himself and let Burke take over. His eyes remained closed.

Burke stroked Mars for several minutes, feeling every inch of his friend's long, thick cock. He rubbed the head, and his fingers came away sticky with precum. Mars remained perfectly still.

Then Burke felt himself moving closer and bending over. His mouth closed over the head of Mars's dick and kept moving, sliding down the shaft. His heart hammered in his chest as he waited for Mars to realize what was happening and stop him, but Mars only rested his hand on the back of Burke's neck, his fingers applying light pressure.

He came a minute later, moaning and lifting his hips as he exploded in Burke's mouth. Burke swallowed the warm load, surprised at how much there was. He waited until Mars's cock stopped twitching, then let it slip from his mouth. He retreated to his own seat, horrified at what he'd just done.

Mars quietly tucked his dick away and zipped his pants up. He took a drink of beer and handed the bottle to Burke. "Man, I am *so* wasted," he said.

Burke pretended to drink but only tipped the bottle back. He didn't want to wash the taste of Mars from his mouth. "Me too," he said.

"Let's get out of here," said Mars as he started the car.

They never spoke about what happened. Burke worried that it would ruin their friendship, but when they next saw one another, Mars acted no differently toward him. Still, Burke sensed that bringing up the subject or attempting to repeat the events of that evening would be a mistake. And so he told himself that it had all been a dream. He accepted the lie because he had to, and because he didn't want to lose Mars's friendship.

But he did lose it when he left for college two years later. Not because either he or Mars ended it, but because it faded away as they moved further down their respective paths and away from one another. There were occasional returns to the past—Mars spent a weekend with Burke in Boston, attending a U2 concert, and Burke was the best man at Mars's wedding to Jane—but then Mars became busy with veterinary school and babies, and Burke became busy with his photography and his first lover. Phone calls became e-mails, which became annual holiday cards. Then even those stopped as time, distance, and absence weakened the bonds of friendship.

Burke had not seen Mars in more than fifteen years, since running into him during a Christmas visit home and promising to get together soon. In all the years they'd never discussed Burke's lack of a girlfriend or wife, and Burke assumed Mars had figured things out on his own. Until seeing Mars in his son's face, Burke hadn't thought about what happened between them in a long time.

He closed the door on the past and brought himself back to the present. The eggs on his plate were now an unappetizing scramble; the toast, soggy with butter. Burke picked up a piece of bacon, took one bite, and dropped the strip on top of the eggs. He was no longer hungry. Pushing the tray away, he lay back and closed his eyes. But no matter how hard he tried, he couldn't get the face of Mars Janks out of his head.

CHAPTER 6

"**Y**our father tells me you're a history buff."

Burke closed *Watership Down* and set it on his lap. He had finished the Merrick novel earlier in the day and, after discovering that his father's house was not equipped with wireless Internet service and the only phone jacks were in the kitchen and his father's office, had grudgingly begun reading about the rabbits of the Sandleford warren. To his surprise, he found himself caught up in the story and was slightly annoyed that Lucy was interrupting at a crucial juncture.

"He would like me to be," he told Lucy, who was standing in the doorway with a large book in her hands. "Actually, I am," he admitted. "Just not as *big* a one as he would like."

Lucy nodded. "I've heard about the great schism," she said, laughing. "Or, as your father puts it, about how you threw away a teaching career for the life of an artist."

"Never mind that I've made a living as a photographer for almost twenty years now," said Burke. "He still hates it that I'm not standing in front of a bunch of bored, pimple-faced kids, discussing the Trail of Tears."

Lucy didn't remark on this statement. Whether this was out of politeness or an unwillingness to get between Burke and his father, Burke was unsure. Instead, she approached the bed and held out the book. "Jerry was a history teacher," she said. "This was his life's work."

Burke took the book and looked at it. "*Sons of the Green Mountain Boys: The Vermont Militia in the Civil War,*" he read. "By Gerald McHenry Grant. Impressive. I have to admit, when I think of the Civil War, I don't immediately think about Vermont."

"Most people don't," said Lucy. "Not even most Vermonters. Jerry was always fascinated by the lesser-known aspects of the war. This was the main reason we moved here, so he could do research for the book."

Burke opened the book and flipped through the pages. It was filled with photographs, maps, and a seemingly endless parade of footnotes. "This is impressive," he told Lucy. "It must have taken him years."

Lucy nodded. "He worked on it every chance he got," she said.

Burke, turning to the front of the book, glanced at the book's copyright information. "This came out only two years ago," he said, surprised. "I thought your husband died five—" He stopped, realizing he might have said something insensitive.

"He did," said Lucy. "I finished it for him. Really it was already done. Jerry was meticulous about his research, and he'd written almost all of the text before his memory got too bad. I just had to pull it all together from the notes he left." She hesitated a moment before continuing. "He was terrified that he would forget about it before it was finished," she said. "After all those years of research, he couldn't bear the thought of the book dying with him. I think it's what kept him going as long as he did."

"So he never saw it like this," Burke remarked, running his hand over one of the pages.

Lucy shook her head. "No. But he knew it was going to be a book, and that's what mattered to him. I promised him I would do it."

"You could have let it go," Burke remarked without thinking. "He never would have known."

"But I would," said Lucy. "Besides, it's a good book. Don't let all the footnotes fool you. Jerry was mad about footnotes, so I left them in, but you can skip right over them. It won't make a bit of difference."

Burke nodded. "I will," he promised. "Thanks for bringing it up."

When Lucy was gone, Burke opened the book again. He turned to the introduction and read the first sentence. "The name Ethan Allen is well known to students of early American history and is recognizable also to those who appreciate a well-turned table leg or an elegantly proportioned hutch."

Burke chuckled at the joke. One of the chief complaints of his history professors at the University of Vermont was that one of the most important figures in the history of the state had been reduced in the minds of the general public to a mascot for a furniture company. It was, as far as they were concerned, yet another slight against their state, which they universally believed to be unappreciated by the larger union. When the state's tourism bureau held a contest to replace the much-derided "I LoVermont" slogan, the history department only half-jokingly launched a campaign for it to be changed to "We are more than maple sugar."

He hadn't thought about that in years. His time at the university had been short. He'd stayed only a year before deciding that teaching history was not his passion. He had discovered photography, thanks to the school's requirement that all freshmen take one class in the arts, and had immediately known that it was what he wanted to do with his life. His father had been less enthusiastic about his son's choice, and at first had refused to pay for any further education unless Burke came to his senses. Burke's mother had played mediator, however, and it was decided that Burke would go to school in Boston to pursue what his father insisted on calling "his new hobby."

For the next three years, whenever he spoke with his father, Burke had endured the same question: "How's the picture taking coming along?" Even when his work began receiving awards and being included in gallery shows, Burke's father had received the news with little enthusiasm, always asking how much Burke was being paid for his work. Eventually Burke had just stopped talking about it altogether, sharing his personal accomplishments with his mother and limiting his discussions with his father to the job he had taken as a staff photographer for a Boston newspaper.

Things had improved over the years. As it became evident that Burke *would* be able to support himself as a photographer, his father had grudgingly accepted that perhaps his son had not made a foolish choice, after all. But there remained in their relationship an underlying sense of disappointment, which no amount of professional success or personal satisfaction could completely overcome.

He wondered if his father had put Lucy up to giving him the book. Was it his father's way of pointing out what Burke could have done with his life? He had come up to see Burke only twice since his arrival, and then for only a few minutes at a time. Although Burke sensed no resentment of his being there, now he couldn't help but question if this was his father's way of saying, "I told you so. If you had just stuck with history, this never would have happened." As if

Burke's decision of twenty-two years before was the first in a chain of easily preventable mistakes culminating in the crash that had landed him in his father's house.

Or, he told himself, maybe Lucy just thought you might be interested in her husband's book.

He tried not to think about anyone's motivations as he read Jerry's book. This was easier than expected, as he quickly found himself caught up in the story. He knew quite a bit about Allen, the Green Mountain Boys, and their role in both Vermont's own struggle for independence from New York and in the larger War of Independence. He was much less familiar with the role the Vermont militia played in the Civil War, and he found this fascinating.

He was so engrossed in the book that when the door opened an hour later, he didn't look up as he said, "This is really good stuff, Lucy."

"Thanks," said a male voice. "I did my best."

Burke looked up. Mars Janks was standing in the doorway to the room. Beside him was the younger version of himself, whom Burke had seen through the window earlier in the day. Burke looked from one to the other. The resemblance was unnerving.

"Hi, Burke," Mars said, stepping forward and holding out his hand for Burke to take.

Burke was momentarily unsettled by the formality of his old friend's greeting but accepted Mars's hand and grasped it warmly. "It's been a while," he said.

Mars nodded. "Too long," he agreed. He turned and motioned his son into the room. "This is my boy, Will," he said.

Like his father had, Will extended his hand. "Good to meet you," he said in Mars's voice.

"Lucy tells me your dad is making you into a vet," Burke remarked.

"I'm trying to," said Mars. "He's got a way with the animals, that's for sure. Old Jack will do anything for him."

"I just know how to talk to him, is all," Will said, his cheeks reddening. "It's no big deal."

"Getting that horse to do anything is a big deal," said Mars. "I swear he's three-quarters mule." He pointed at Burke's leg. "Heard you had yourself an accident," he said.

"No, I just wanted to spend a couple of months in the country," Burke joked.

Mars laughed. "Be glad you're not a horse," he said. "We'd have to put you down."

Burke laughed at the poor attempt at a joke. He was trying not to stare at Will. Mars had matured into a handsome man, but looking at Will took Burke right back to high school. Where Mars had grown into himself, Will was still finding his way. His awkwardness reminded Burke of his own at that age. It also reminded him of that night in Mars's car. He looked away.

"So, is Old Jack going to be all right?" he asked a little too loudly.

"He'll be fine," said Mars. "You know how it is. The older you get, the more you have to watch what you eat."

Burke didn't bother to laugh this time. He looked at Will and caught him grimacing at his father's poor attempt at humor. Will in turn saw Burke watching him and gave a lopsided smile, one side of his mouth rising up as he shook his head. Burke felt something in his belly jump at the sight.

"Well, we should be going," said Mars, oblivious to the joke being shared at his expense. "We've got to check on Sam Barton's ewe. Poor girl's got mastitis."

"Sounds painful," Burke said.

"I'll come by again soon," Mars assured Burke. "We can talk about the old days."

He's talking as if we're in our seventies, Burke thought. *Like his life is all but over.*

"That's a good book."

Will's comment drew Burke's attention. "This one?" he said, holding up Jerry's book.

Will nodded. "It's interesting. I mean, if you're into Vermont history."

"Will plays around in one of those reenactment groups," Mars explained.

"It's the Eighteenth Vermont Regiment," Will corrected. "And it's not a reenactment group, although we do that sometimes. It's mostly about preserving the history of Vermonters who fought in the Civil War."

"Sounds interesting," said Burke. He felt sorry for the young man.

Mars clearly didn't think much of Will's activities. "Maybe you can help me get up to speed on this. I'm afraid my knowledge of Vermont war history ends with the capture of Fort Ticonderoga."

"Sure," Will said, flashing the endearing grin again. "Maybe later this week?"

"I'm not going anywhere," said Burke, indicating his leg. "I'm a captive audience."

"Now you've done it," Mars told Burke. "Once he gets started, there's no shutting him up about this stuff. He'll talk your ear off if you give him a chance."

"That's all right," Burke replied. "I've got two of them. I can afford to lose one." He looked at Will. "You come by any time you want to."

After Mars and Will left, Burke was surprised to find that he was exhausted. Had seeing his old friend really been stressful? He hadn't felt anxious or nervous, or at least hadn't been aware of it if he had, but now he felt the way he did when he had to make small talk with people he didn't know.

Then again, Mars really wasn't the guy he'd known in college. He'd changed somehow, become practical and—it was the only way Burke could think of to describe him—grown up. Burke didn't know this Mars.

On the other hand, Will was someone he recognized. In him he saw the Mars of twenty-five years ago, the young man with good looks and a devil-may-care attitude. He could imagine riding around in the old Volvo with *that* Janks boy.

What are you doing? he asked himself. *He's half your age.*

"Don't be ridiculous," he argued. "It's not like that. He just seems like a nice kid."

He tried to get back into the book, but the weariness soon overtook him. Combined with the warmth of the afternoon, the sun coming through the window, and the gentle bleating of the sheep outside, it was impossible to resist. He told himself he would close his eyes for only a few minutes. He didn't want to sleep the day away and then be up all night.

His resolve lasted all of thirty seconds. Then his breathing slowed, his thoughts dimmed, and he slept.

CHAPTER 7

When he woke up, it was dark. For a moment he couldn't remember where he was. He had been dreaming about the first day of high school. He couldn't find his locker, then couldn't remember the combination when he *did* find it. When the bell rang, rebuking him for being late to his first class, he'd woken up.

Slowly the room came into view and the anxious feeling dissipated. He hated that dream. It was one he had fairly regularly, usually when he was stressed out about a project. Sometimes it took another form and he was—for reasons that were unclear—back in high school after having already graduated from college. He was looking for the student affairs office so that he could prove that he didn't belong there, but it was always around another corner or down another hallway, just out of reach.

It's because you're in your old room, he told himself as he sat up and turned on the light on his bedside table. It illuminated a plate with a sandwich on it. A note lay beside the plate.

Don't want to wake you.

Dinner was grilled lake trout. Don't think it would be good cold, so here's a sandwich.

Dad

Burke picked up the sandwich and lifted the top piece of bread. It was peanut butter and jelly. Strawberry, by the smell of it. He took a bite and chewed, only to discover that the peanut butter was of the crunchy variety. He forced himself to swallow what was in his mouth, but the rest of the sandwich was returned to the plate.

"Who uses crunchy peanut butter?" he asked the room. "You might as well eat squirrel shit."

His father should have known he didn't like crunchy peanut butter. On the rare occasions when Burke's mother had gone away without them, it had been up to his father to feed them. Usually Burke's mother had made and frozen enough meals to last the duration of her absence, but occasionally Burke's father had found defrosting and reheating one of her dishes too taxing, and had resorted to sandwiches. Burke had always requested peanut butter, and it had always been smooth.

"Of course, he probably never even looked at the jar," Burke mused.

He wasn't hungry, anyway. But he was awake. He looked at the clock. It was 2:26. The air was heavy and still, as if the whole world was holding its breath. He knew he wouldn't be able to fall asleep, so he reached for *Watership Down*. He'd always liked reading late at night, anyway. It made the experience feel more like an adventure somehow.

Then he remembered Jerry's book. Someone—most likely his father—had removed it from the bed and placed it on the bedside table. The sandwich plate was atop it. Burke lifted the plate and slid the book from underneath it. Opening it to where he'd left off, he continued to read.

> *The majority of the information we have on the private lives of the men who fought in the Civil War comes from the letters they wrote to loved ones back home. Although it seems unlikely given the chaotic nature of life during wartime, the delivery of mail to and from troops on the move was carried out with surprising efficiency. And as recipients on both ends of the exchange more often than not kept the letters they received, there exists a rich store of firsthand accounts of the events of that period.*
>
> *Equally important, these letters provide a very personal glimpse into lives turned upside down by the division between the states. Often filled with sorrow and joy*

*in equal parts, they were generally written either to bol-
ster the spirits of sons, husbands, and brothers serving the
cause far from home or to reassure loved ones anxiously
awaiting a soldier's return that a reunion was surely not
far off.*

*Perhaps most poignant are the letters sent between
husbands and wives or between affianced couples. These
are often unusually intimate in tone, almost assuredly
because the senders never knew if the letter might be the
last words spoken to a loved one. Although inarguably
romantic in tone, the majority of the letters of this type
are remarkably without the sentimentality that charac-
terizes most love letters, as if the ever-present threat of
death made it possible to speak plainly what was contained in the heart of the author.*

The following pages contained photographs of letters sent and received by soldiers in the Vermont militia. Most were unreadable, the
spidery handwriting difficult to decipher. Fortunately, next to each
letter appeared a transcription of the contents. Burke read through
some of them.

He found himself drawn particularly to a letter identified as being
written by one Amos Hague, a soldier in the 3rd Vermont Infantry, to
his fiancée, Tess Beattie, back home in Sandberg. For one thing, he
could actually read it. For another, it included a sketch—remarkably
well done—of a sweet flag plant. Curious to see what the sketch had
to do with the letter, Burke began to read.

My beloved T:

*How long has it been since I last saw you? It seems an
eternity, though I know it is less than three months' time.
Much has transpired since I last wrote, but I will not
waste words or time on descriptions of war, except to re-
port that last night my good friend William Holburne suc-
cumbed to fever brought on by an infected wound. I have
spoken of William to you before. He was a young man of
only eighteen years, gentle and full of spirit. I considered
him my brother and sought to look after him as much as
I could. I feared this day would come, as the very young*

seem always to draw the eyes of the Fates upon them, but now that it has, I find myself unable to grieve the loss of him. It is but one more thing this war has taken from us, the soothing power of tears. Or perhaps I am simply afraid that should I allow myself to mourn, I shall never stop.

I comfort myself with thoughts of you. Our last kiss lingers still on my lips, and the taste of you relieves both thirst and hunger. Two days ago, while marching to our current encampment, we passed through a marshland where I plucked sweet flag and tucked it into my haversack. At night, in the darkness of my tent, I crush it 'tween my fingers and hold them to my face. The scent remains for an hour or more, during which I recall afternoons lying with you in the grass. I hear your laughter and feel your sun-warmed skin beneath my hands. Whispering your name, I fall asleep and dream.

It is just past dawn. We will be moving on shortly, to where, I do not know. I know only that it takes me another step, another mile away from you. I pray that soon the day will come when I turn my face homeward. Then I will not walk but run to you as swiftly as these feet will carry me.

Your devoted companion,

A

Burke ran his fingertips over the drawing of the sweet flag. It was detailed enough that he could almost feel the hundreds of tiny bumps on the spadix that rose up from between the leaves of the plant. It seemed such an odd thing for a soldier to focus on. Then he reminded himself that the soldiers had been other things first, farmers and teachers and shop owners, who had been called up to fight for the North. He wondered what Amos Hague had been before he'd put on the uniform of a Yankee soldier, and what he'd gone back to following the end of the war.

He searched the book for more letters written by Amos Hague but found none. Nor was there any information on the man, apart from the fact that he had been part of the 3rd Vermont Infantry. From other chapters in the book, Burke learned that the unit was instrumental in several key battles of the war, including encounters at Gettysburg, Antietam, and Fredericksburg. Amos's role in these skirmishes, however, went undocumented.

Burke read until his eyes grew heavy. As the first lines of dawn cracked the dark face of the night, he fell asleep again. He found himself standing in a field. The grass, green and high, was stained with blood. Around him lay fallen soldiers, some dead, some near death. A few were merely wounded.

Burke himself was unscathed, as if he had just that moment materialized out of thin air. A man, his leg shredded below the knee and the life quickly draining from him, lifted a bloodied hand and pointed at Burke with trembling fingers. His mouth opened, but no sound came out.

Then Burke heard his name called. He turned, searching for the voice, and saw a young man lying not far off. The front of the soldier's uniform was stained with blood, and he was pressing his hand to his chest. Once more he called Burke's name, his voice faltering.

Burke tried to run to the boy but found that his feet refused to move. He wanted to take the soldier in his arms and comfort him in his last moments, but could only stand and watch in horror and despair as the stain on the young man's uniform grew larger and the light in his eyes flickered out.

He awoke with a gasp. For a long, terrifying moment he thought he was unable to breathe. Then his lungs drew in air, and the terrible weight was lifted from his chest.

"Good morning," his father said. He was standing at the foot of the bed, regarding his son with a bemused expression. "Sleeping in today, are you?"

Burke looked around. "What time is it?" he asked.

"Half past seven," his father answered.

Burke groaned. "That's sleeping in?" he said.

"How's the leg?"

"Still broken," said Burke.

His father nodded. "I can see that," he said.

"It *hurts,*" said Burke. He was tired and irritated, and it felt as if his father was teasing him.

"Means it's healing," his father said. "We need to get you up soon, get the muscles working again."

"Swell," said Burke. He noticed the cup of coffee in his father's hand. "I don't suppose there's any more of that?" he asked.

"Whole pot of it," his father told him. "Want to come down and have a cup?" He chuckled at his joke. "I'll bring you up some with breakfast. You should be hungry. I see you didn't eat your supper."

Burke glanced at the forgotten peanut butter sandwich. It looked none the fresher, despite a night of rest. "I should have told you, I apparently developed some kind of an allergy to peanuts," he lied. For some reason he wanted to spare his father's feelings, although he had no reason to think he would be offended.

"Good thing you had only a bite, then," said his father. "Figured it out before it was too late."

"Yeah," Burke said. "I guess I wasn't paying much attention when I picked it up."

"I assume you've got no allergy to pancakes?" his father asked as he picked up the plate.

"No," Burke replied. "Pancakes are fine."

His father walked to the door. "I'll be back in a bit," he said. "I've got to meet Mars out at the barn first."

"Mars is here this early?" Burke asked.

His father chuckled. "A country vet never sleeps," he said. "I guess you've forgotten what it's like out here after all those years in the city."

"I'm not sure Boston's *the* city, but it's certainly a pretty nice one," Burke said, unable to contain his irritation.

"Mars has made a nice life for himself here," his father said. "His son seems likely to stick around, too." He paused. "Anyhow, I'll be back shortly. Lucy's gone off to run some errands, so it's just us fellows this morning."

Errands? Burke thought. *At seven thirty in the morning? What's wrong with these people?*

His father retreated downstairs, leaving him to stare out the window. Now that he was more awake, Burke noticed Mars's pickup parked outside. A minute later he saw his father walk across the yard as Mars emerged from the barn. The two men shook hands. Burke's father said something, and Mars turned his head and looked up at the window of Burke's room. For a moment his eyes seemed to look right into Burke's. Then he laughed. So did Burke's father.

Anger rushed in. Burke was clearly the subject of their amusement. Probably his father was telling Mars how his lay a bed, city-boy son had slept the day away, while they had already tilled the field, milked the cows, and raised a barn.

Then there was his father's comment about how great Mars's life was. *Compared to mine is what he meant,* Burke thought. And what was that about Will staying in Vermont? He knew his father thought that he'd made some bad choices in his life, but did he really resent so much that Burke had left Wellston? Had he really expected his son to stay and become—what—a farmer? A schoolteacher? A country vet?

Apparently so, he concluded. And did he really think it was fair to compare his life to Mars's? Burke bristled at the idea. But was it really so unexpected? After all, he and Mars had both been raised there. Why had one of them left and one of them stayed?

Burke knew the answer to that question. He'd *had* to leave, not only because he wanted to see what else the world had to offer, but also because staying in Wellston would have meant forever hiding who he was. Mars could stay because he was one of them. He fit in. He was everything Burke wasn't.

This realization irritated Burke more than he expected it to, not because he wished he had Mars's life, but because he resented that it was a life Mars was afforded because he played by the unwritten rules of small-town life. He hadn't fought for it, hadn't risked anything, hadn't risked alienating anyone by daring to break out.

And now he's the one down there laughing with my father, while I'm up here playing the prodigal son, he thought. It wasn't the way the story was supposed to end. In his version he would have come home triumphant, having conquered the world, found love, and achieved fame and fortune. Instead, he couldn't even take a piss without someone's help.

Whoever said there's no place like home was never a middle-aged gay man laid up in his childhood bedroom, waiting for coffee, while his high school crush joked about him with his father, he concluded. *Because* that *story doesn't have a happy ending.*

CHAPTER 8

"Are you *trying* to kill me?"

Burke leaned against the hallway wall. The pain in his leg was excruciating. His head throbbed, and for a moment he thought he might pass out.

"The doctor says you need to start moving around," Lucy said.

"The *doctor* is a vet," Burke argued. "And I'm not a calf."

"Well, you're certainly acting like one," said Lucy. "Honestly, you'd think I'd asked you to play hopscotch, the way you're carrying on."

"It *hurts,*" Burke insisted. "I want to go back to the bed."

Lucy shook her head. "To the end of the hall and back," she said. "Now."

Burke gritted his teeth and steadied himself on the crutch. Had both his arms been usable, it would have been difficult enough, but with one in a cast, it was almost impossible. He had to put his weight on the single crutch and hop forward on his left leg, then shift his weight to that leg and bring the crutch even with that foot. On his first attempt the injured leg clanked against the crutch, making him yelp.

"See?" said Lucy. "That wasn't so bad."

"For you," Burke snapped. "For me, it was fucking horrible."

"Language," said Lucy. "Don't let your father hear you talk like that."

"Why?" Burke asked. "Is he going to wash my mouth out with soap?"

"I imagine you were a difficult child," Lucy mused as Burke attempted once more to move forward. "Your mother must have had quite a time with you."

"My *mother* never would have tortured me like this," said Burke.

"Oh, I'm sure she would have," Lucy said. "She'd have known it was what you needed."

After another painful five minutes they reached the end of the hall. Burke, relieved, turned around. "Happy?" he asked Lucy.

"Very," she said. "Now, I suppose you want to get back to bed."

"That's the general idea," Burke answered as he began the long trek back to his room. Although it was fewer than twenty feet, it might as well have been a mile. To his surprise, however, he seemed to be moving more quickly than he had on the outbound journey.

"Like a horse to the barn," Lucy joked as Burke employed the awkward forward-step-swing maneuver.

"Can we stop with the livestock references?" said Burke. The door to his room was not far off, and he covered the remaining six or so feet with only a few stops.

"While you're up, we should probably change those shorts," Lucy suggested. "You've worn those for three days now."

"I asked Gregg to pack some sweatpants," Burke said. "Those should fit over the cast."

Lucy went to the dresser and opened one of the drawers. She looked through the clothes and pulled out a pair of sweats. Then she looked at Burke thoughtfully. "Probably time to change the underpants as well," she said.

"I'm good in that department," Burke said quickly. "But thanks."

"Suit yourself," said Lucy. "Now, let's get those shorts off."

Ten minutes later Burke was propped up in bed, wearing the sweatpants and a white T-shirt. His leg had stopped aching, and apart from wishing he could wash his hair, he felt almost human.

"I think I may be up for a shower later," he announced.

"Excellent," said Lucy. "Another few days and we'll have you downstairs."

"That would be nice," Burke said. "I'm starting to feel like one of those princesses locked in a tower by her evil stepmother."

"So that's how you see me, is it?" said Lucy, feigning offense.

"Exactly like that," Burke replied. "And you know what happens to evil stepmothers."

"They get all the money and send the kids to boarding school," said Lucy. "Not bad work, if you can get it."

Burke laughed. Then he said, "Are you and Dad going to get married?"

Lucy turned from the dresser, where she was rearranging things, and cocked her head. "Do you want us to?" she asked.

"No," Burke answered quickly. "I don't mean *no*," he added. "I mean, I don't care one way or the other. I was just wondering."

Lucy shut the dresser drawer. "I don't think so," she said.

"I'm sorry," said Burke, afraid he'd embarrassed her. "I just assumed he might have asked by now."

"Oh, he's asked," said Lucy. "Several times. But I told him I don't want to be married."

Burke, surprised by her answer, couldn't help but ask, "Why not?"

Lucy sat at the end of the bed. "This may sound strange," she began, "but it's because of the gay marriage thing."

"You're protesting by not getting married?" said Burke. "But gay marriage is legal in Vermont."

Lucy shook her head. "I'm not protesting," she said. "Although I do think everyone should be able to marry the person they love, and I don't see why anyone cares."

"Then I don't understand," said Burke.

"Part of the reason for wanting gay marriage is so that partners have legal rights," Lucy said. "And that makes sense. But personally, I think the main reason is that they want their relationships validated— seen as equal to the marriages the rest of us have been able to have basically forever. I understand that as well. It's important that we all be treated equally."

"But?" Burke asked when she didn't continue for a moment.

"But marriage isn't about what other people see or think or feel," Lucy said. "It's about what the people marrying each other feel. I love your father very much, and I don't need a piece of paper or the blessing of the state to prove that. I want to be with him because I don't want to be with anyone else, and I want him to be with me for the same reason. I've been married," she added. "And it was wonderful. But it was never about what anyone else thought."

"And you decided this because of gay marriage?"

"I started thinking about it during all the debates," said Lucy. "Then when your father asked me to marry him the first time, I had to make a decision."

"What does Dad think about this?"

Lucy laughed. "He's horrified. Says we're living in sin and scandalizing the whole town."

"That sounds like Dad, all right," Burke said.

Suddenly the joy on Lucy's face turned into something else. "I know it hurts him," she said softly. "He doesn't entirely understand why I can't do this one thing for him. I'm sure he fears that it *means* something." She looked at Burke. "And sometimes I wonder if I'm not being selfish."

"I think you're doing what you feel is right," Burke said.

"I like to think so," said Lucy. "Still, it seems ungrateful to not take part in something so many other people wish they had the right to take part in."

"I don't know why anyone wants to get married," said Burke. "I think the whole thing was cooked up by lawyers so they can get rich off of divorce."

"You don't want to get married?" Lucy asked.

"You need a boyfriend for that," said Burke. "And I'm not so good at keeping those around."

"Which explains why you're here," Lucy said.

"Which explains why I'm here," Burke agreed.

"But this Gregg fellow—"

"Says that I'm overbearing," said Burke.

Lucy patted Burke's foot. "I can't imagine why," she said sweetly.

"Gregg and I gave it a try," Burke told her. "It just didn't work out."

"And he's the only man in Boston?" asked Lucy.

"All the other ones think I'm overbearing, too," said Burke.

"Maybe you should try Chicago," Lucy joked.

"Am I interrupting something?"

Burke's father entered the room. He was carrying a large cardboard box, which he set down next to Burke on the bed. "I thought you might be interested in these," he said.

Burke looked at the box, which, judging by the streaks of dust on it, had recently been removed from either the cellar or the barn. "What is it?"

"Just some things that belonged to your grandfather," his father told him.

Burke lifted one of the flaps holding the box closed and peered inside. The box was filled with half a dozen old cameras and assorted pieces of photographic equipment. He reached in and picked one out. "A Kodak Brownie Hawkeye," he said, holding up what was essentially a square plastic box. "Very old school."

He removed the other cameras, setting each one on the bed and identifying it. "Zeiss Nettar," he said. "Duaflex II, Yashica-Mat, Leica IIIf. These all look like they're in good condition."

He lifted out a square black box with no identifying marks on it. Removing the cover, he stared at the contents for a long time, hoping that what he was seeing was real. He almost didn't dare to touch it but couldn't resist picking it up. "This is a Hasselblad 1600F," he said, awed by the find. He turned the camera over, inspecting it. "And it's in perfect condition." He looked at his father. "This was Grandpa's?"

His father nodded. "I found them in his house after he died. Never even knew he had them."

"Why didn't you tell me about them?" Burke asked.

His father shrugged. "Guess I didn't think much about them," he said. "Just a bunch of old cameras. Everything's digital now. I didn't know you'd be interested."

"I would have been *very* interested," Burke said sharply. "Do you know how rare this camera is?" He held up the Hasselblad. "You almost never see them, and certainly not in this condition." He indicated the other cameras. "And these are all great, too. I wish you'd told me about them sooner."

"Like I said, it never occurred to me anyone would be interested. I was about to put them up on this auction site Lucy told me about."

"On eBay," Lucy told Burke.

"Figured we could get a couple dollars for them," said Burke's father.

"Yeah, well, you would have made some collector *very* happy," Burke said. He couldn't believe his father had almost practically given away such gorgeous cameras. Any one of them was a prize, even the Hawkeye, which was a common find for under ten bucks but which was still a beautiful little piece.

"You might as well have them," his father said. "I can't be bothered to figure out how to sell them on the computer, anyway."

"Hooray for being a Luddite," Burke whispered under his breath. "Thanks, Dad," he said more loudly. Then he thought of something. "How come Grandpa never talked about being a photographer?"

"I don't think he really was one," his father answered. "He was always getting into one hobby or another, but never long enough to really do anything with it. I imagine this was just one of his fancies. You take after him in that way."

Burke resisted sharing the response that first came to mind. Instead, he picked up the Zeiss and pressed the delicate little button that opened the case. The bellows extended smoothly. He moved the levers that set the aperture and shutter speeds, and both seemed to function as they should. The unassuming cardboard box really had yielded up a load of unexpected treasures.

"I wonder where I can get film around here?" he thought aloud.

"I'm sure we can find someplace," Lucy assured him.

"I can always order some online," said Burke. He'd set down the Zeiss and was looking at the Yashica-Mat. It was a stunning camera, its black metal housing solidly fashioned and its twin lenses nearly perfect in design. He couldn't wait to run a roll of film through it. For the first time since the accident he felt himself excited about something.

His father turned to leave. "Glad to see you like them," he said. "If I find any more, I'll bring them up."

Any more? Burke thought. *Any more and I'll have a heart attack.* The Hassy alone was enough of a find. He could live on the excitement from that for years.

"Was he really going to sell these on eBay?" he asked Lucy, who remained seated at the end of the bed.

She nodded. "He didn't think they were worth anything."

"Why didn't he even tell me about them? I'm a *photographer,* for Pete's sake. Didn't it even cross his mind that I might be interested in vintage cameras?"

"He doesn't do it on purpose, Burke," said Lucy.

"I don't know," Burke countered. "Part of me thinks he does. I mean, look at these." He indicated the cameras scattered around the bed. "These are in perfect condition. But he never said a word."

The more he thought about it, the madder he became. How dare his father keep these from him? There was no way it hadn't been done deliberately.

"Maybe they remind him too much of his own father," Lucy suggested.

"Why would that bother him?" said Burke. "They always got along."

"I don't know," Lucy said. "It's just a thought. When our mother died—our father had passed many years before—my sister and I cleaned out her house. I remember finding a china kitten in a box of odds and ends. Its head had clearly been broken and glued back on.

I distinctly remembered it always being on our mother's dressing table. I used to sit on the floor and watch her put on make-up, and the kitten always sat next to her bottle of Oil of Olay. Seeing it made me think of those times, and I wanted to keep it, but my sister and I had agreed that we would discuss each item before we took it for our own. So I showed her the kitten and asked her if she wanted it. I was surprised at her reaction. She said she'd hoped never to see that figurine again. When I asked her why, she said that one time, during a fight, our father picked the kitten up and threw it at our mother. It missed her and hit the wall, which is how it had broken. Later our father fixed it, and apparently our mother forgave him, but to my sister that kitten was nothing but a reminder of a time when she was frightened of our father."

"Did you keep it?" asked Burke.

Lucy nodded. "It's still on my dresser. And when I look at it, I don't see my parents arguing. I see my mother getting ready to go out somewhere wonderful. But for my sister it's a painful reminder of something she would rather forget."

"I still don't know why Dad wouldn't want to think about my grandfather," Burke said.

Lucy stood up. "You never know what people are thinking," she said as she gathered up the cardboard box and set it on the floor. She looked at Burke. "Not unless you ask."

CHAPTER 9

Even with Old Jack standing still, Burke was having difficulty focusing the camera. Mostly this was because he had to balance on the crutch while trying to work the camera knobs with one hand. He could do one or the other but hadn't quite gotten the hang of doing both. So far he'd wasted two shots, and with only ten on the roll, he didn't have any more to spare.

The fact that he was outside at all was a testament to the power of the cameras to inspire him. After finding no stores that carried the kind of film he required, he had placed an order for some with an online store. Well, Lucy had placed it, as Burke still wasn't up to attempting the stairs. But he'd spent the two days waiting for the film to arrive getting himself comfortable with going up and down stairs again, until he was able to do it with a minimum of anxiety.

Now he was standing in the paddock, holding the Yashica-Mat in his hands and trying to focus. Old Jack, completely uninterested in his role of model, flicked his tail and whickered softly. Burke had brought an apple for him, but fishing it from his pocket was currently impossible without either falling over or dropping the camera.

"Need some help?"

Will Janks opened the paddock gate and came inside. He was dressed in jeans and a Modest Mouse T-shirt, looking as if he'd just come from a concert. He walked slowly over to where Burke was doing his balancing act and, without prompting, reached into the pocket of Burke's hoodie and withdrew the apple. "Is this what you're looking for?" he asked.

"That's it," Burke said. He was trying not to think about how Will's hand had brushed against his stomach.

"Want me to feed it to Jack?"

Burke nodded. "I'm trying to get some test shots," he explained. "I want to see if the camera is working."

Will walked over to the horse and rubbed him behind his ears. Old Jack, smelling the apple, nuzzled Will's neck.

"Just a second," Burke instructed. He rested the camera on his arm cast and fiddled with the focusing knob until the fuzzy images of Will and Jack became crystal clear. "Okay, give him the apple."

Will held the apple out to Old Jack, who immediately reached for it. Will, turning to Burke, smiled as the horse's mouth touched his fingers.

Burke released the shutter and advanced the film. "One more," he said.

Will grinned. "Tell it to Jack," he said. "I can hold on to this apple only for so long."

Burke took the second photo just as Old Jack took what was left of the apple into his mouth and Will threw his head back, laughing. "That's great," Burke called out. "Thanks."

"When will you know if they came out all right?" Will asked.

Burke sighed. "Good question," he said. "Normally, I would develop them myself, but obviously I can't do that here. I'll have to send the film out. So we're looking at two weeks or more."

"I bet there's a place in Montpelier that can do it," Will said. "I can search around if you want."

"Thanks, but that's too much trouble," said Burke. "Besides, I'm kind of fussy about who develops my film. I'll figure something out."

"What do you need to do it yourself?" asked Will.

Burke thought for a moment. "Not a lot, actually," he said. "I'm shooting black and white for now. I could develop that myself, no problem. And if I had a scanner, I could just scan the negatives in."

"UPS does deliver out here, you know," Will said.

Burke nodded. "Maybe," he said. "Right now I just want to take a bunch of pictures. I'm still getting used to being a monopod."

Will looked around. "No offense to Old Jack, but there's not much to take pictures of around here," he said. "I know a place that would be great, though."

"Yeah?" Burke said. "Where's that?"

"Old farm about half an hour from here," Will told him. "There's not much left but some stone foundations, but it's real pretty."

"Thanks," Burke said. "But half an hour in a car and walking around an overgrown farm with a bum leg doesn't sound like the best idea. I think I'll just stay around here for today."

"Come on," Will coaxed. "It's a beautiful day, you've got a chauffeur, and I promise you it will be worth it. Best pictures you've ever taken."

"I don't know," said Burke hesitantly. "It sounds like a recipe for disaster."

"All right," Will said. "I give up. Stay here and shoot the same old horse over and over. That sounds like a lot of fun."

Burke looked at Old Jack, who stared back sullenly. The prospect of looking at that face all day was suddenly very depressing. "Okay," he said. "But you have to promise to catch me when I trip."

"You got it," Will promised. "I'll go tell Lucy what we're doing. Can you get in the truck by yourself?"

Burke looked at the pickup parked behind them. "No chance," he said.

"Then just stay put," Will said. "Do you want me to get anything from the house?"

"Yeah," Burke said. "There's a bunch of film up on my bed. Grab five rolls of the Efke R100. The boxes are green and gray. You can't miss them."

"Efke R100," Will repeated. "Got it. Be right back."

As the young man trotted toward the house, Burke made his way out of the paddock. With the camera hanging by its strap around his neck, he was able to move with a little more confidence. But there was no way he was getting into Will's truck without assistance, so he stood beside it, leaning on the truck bed and waiting for Will's return.

Five minutes later Will was back, the requested film in his hand. "Lucy says if I break you, I have to buy you," he said as he opened the passenger-side door. "Since I'm pretty much broke, I guess I'll have to take good care of you."

"How should we do this?" Burke asked, eyeing the truck seat, which seemed impossibly high.

"Like this," said Will, putting one arm around Burke's shoulders and the other under his thighs. Burke felt himself lifted up, but before he could express surprise, he was sitting in the truck and Will was putting the crutch in the back and shutting the passenger-side door. He walked to the other side of the truck and got in. "There," he said as he started the truck. "That was easy. Put your seat belt on."

The ride wasn't nearly as unpleasant as Burke had feared. Will drove slowly, the road was smooth, and Burke's leg remained stable. Only once or twice did he feel a twinge of pain, and even those were mild compared to what he'd felt on the drive up a week before. He hoped it meant he was healing more quickly than expected and could go home sooner than the doctor had predicted. That thought alone brightened his mood considerably.

"It might get a little rough now," Will said as he turned off the main road and onto what amounted to little more than a dirt track. But even this was not bad. When finally Will brought the truck to a stop, Burke was almost tempted to try getting out on his own. But his crutch was in the back, and Will was at the door before he could do anything, anyway. A moment later he was standing on the ground.

"So where's the farm?" he asked as Will got a backpack from behind the seat and put the film into it.

"You're looking at it," Will replied, nodding in the direction of a field of grass. "What's left of the house is over there." He pointed, and Burke followed the line of his hand to what looked like a low stone wall. "There's a pond on the other side of that rise," Will added.

Will set off into the grass, making a path through it for Burke to walk on. The grass was only knee height, and it parted easily. Still, Burke knew that it could be slippery, and he made sure to move slowly. And Will was always there, never more than a foot or two away, watching him.

The area around the foundation was bare, the stone walls forming a kind of island in the sea of grass. Wildflowers, mostly brown-eyed Susans, grew out of the cracks. Tired from the walk, Burke lowered himself onto one of the walls and looked around. The walls made a basic rectangle, the long sides no more than thirty feet and the short ones perhaps twenty. The space between them was empty except for some rotting timbers and a section of flat rocks scorched black. *That's where the hearth was,* Burke thought.

"Whose farm was this?" he asked Will.

Will shrugged. "I don't know," he said. "I never really thought about it."

Burke surveyed the area. "You say the pond is over there?" he asked, nodding at a point west of the house.

"Want to see it?" Will asked. "It's beautiful."

Burke stood up and once more followed Will through the grass. They walked away from the road, toward a small stand of trees. For a moment Burke thought they wouldn't be able to get past the trees, but then a path appeared between them, narrow and winding. They passed through the trees, and Burke saw the pond before them, its water shining gold beneath the sun. He realized that the trees curved around the edge of the pond, concealing it from view.

"It's like we walked through some invisible door into another world," he said.

"I told you it was beautiful," said Will.

The pond was not terribly big—perhaps forty feet across. It formed what appeared to be an almost perfect circle. On the far side an enormous rock broke the surface, its top rising a foot or two above the water. Two red-eared sliders sunned themselves on it, oblivious to their observers.

On the side where Burke and Will stood, the trees cast shadows over the ground. Here the grass gave way to earth, creating a short stretch of beach. A log, placed sideways, formed a low bench. Burke went to it and sat down. Will joined him a moment later.

"Have you gone in the water?" Burke asked him.

"A couple times," said Will. "My guess is the pond is fed by an underground stream. The top couple of feet are nice and warm, but when you dive down, it gets really cold." He flashed a smile. "It's a good place for skinny-dipping."

"I'll have to take your word for it," said Burke. "This cast is not going near that water. With my luck, I'd sink straight to the bottom."

"Well, I didn't bring you all the way out here to sit and stare at a couple of turtles," Will said.

Burke turned to him. "Then why *did* you bring me out here?" he heard himself ask. He hadn't meant for the comment to sound provocative, but it did. *What's wrong with me?* he wondered. It was as if something about the place had enchanted him.

"To take pictures," Will said. He held up the backpack containing the film. "Remember?"

Burke laughed. "Actually, I did forget," he admitted. "I was too busy admiring the scenery."

"What do you want to shoot?" Will asked. "You've got trees, water, and a rock. Take your pick."

"I don't know," Burke said, flipping open the Yashica-Mat's view-finder. "Let's see what the glass eye thinks is interesting." Without getting up, he slowly panned the camera along the shore of the pond, watching the image reflected in the camera's eye shift and change. Several times he paused, thinking he might have found something, but each time he decided not to trip the shutter.

"What are you doing?" Will asked, peering at Burke as if examining a strangely behaving dog.

"Cutting out everything but the picture," Burke explained. "When you try to see with your own eyes, there's too much. Things get lost. But the camera's eye sees only one small part of the world at a time." He moved the camera another inch. "There," he said. "That's it."

"What's it?" Will said, looking at the direction in which Burke was pointing the Yashica-Mat.

Burke didn't answer. He was busy focusing and composing the image. When he had it, he pressed the shutter release. "That one will be good," he said happily as he advanced the film.

"But *what* was it?" Will demanded.

"Grass," Burke answered. "A dragonfly. Water." He shrugged. "You'll have to wait and see." It was always impossible for him to describe his best photographs in words. There was just something about them, some inner essence—he hated that term, but it was the best description he could come up with—that lit up the photo from within and brought it alive. It didn't matter if he was shooting people or land-scapes, dogs or carnivals. His best pictures were alive.

He took several more photos while sitting, then asked Will to help him move to a place where he could stand. "Maybe I could kind of lean against you," he suggested. "That way my weight isn't on my arms."

It was awkward, but it worked. Burke finished the first roll of film and removed it from the camera, replacing it with a fresh one. He was seeing more and more things now, which was the way it often happened. Sometimes he would decide a subject had nothing to show him, only to find after a few shots that there was much more there than he'd first seen. He shot three rolls around the pond be-fore he felt he'd seen everything there was to see for that visit. Also, his leg was starting to ache.

"We should probably go," he told Will. "I think I might have had too much excitement for one day."

"You're the boss," Will said. "Let's roll."

They returned down the path, which seemed longer and more difficult to walk than Burke remembered. He was definitely tired, although at the same time he was filled with a buoyancy he hadn't felt in some time. He was excited about seeing the pictures, and he was happy that he was excited.

They reached the grass and headed back toward the house, intending to intercept their original path from the truck. They were almost there when Burke moved his crutch forward and felt it slide out from under him. He started to fall, his body twisting around as he tried to plant the crutch and hang on.

Will caught him, grabbing Burke under the arms and holding him up. His hands laced behind Burke's back so that they were face-to-face, their chests touching. Burke looked into Will's eyes as the wild beat of his heart returned to normal.

"I said I'd catch you," Will reminded him. Then he leaned forward and kissed Burke's mouth.

CHAPTER 10

UPS delivered the boxes three days later, one from Gregg and the other from B&H Photo in New York. The driver brought them to the porch, where Burke met him and signed for them. His father then carried them into the dining room, where he set them on the table. "What's all this?" he asked.

"Photography stuff," Burke answered as he opened the box from Gregg. He had stayed on the phone with Gregg while his friend packed the box, telling him everything to include in the shipment, but he still went over everything again. It was all there.

"Can you take this stuff upstairs for me, Dad?" Burke asked after checking the packing list from the second box and matching it to the contents.

"What are you doing? Setting up shop?" his father said.

"I'm just going to develop some film," Burke explained as he followed behind. He had gotten good at managing the stairs and now went up and down several times a day.

"Don't you need a darkroom for that?"

"I've got one," Burke told him.

His father set the first box down on the bed. "You do?" he said doubtfully.

Burke reached into the box and pulled out a black cloth bag that appeared to have two arms sewn onto it. "Right here," he said. "You want to see how it's done?"

"I do," his father said, sounding genuinely interested.

"Bring up the second box," Burke instructed him. "I'll get everything ready."

As his father went to fetch the other box, Burke unpacked the contents of the first box. Most of it was taken up with the photo scanner he'd asked Gregg to send him. He set this aside for later use and concentrated on the project at hand. By the time his father returned, Burke had laid out on the bed a pair of scissors, a metal film reel, and what looked like an oversize martini shaker.

"Looks like you're going to perform surgery," his father remarked as he put the second box on the floor.

"This is more fun," said Burke. He took a roll of exposed film and placed it inside the black bag along with everything else he'd set out. Then he sealed the bag and stuck his hands into the arms on either side. "This is a changing bag," he explained. "You use it for changing film when there's nowhere dark to do it. But you can also use it as a darkroom." He felt for the roll of film and held it with one hand while he released the bit of tape holding the end closed. This he trimmed away with the scissors.

"I'm spooling the film onto the reel," he told his father as he threaded the end of the film into the receiving slot on the reel. When it was secure, he turned the reel forward and back, working the film onto it. He was careful to hold the film by the sides so as not to touch its surface. "That shaker thing is called a developing tank," he said as he took the tank and placed the film reel inside. He placed the top on it and screwed it down tight. When he was sure it was secure, he pulled his hands free and opened the bag, removing the developing tank. "Now, this becomes our darkroom," he told his father.

"That?" his father said dubiously. "It's a can."

"Basically, yes," Burke admitted. "It's what you put in the can that makes a difference."

"I'm guessing that's what's in this box here."

"Right," said Burke. "You can watch if you want to, but it's basically a lot of pouring, turning, and more pouring. It might be easier if you come back for the fun part."

"Call me when it's done," his father said. "And try not to blow anything up."

"All the chemicals are harmless, Dad," Burke assured him. "Oh, would you mind putting that box in the bathroom for me?" In the excitement of developing the film, he'd forgotten all about his leg.

After depositing the box on the lid of the toilet seat, Burke's father left. Burke, who had developed thousands of rolls of film, performed the steps of the developing process almost without thinking about it. He filled the tank with water from the tap, pouring it into the ingeniously designed opening which allowed fluids to enter and leave without letting in light. He then let the tank sit while he mixed the developing fluid with water in a graduated beaker. When it was ready, he poured the water from the tank and replaced it with the developer.

Now came the tedious process of monitoring the time and agitating the tank for ten seconds every minute. As he did this, he thought back to what had occurred three days before. It was an understatement to say that Will's kiss had taken him by surprise. At first he'd thought that he was imagining it, or that maybe it was an accident, a peculiar result of his stumbling into Will's arms. But when it continued, and when Will's tongue probed gently at his lips, he'd accepted that it was really happening.

Kissing had been the extent of it, although both of them had become obviously aroused and Burke had sensed that Will wanted more. But it was too strange, too sudden, and Burke had stopped it. Will had surprised him by not seeming either embarrassed or angry, and the ride home had been only marginally uncomfortable. At the house Will had helped Burke out of the truck, walked him to the front porch, and reminded Burke to let him know when the pictures were ready, as he was curious about them. Then he'd gotten into his truck and waved good-bye, as if they'd just returned from the movies.

He watched the timer, turning the developing tank on schedule. He still didn't know what he was going to do about Will. *Why do you have to* do *anything?* he asked himself. *If Will isn't bothered by it, why should you be?*

This was a good question. The immediate answer was that Will was half his age and the son of his former best friend, with whom he'd been half in love and to whom he'd given his first blow job. That was not an insignificant detail and couldn't just be brushed aside. But if he *could* set it aside for a moment, that made things easier. The "half his age" thing was a bit worrisome, true, but it wasn't as if they were setting up house together.

The timer dinged, and Burke upended the developing tank, emptying it into the sink. *It's not like you never hooked up with guys twice your age when you were in your twenties,* he reminded himself as he filled the tank with stop bath and agitated it for thirty seconds. *And you didn't think it was strange.*

No, he hadn't thought it was strange. But he had been the younger man. Now he was the older one, and the realization that Will was born when Burke was already twenty was difficult to get past. While Will was learning to walk and talk, Burke was already making love with other men. Had Burke seen Will being pushed along in his stroller by his parents, he would hardly have looked at the infant making googly eyes at him and thought about how one day they would be making out.

That's just wrong, he thought as he turned the developing tank over. *But he's not a child. He's a grown man. And he's the one who kissed you, remember.*

He wondered if he would feel differently if Will weren't Mars's son. He thought he probably would, but there was really no way to know. Of course, if Mars found out about it, things would probably get ugly. He doubted Mars had any idea his son was into other men. But maybe he did. Maybe in the years since high school he'd learned to accept things like that.

Burke poured fixer into the developing tank and agitated it for thirty seconds. He emptied the fixer back into the bottle to reuse it, then unscrewed the lid of the developing tank and removed the reel. He inspected the film, decided it looked fine, and replaced the reel. He set the developing tank beneath the tap and turned on the water, letting it fill the tank halfway. Replacing the lid, he agitated the tank for thirty seconds, then emptied it and once again filled it halfway.

He repeated this process for ten minutes, during which he continued arguing with himself about the wisdom of maybe pursuing something with Will Janks. With every emptying of the developing tank, he talked himself out of it, and with every refilling, he changed his mind. By the time he was finished rinsing the film, he was exhausted, not from the physical effort of developing the film, but from the mental effort expended in fretting over a kiss.

After the final emptying of the developing tank, he added a few drops of wetting agent and allowed it to sit for half a minute, tapping the sides of the tank to remove any bubbles that might have formed on the surface of the film. Then he removed the reel, gently twisted its two halves apart, and pulled the film free. To one end he attached a weighted film clip, and to the other an unweighted one. Then he hung the strip from the shower curtain rod and left it to dry while he went downstairs.

"Is it soup yet?" his father asked when Burke walked into the kitchen. Lucy was sitting at the table, doing a crossword puzzle in the newspaper, while Burke's father rinsed a chicken in the sink. Burke couldn't help but notice that several small reddish feathers remained on the chicken's body.

"That isn't one of yours, is it?" he asked his father.

"Killed not half an hour ago," his father answered.

Burke looked away. It was years since he'd endured the horrors of chicken killing: the blood, the smell, the warm innards, which had to be scooped out by hand, the feathers, which had to be plucked off and which stuck to everything. For years after leaving the farm, he'd avoided chicken altogether, and then he'd eaten it only when it was smothered in sauce or otherwise unrecognizable. It had taken a long time for him to look at a roast chicken without getting queasy, and he'd been relieved to find on his first night back that he could eat it again.

"The film is hanging up to dry," he said, trying not to think about the chicken. "It takes about six hours."

"We'll be asleep by then," his father said.

"Don't worry," said Burke, looking at Lucy and winking. "I'll wake you up."

He managed to make it through dinner, although the chicken leg on his plate was largely intact when he scooped the remains into the trash. And true to his word, his father was in bed and asleep by nine o'clock, although Lucy stayed up and played cards with him until a little after ten.

By eleven the film was dry and he had cut it into manageable strips. He'd already hooked the scanner up to his laptop, and now it was just a matter of scanning the film. He put the first strip in and waited as the machine transferred the images to his computer. It took some time, and he was impatient. But finally the first three photos were processed.

They were beautiful. The Yashica-Mat's lenses appeared to be clean, with no mold or dust to mar the photographs. Each of the square images was lovely in its simplicity. The rock with the turtles. A grouping of wildflowers. A single leaf floating on the water, a dragonfly riding it like a raft. Burke was more than pleased, both with the camera and with his eye.

He fed another strip of negatives into the scanner, then another.

In the space of an hour he had scanned the entire first roll. And there were three more waiting to be developed. He couldn't wait.

As the last group of images appeared on the screen, he looked at them. The last one caught his attention. It showed Will's face reflected in the surface of the water. Burke didn't remember taking it, and he was startled by its unexpected beauty. Will wore an expression of total happiness.

But something was wrong with the picture. When he looked closer, he saw that there was a large cloudy spot to the right of Will's face. At first he thought it might really be a cloud, or perhaps ripples in the pond, but on closer examination it was definitely something wrong with the film itself.

He attributed the aberration to the processing. It was the last frame on the roll, and sometimes, despite taking all the usual precautions, those photos suffered from exposure to light. And really, it made the image even more arresting. Will's face was in perfect focus, and the cloudiness beside it only emphasized his beauty. Burke found himself staring at the young man's face and thinking about their kiss.

A minute later he had made up his mind.

CHAPTER 11

"It's a plant." Burke's father stared at the laptop's screen, peering over his glasses at the photos as Burke brought them up.

"It's not *just* a plant, Ed," Lucy said, looking at Burke and shaking her head. "It's about the *feeling* of the image."

Burke's father snorted. "Well, it *feels* like a plant." He turned to his son. "I'm not saying it's not pretty. But it's a plant."

"It is indeed," Burke agreed. He was trying very hard not to be irritated with his father. The photos were some of the most interesting ones he'd taken, and he was excited about them. But to his father, they might as well have been snapshots of the back garden.

"These remind me of Sugimoto," Lucy remarked. "The sparseness is really lovely."

Burke was impressed that she knew the work of the Japanese photographer. He was one of Burke's favorites, and secretly he'd always hoped to achieve the same aesthetic with his work.

"I guess I just don't get art," said Burke's father, standing up. "It's too much for this farm boy's brain."

"You make it sound like you're a country bumpkin, Dad," Burke teased. "In case you've forgotten, you do have a degree in finance. You make it sound like you've been working the land for fifty years, instead of helping people invest their money and making yourself a tidy little pile in the process."

His father made a vague sound. "I should probably get back to work."

"Sure, Dad," said Burke. "Those sheep won't graze themselves."

With his father gone, Burke relaxed. Lucy understood what he was doing. It would be nice if his father showed a little more enthusiasm, but Burke had long ago given up on that happening. His mother had enjoyed what he did, and she hadn't really understood it, either, but his father was hopeless. Sometimes it felt to Burke that he was deliberately trying *not* to understand his son's work.

"Don't let him bother you," said Lucy. She was scrolling through the pictures, looking at each one intently. "He's just afraid of looking foolish."

"It's not like I'm asking him to explain the origins of the universe," Burke replied.

Lucy turned to him. "Do you know he doesn't read fiction?" she said. "None. Won't even try. I tried to get him to read *Life of Pi* when my book group read it. He said he didn't see any point in made-up stories. I know he was afraid he wouldn't understand it."

"Now that you mention it, I haven't ever seen him read a book," said Burke. "I guess I never noticed. Mom was always reading. She read enough for both of them."

Lucy looked thoughtful. "Maybe that's part of it, too," she said. "Maybe books remind him of her." She had stopped at one of the photos on Burke's laptop. "This one is beautiful," she said.

Burke looked over her shoulder. She was looking at the picture of Will.

"He's such a handsome young man," Lucy said.

"You think so?" said Burke.

"Oh, all the girls are after him," Lucy told him.

Burke hesitated before asking, "And none have landed him?"

Lucy nodded. "He has a girlfriend," she said.

Burke felt his stomach drop. *He has a girlfriend,* he thought. The news upset him more than he would have thought.

"Donna Lewis," Lucy continued, still looking at the photo. "Nice girl. She was Maple Syrup Queen last summer. This almost looks like a face."

"What?" said Burke.

"This," Lucy said, pointing to the cloudy area on the photograph. "It looks like a face. Well, a little bit, anyway. There's the nose, and that could be a mouth. It's missing eyes, though."

Burke peered at the photo. Now that Lucy had mentioned it, the cloudiness did resemble—in a very primitive way—a head. It was as if someone were standing behind Will, looking into the water with him.

"That's kind of creepy," said Burke.

"I used to love finding shapes in the clouds when I was a girl," Lucy said.

"That's not a cloud, though," Burke told her. "It's just bad processing."

"Really?" Lucy said. "It looks so natural."

Burke straightened up. "Some of the most interesting art is accidental," he remarked. He was still thinking about Donna Lewis. He wondered what she looked like, and pictured a thin, giggly girl with blond hair and huge breasts. He pictured Will kissing her.

"When will you develop the others?"

Lucy's question broke the spell, and the image dissipated. "I did it this morning," said Burke. "They're hanging up to dry."

Lucy smiled. "You're certainly getting around well," she said.

"Yeah," Burke agreed. "It's not nearly as bad as I thought it would be."

"And here I was hoping you'd be with us all summer," said Lucy. "It's selfish of me, I know. But I like having you here, and I know your father does, too."

Burke didn't argue this point. He knew Lucy was just being nice, at least about his father being happy to have him there. *He's probably as anxious to be rid of me as I am to be out of here,* he thought.

"I'm supposed to go to a doctor in Montpelier this week," Burke told Lucy. "To see how the leg is healing. Dr. Liu set it up. We'll see what he says."

Lucy stood up. "I hope it's bad news," she said, patting his cheek. "I'll go make you some breakfast."

"I thought you made Dad do all the cooking," said Burke.

Lucy smiled at him. "I make the occasional exception," she said. "Don't tell your father. He's just looking for an excuse to hand over that particular duty."

She went into the kitchen, and Burke shut the laptop down. He was thinking of Will again. The young man was supposed to come by to look at the photos later. Burke had been excited about showing them to him. Now the thought just made him sick.

Don't be stupid, he chastised himself. *It's not as if the two of you are lovers. Why are you so upset?*

He had no answer for this question. He just knew that he was. He didn't want Will to have a girlfriend. *It's like Mars all over again,* he thought. *We're going to pretend nothing ever happened.*

He went upstairs and checked on the film. It was almost dry enough to scan. But now he didn't care whether he scanned it or not. The news about Will had sapped a lot of his excitement about the photographs. "Maybe Dad is right," he said to the empty bathroom as he looked at the strips of film hanging from the curtain rod. "Maybe they're just pictures of plants."

Lucy called him down for breakfast a few minutes later. She'd made eggs and bacon, all of it perfectly cooked. Burke ate, but without enthusiasm. He felt guilty about not enjoying the food more, but his bad mood was getting worse. "This is great," he told Lucy, his voice overly enthusiastic.

He was finishing the last of the bacon when Will appeared outside the kitchen's screen door. "Knock, knock," he said.

"Will!" Lucy said. "Come in. Can I get you some coffee?"

"No, thanks," Will answered. "I've already had three cups this morning. Any more and I'll get twitchy." He looked at Burke. "How'd they come out?"

"They're *wonderful,*" Lucy told him.

"Yeah?" Will said, waiting for Burke's verdict.

"Come upstairs," said Burke. "See for yourself." He went up the stairs ahead of Will, his irritation growing with each step. As soon as they were in his room, he turned around. "What are you doing?" he asked.

Will, confused, furrowed his brow. "Coming to look at pictures?" he said.

"What would Donna think about you kissing me?" Burke said.

Will shut his eyes and sighed. "Who told you about her?"

"That doesn't matter," said Burke. "The real question is, why didn't *you* tell me about her?"

Will turned and shut the door to the room. "I was going to," he told Burke.

Burke sat down on the bed. Suddenly his leg hurt. He didn't say anything in response to Will's words. He just waited for him to continue.

"Donna's just a . . . ," he began.

"A what?" asked Burke when Will didn't finish the sentence. "A friend?"

"No," Will said. "She's more than that."

"Does she know you kiss other men?"

Will's face flushed. "You don't understand," he said.

"I think I do," Burke countered. "You like banging girls, but you've wondered what it might be like with a guy. You thought you'd give it a try. So tell me, was it what you expected?"

Will ran his hands through his hair. "That's not it," he said. He paced back and forth, seemingly trying to find the right words. "I know I like guys, okay? I mean, I haven't really done much, but I know I like it."

"But?" Burke asked.

"But my dad," said Will. "This place. You don't know what it's like."

Burke laughed. "No, I don't know anything about that," he said. "I only grew up here with your father." He resisted adding that he and Will's father had engaged in a little man-on-man action of their own. *Like father, like son,* he couldn't help thinking.

"You got out," Will continued. "I don't know if I can. I *want* to. I just don't know if I can do it."

"Why?" said Burke. "Does your dad lock you in at night? Are you forbidden to leave the county? Come on, Will. You're a grown man. You can do what you want to."

Will shook his head. "They expect me to be a certain way," he argued. "If my father thought I was . . ."

"So you're going to hide your whole life?" said Burke. "You're going to marry Donna, have a couple of kids, and play country vet forever? Maybe sneak off every now and again for a blow job or a quick fuck in a men's room, or hook up with some guy online? This isn't 1956, Will. In case you hadn't noticed, a lot of people manage to escape the *expectations* their families have for them."

Will sat beside him on the bed. "I know that," he said.

"But it's different for you, right?" said Burke. "You're different. Things are *harder* for you."

"Why are you being such a dick?" Will asked.

Because you're doing the same thing to me that your father did, Burke thought. *Because I know what's going to happen to you if you don't get out of this place.* "I'm not being a dick," he answered. "I'm reacting the way people do when they find out they've been lied to."

"I didn't lie," Will objected.

"Right," said Burke, nodding. "You just didn't tell me. The sin of omission is still a sin, Will. You let me think that maybe—" He stopped as he realized what he was about to say.

"Maybe what?" asked Will.

"Nothing," Burke said. "You let me think something that isn't true is all."

There was a long silence as neither of them spoke. Outside Old Jack whinnied. The bed shook as Will laughed. "I think he's feeling better," he said.

Burke knew Will was trying to break the tension, but he wasn't ready to let him off the hook. His irritation at being deceived had grown into a larger disappointment over Will's apparent inability to claim his life as his own. The young man was allowing himself to be bullied into hiding who he was. *No, it's worse than that,* he thought. *He's doing this to himself.*

"What did your parents say when you told them?" Will asked after a moment.

"Told them what?" asked Burke.

"That you're . . . you know."

He can't even say the word, thought Burke. "Gay," he said. "The word is *gay.*"

"I know what it is," Will said.

"Then say it," said Burke. "If you can't even say it, you'll never be able to be it. Or maybe that's what you want. Maybe you think that if you never say the word, you'll never have to deal with it. Good idea. But it doesn't work that way."

"Gay!" Will said sharply. "Gay. There. Are you happy? I said it."

"You forgot the 'I am' part," Burke said. "'I am gay.' Say that."

"Fuck you," Will spat. "I don't owe you anything. And you haven't answered my question."

"What did my parents say?" Burke was suddenly embarrassed. "They didn't say anything. I never told them."

"They don't know?" said Will. "Your dad doesn't know?"

"Of course he knows," Burke answered. "My mother knew, too. We just never talked about it. I kind of let them figure it out on their own."

"And you're telling me how I should live *my* life?" said Will.

"Things were different then!" Burke argued.

"Oh yeah?" Will countered. "How? It wasn't 1956."

Burke started to snap back but stopped. To his surprise, he laughed. "You're right," he said. "You're right. I don't really have an excuse for that. I guess I was just scared."

"Then don't expect more from anyone else," said Will. "It's not fair."

"Maybe not," Burke agreed. "But is it fair to Donna to let her think you're someone else? More important, is it fair to you?"

Will didn't answer. He was looking at the floor, his hands folded in his lap as his thumbs tapped against each other anxiously. Seeing this, Burke felt bad for pushing him so hard. *What he needs is someone who doesn't judge him,* he thought. *What he needs is a friend.*

"I'm sorry," he said quickly.

After a moment Will nodded. "Me too," he said.

Burke picked up the laptop and opened it. "Let's look at some pictures," he said.

CHAPTER 12

"Here's everything," Lucy said, setting a cardboard box on the kitchen table. "Took me a while to find it. I'd stuck it in with the boxes of china in the cellar. I don't know why."

"When are you just going to move in here?" Burke asked as he opened the box. "You're here all the time, anyway."

"You really do sound like your father," said Lucy. "'Why don't we get married?' 'Why don't you move in?' You Crenshaw men really are a pushy bunch."

"Sorry," Burke said. "But it does seem like the logical thing to do."

"Life isn't always logical," said Lucy. "I like having my own house. I like knowing it's there."

"You mean you like having an escape route," Burke teased.

"Yes," Lucy admitted. "I do. I spent most of my life with one man. I may spend the rest of it with one man. But you never know."

"Good for you," Burke said. He lifted a smaller box out of the larger one. "Here we are," he said, removing the lid and finding a stack of photographs.

Intrigued by the pictures in Jerry's book, he'd asked Lucy if she still had the originals. To his delight, she did. Now she'd brought him all of Jerry's original materials. He flipped through the photos, amazed at how clear most of them were. At the time of the Civil War, photography was still in its infancy, yet some of the images were strikingly vivid.

"Where did he get these?" Burke asked Lucy.

"Oh, all kinds of places," Lucy answered. "The Library of Congress, the Center for Civil War Photography, the Henry Sheldon Museum in Middlebury. Some he got directly from people whose family members were in the army. The source should be written on the back of each photo. Jerry was very good about that kind of thing."

Burke flipped over the photograph he was currently looking at, a battlefield scene depicting the aftermath of a confrontation. "The Civil War Photography Project," he read. "Photograph by Alexander Gardner."

"I wanted to use all the photos in the book, but it would have been too expensive," Lucy said. "I had to choose the ones that would reproduce the best. It's too bad, because there are some wonderful personal ones in there."

Burke looked through some more pictures. Many he'd seen in Jerry's book, but many more were new to him. Mostly they were battlefield scenes, but there were also photographs of individual soldiers. These were most interesting to him. The expressions on the faces of the men fascinated him. Some looked into the camera with tired eyes, as if submitting to an ordeal, while others faced the lens defiantly, their faces proud and determined.

Then he came to a photo that was different from anything else he'd seen. It was a picture of two men and a woman. The woman was standing in the middle. Her dress was plain, and her hair was pulled into a bun. The man to her left was dressed in the familiar uniform of a Northern soldier. He had a short beard, strong features, and eyes that looked straight ahead. His arm was around the woman's waist. On the woman's right was the other man. Younger than the first, and without a beard, he was dressed in dark pants and a checked shirt, open at the neck. But instead of looking at the camera, his head was turned so that he was looking at the woman beside him.

No, Burke thought as he examined the photograph more closely. *He's looking at the other man.* All three were standing in front of a large tree. In the distance behind them was a small house.

At first he thought the younger man might be the couple's son, but he was clearly not much younger than they were. He turned the photo over to see if the subjects were identified. Unlike the other pictures, which were neatly labeled, this one had only a note scrawled in pencil: "A. Hague and T. Beattie."

"Amos Hague," Burke said. "The fellow who wrote the letter."

Lucy turned from the sink, where she was washing strawberries. "Isn't that a lovely photo?" she said. "It's a pity I couldn't use it."

"Why didn't you?" Burke asked.

"I don't know where it came from," Lucy replied. "And I'm not certain the identification is correct."

"But it says it's Amos Hague and Tess Beattie," said Burke.

"Look more closely," Lucy said. "There's a question mark after their names."

"Is this Jerry's handwriting?"

"Could be," said Lucy. "It's similar, anyway. The other problem is that second fellow. There's nothing about him."

"And you don't know where the photo came from?"

Lucy shook her head. "It's a bit of a mystery," she said.

Burke turned the picture over again and looked at the man who might or might not be Amos Hague. He tried to imagine him writing the things in the letter. Then he tried to imagine the young woman—presumably Tess—reading them. Despite the intimacy of their pose, Burke had a difficult time imagining them exchanging such romantic words. Amos Hague the soldier didn't look like a man who would crush sweet flag between his fingers because the smell reminded him of his woman at home.

Then again, they all looked like that in photos back then, he reminded himself. The overly formal style was ubiquitous, as though the subjects were all afraid of revealing their true selves. Only the younger man in the photograph seemed to be at ease, and he was looking away from the camera.

"Do you think he's going off to or coming back from war?" Lucy asked.

"Amos?" Burke said. "It's hard to tell, isn't it? I'd say going off to. They all look very stoic about the whole thing."

"I can't decide," said Lucy. "Not that it matters. It's still a striking image."

"In the book it says Tess is from Sandberg," Burke said. "Do you know if Amos was as well?"

"I don't," Lucy answered. "I meant to find out what became of them, but there were so many other things to do, and I just never did. That letter is the only other thing connected to Amos Hague, so I didn't have much to go on."

"And where did that come from?" asked Burke.

"The Sheldon Museum, if I remember correctly," Lucy said. "They have quite a collection of correspondence there. Anyway, the source should be noted in the book."

She finished rinsing the berries and wiped her hands on a dish-cloth. "Here," she said, bringing Burke a strawberry. "Right out of our own patch."

Burke bit into the fruit. "Sweet," he said. "Usually the homegrown ones are kind of bitter."

"It's all the manure," said Lucy. "It makes them tastier."

Burke grimaced. "Thanks," he said. "Now I can never eat another strawberry as long as I live."

"Nonsense," said Lucy. "Manure's natural. It's better than all those chemicals they spray on them. Besides, it's Old Jack's manure, and he's family."

"You're something else," Burke told her. "You know that?"

Lucy bit into a strawberry. "I've been told," she said.

"Did Jerry serve in any of the wars?" asked Burke.

"Korea," Lucy told him. "He was a communications specialist. We met not long before he joined the army. I was still in high school when he left."

"It must have been difficult," said Burke.

"Not as difficult as explaining to my parents how I got pregnant," said Lucy.

Burke looked up, surprised. "Pregnant?" he said. "But—"

"I lost the baby," Lucy interrupted. "There were complications. It was a long time ago."

"I'm sorry," said Burke, not knowing what else to say.

"I remember telling my father that I *had* to sleep with Jerry be-cause he might be killed over in Korea," Lucy said. "I think that actu-ally made sense to him, because he wasn't nearly as upset as I thought he would be. Although he did write to Jerry, telling him we would be getting married the instant he came home. Unfortunately, that was the first Jerry had heard about there being a baby, too. It took a cou-ple of letters back and forth to get it all sorted out. And my mother went out and bought me a wedding ring at Woolworth's and made me tell everyone that Jerry and I had eloped."

"And how old were you?" Burke asked.

"Sixteen," said Lucy. "Almost seventeen. I know it sounds awful, but secretly I was terribly pleased about it. I loved Jerry, and I wanted to have his baby." She laughed. "This was before women started looking at their vaginas in hand mirrors and Gloria Steinem told us we could be more than just mothers," she said. "When I lost the baby, I was devastated. I thought I'd failed Jerry somehow."

"I can't even imagine," Burke said.

"I remember my mother telling me that God had a reason for taking my baby," said Lucy. "Some nonsense about needing more cherubim or something like that. I hated her so much at that moment. She couldn't just say, 'This is a horrible thing that's happened to you, and I wish I could make it better, but I can't.' She had to pretend it was all for the best. And, of course, we never talked about it again."

"Family secrets," Burke said.

"How did we start talking about this?" Lucy asked. "Oh, yes, the photograph." She picked it up and stared at it for a moment. "I think he's leaving," she said. "For one thing, his uniform is too clean. For another, the girl looks as if she's expecting the worst. In my day she would have been grinning from ear to ear, pretending everything was just fine." She set the photo down. "No wonder so many of us became alcoholics," she said thoughtfully.

"Who's an alcoholic?" Burke's father asked as he came through the screen door.

"All women my age," Lucy answered. "And it's because men your age drove us to it."

Burke's father turned on the water and began washing his hands. "Well, I apologize for that," he said.

"It's all right," said Lucy. "You didn't do it on purpose."

Burke's father turned around, drying his hands on a dish towel. "More photos?" he asked.

"These are from the Civil War," Burke explained. "We were just looking at them." He handed his father the picture he and Lucy had been discussing. "What do you think is going on in this one?"

His father looked at the photo, peering over the top of his glasses. "I think that young man on the right is very happy that the one on the left is going off to war, because it means he'll have that pretty young lady all to himself."

Burke and Lucy exchanged glances. "That never occurred to me," Lucy said.

Burke's father chuckled. "That's because you're not a man," he said.

But I am, Burke thought, *and it didn't occur to me, either.* "You think he's jealous of Amos?"

"Who's Amos?" his father asked. "The soldier? Yes, I think he is. I think both gentlemen have an interest in that young lady. What's her name?"

"Tess," Burke told him.

"I think both gentlemen have an interest in Tess. As Amos has his arm around her, my guess is he's the one with a claim on her. The other fellow . . . What's his name?"

"We don't know," said Lucy.

"Let's call him George," said Burke's father. "George there is hoping that Amos will go away and get himself killed. I don't know what Tess is hoping. You never can tell with women."

"An interesting theory," Burke said. "Maybe you're right."

"Doesn't much matter, does it?" his father said. "They're all dead."

Lucy looked at him, shaking her head. "You're an incurable romantic, you know that?" she said.

"I do my best," said Burke's father. He looked over at Burke. "I spoke to Will this morning. He's going to drive you to your appointment in Montpelier tomorrow."

"Will?" said Burke. "Why?"

"Says he has to go there, anyway, to pick up something for his father. It saves me a trip, and I didn't think you'd mind."

"No," Burke said. "It's fine. I just don't want to put anybody out." *Which, apparently, I am,* he thought. *I'm only too happy to save you a trip.*

"He'll be by around eight," his father said. "That should give you plenty of time."

It certainly should, thought Burke. Despite the fact that his anger at Will had diminished, he still didn't relish the idea of spending a couple of hours with him in such close quarters. But apparently Will felt otherwise, as he'd volunteered for the job. Burke hoped everything would be okay. *You're the grown-up,* he reminded himself. *It's up to you.*

He looked at his father. "I'll be ready," he said.

CHAPTER 13

D r. Radiceski clipped the films to the light box and flipped the switch, revealing Burke's bones. He pointed to an obvious fault line. "You've been putting too much pressure on it," he said. "Didn't Dr. Liu tell you to stay off it?"

"She might have," Burke mumbled.

The doctor raised one eyebrow. "I thought she might have," he said. "You should have listened to her. I'm afraid you'll have to have that cast on for longer than we—and especially you—had hoped."

"How much longer?" asked Burke.

"I'm estimating another six weeks," the doctor answered.

"Six weeks?" Burke said, groaning.

"That's only two weeks longer than we originally planned," Dr. Radiceski told him. "It's your own fault for rushing things. Try to take it easy."

"I don't want to take it easy!" Burke said. "Taking it easy is making me nuts. Did I tell you I'm staying with my father? You have no idea."

"Oh, I do," the doctor said. "*My* father is staying with *me* while he recuperates from a broken hip. Believe me, that's no day at the circus. My partner keeps threatening to put on the naughty nurse costume he wore last Halloween, just to see if it gives Dad a heart attack."

"Does your partner look good in a naughty nurse's uniform?" Burke asked.

"He's a bear," Dr. Radiceski said. "What do you think?"

Burke laughed in spite of himself. "That's a mental image I didn't need," he joked.

"The white patent pumps are the worst part," said the doctor.

"Can I ask how your father is with the whole thing?" said Burke. "You know, living with you and your partner."

"He's fine with it," Dr. Radiceski said. "He's actually an Episcopal priest. Vermonter born and bred. Doesn't think either the government or God should interfere in your personal life. In fact, he officiated at Buck's and my wedding."

"Nice," Burke said.

"How about your father?" the doctor asked. "Is he okay with you and your partner being there?"

"Partner?" said Burke, confused.

"The fellow in the waiting room," Dr. Radiceski said.

"He's not . . . We're not together," Burke told him. "He's just a friend. I'm not with anyone right now."

"That's too bad," the doctor said. "Well, stay off the leg, and come back in two weeks for another X-ray."

What does he mean, too bad? Burke wondered as he got up. *He said it like he was telling me I have cancer. When did being single become a disease?*

He walked to the waiting room, where Will was sitting, looking at a copy of *Highlights* magazine. He looked up when Burke came in. "I can find only six differences between the two pictures," he said, showing Burke the puzzles page at the back of the magazine. "They claim there are seven, but I think they're just fucking with me." He set the magazine down. "Everything okay?"

"Six more weeks," Burke said shortly. "So no, not okay."

"Ouch," Will replied. "Sorry. Well, I went and picked up the vaccines Dad needs, so we can head home. Or we can hang out in town for a while if you want to. The vaccines are on ice in a cooler. They'll be fine for a few hours."

Burke weighed his options—going back to his father's house and lying around, or spending some time in an actual city. "Let's stay," he said. "Maybe we can find some real coffee."

They left the doctor's office and walked down the street. "You look like a monkey," Will remarked as Burke did the peculiar step-swing-step movement with the crutch.

"Thank you," said Burke. "That's exactly how I feel."

"Come on," Will said. "Six weeks isn't that long. Besides, it gives us more time to hang out."

"Why?" asked Burke. His bad mood was getting worse as they walked, and the question sounded harsher than he meant it to.

"I don't know," Will said. "Because I like you?"

Burke stopped. "Look," he said. "I like you, too. But we have a problem here. I had a pretty good time kissing you, and I think you liked it just as much as I did. Then I find out you have a girlfriend, and you tell me that you can't ever be who we both know you are. That makes things a little difficult, don't you think?"

"I did like it," Will said. "And I wouldn't mind doing it again." He gave Burke the half grin that made Burke weak in the knees. "Wouldn't you?"

"What about what's-her-name . . . Donna?"

Will shrugged. "What about her?"

Burke shook his head. "Don't you think she might be just a little bit upset if she knew her boyfriend was cheating on her with another man?"

"Honestly? I think she'd be more upset if you were another girl," Will said.

"I need to sit down," Burke said. "Let's find a coffee shop or something." He saw a Starbucks a block away. "There's civilization," he said, thinking of Gregg.

They walked to the shop, and Burke took a seat at one of the outside tables and sent Will inside to get drinks. It was pleasantly warm, and the table was in the shade. Burke felt himself calming down as he watched people coming and going. They all seemed impossibly young, and he suddenly felt very old. When Will appeared, set a latte in front of him, and handed him some bills and coins, saying, "Here's the change, Pop," Burke responded with, "Keep it up. You're not too old for a spanking."

"Oh, that sounds fun," Will replied.

"Have you ever even done it with a guy?" Burke heard himself ask. "And by *it,* I mean anything involving a dick and an orifice."

Will blushed. "Sure," he said.

"Details," Burke demanded.

Will sipped his coffee. "This is kind of embarrassing," he said.

Burke didn't give him the out he was looking for. Instead, he just stared at Will until the young man shook his head.

"Okay," Will said. "I got a blow job from this guy at baseball camp in tenth grade."

"That's it?" said Burke. "One blow job?"

"And I jacked off with a guy in the bathroom at Home Depot once," Will told him. "He was doing it when I walked in, and it just kind of happened."

"That's not exactly an extensive résumé," Burke said. "I assume you've done more than that with Donna."

Burke shook his head. "She's a virgin," he said. "Seriously," he added when Burke gave him a look of disbelief. "She wears one of those stupid purity rings."

"I suppose that makes things easier for you," said Burke. "But what are you going to do when she wants to get busy?"

"I've done it with other girls," said Will. "I just think about . . . other stuff. It's not that hard, really."

"And that's what you want to do for the next fifty or sixty years?" said Burke. "Think about other stuff?"

"Do we have to talk about this shit again?" Will asked.

"I'm just trying to figure out what it is you want," said Burke.

"Okay," Will said. "I'll tell you what I want. What I *want* is to go to New York and be an actor. But that's not going to happen. And what my dad wants is for me to be a vet. But I couldn't get into vet school. So what I'm *going* to do is stay in Dullston and help him out until I find something else to do."

Burke had to laugh at Will's nickname for the town. "Your dad and I used to call it Dullston, too," he said. "Did you get it from him?"

Will shook his head. "To hear him tell it, Wellston is the best place on earth," he said. "He used to think it was boring?"

"All he talked about was getting out," said Burke. "I guess that changed. So, you want to be an actor?"

Will shrugged. "I'd like to," he said. "I did a couple of plays in school. But like I said, that's a stupid dream. There are a million guys who want to be actors."

"And some of them make it," said Burke. "The difference between you and them is that they *believe* they can. You're giving up before you've even tried."

"I did try," Will replied. "When I didn't get into vet school, I told my parents I wanted to move to New York. It didn't go over well."

"But it's *your* life," Burke insisted. "And you only get one. Don't you want to do something with it?"

"Maybe I should be a model," said Will, grinning. "I look pretty good in that picture you took of me. Too bad about the splotchy thing. But we can always take more."

"We'll see," said Burke. He was in no mood to indulge Will's play-fulness. It annoyed him that he wasn't taking his own life seriously.

"I don't get why you care what *I* do with my life," Will said.

"I care because things are supposed to be different for you," said Burke. "You're supposed to be who you are instead of hiding it. You're supposed to be proud of it. You're supposed to get married, for fuck's sake. This is what people my age dreamed about, and you're going right back in the closet."

"I guess I don't see it that way," Will said.

"Apparently not," said Burke. "But can you see why it pisses me off?"

"I guess," Will admitted. "But it's still my life."

Burke leaned back in his chair. "Fair enough," he said.

"Why don't you have a boyfriend?" Will asked.

Burke looked at him. "Why do you think I don't have one?"

"Because you think you know everything?" Will suggested.

"Maybe I do know everything," Burke countered.

"Do you even want a boyfriend?"

Burke thought for a moment. "I don't know anymore," he admit-ted. "When I was your age, I did. I thought I'd find the right guy and we'd be together forever, like my parents. But I found out it doesn't work that way, at least not for most of the guys I know. I'd find some-one, and we'd be happy for a while. Then one of us wouldn't be happy, and that would be the end of it."

"Sounds great," said Will. "And that's what you think I'm missing out on?"

"It doesn't have to be that way," Burke said. "At least, I don't think it does. I know some couples who have been together for a long time."

"How many?" Will said, pressing.

"Enough to think it's not impossible," said Burke.

"What about kids?" asked Will. "Didn't you ever want kids?"

"You don't need to be married to a woman to have kids," Burke said. "You can always adopt."

"I just asked if you ever wanted them," said Will. "I know you can adopt. Christ, Angelina Jolie has enough for a soccer team."

"I guess maybe I would have liked to have kids," said Burke. "Like I said, it wasn't really an option when I was your age."

"It's not like you're ancient now," Will pointed out. "Even if you adopted now, you'd only be what, seventy, when it graduated from high school?"

"Nice," Burke said. "Smart-ass."

Will grinned. "I'm just pointing out that maybe I'm not the only one who's afraid to have the life he wants."

"At least you're admitting you're afraid," said Burke, ignoring the implication of Will's statement. "That's a start."

"We can't all be Neil Patrick Harris," Will remarked. He looked at his watch. "You ready to go?"

"No," Burke said, shaking his head. The idea of getting in Will's truck and going back to his father's house was about as appealing as going back to jail after escaping for an afternoon. "But I suppose we should."

"You'll survive," Will told him as he helped him up. "And on the way home you can tell me about your first time."

Burke laughed, thinking again about the night with Mars. "How about I tell you about my second time?" he said. "That's a better story."

CHAPTER 14

The Sandberg Public Library was a small brick building that sat between the Dew Drop In Diner and, appropriately enough, a used bookstore. It was on Sandberg's Main Street, which wasn't saying a great deal. Although much larger than Wellston, Sandberg was still not what could be called a metropolis. It had the benefit of being very near both a fairly popular skiing resort and an equally popular lake, however, and therefore enjoyed a brisk tourist trade. Burke had never seen so many maple sugar and moose-emblazoned products in one place. *Now I know where it all comes from,* he thought as he hobbled past shop windows promising 20 percent off all garden items. He wondered if that included the delightful wooden cutouts painted to resemble very large women bending over and displaying their bloomers.

His father had dropped him off and was due to return in an hour, after running some errands for Lucy. That didn't give Burke a huge amount of time, so he headed straight for the library. Pushing open the heavy wooden door, he stepped into a room that looked as if it hadn't changed in a hundred years. Large, heavy wooden shelves lined the walls, while the center of the room was occupied by several equally large and heavy tables, the tops of which were worn smooth from countless elbows. Even the air seemed ancient—warm and filled with dust motes that floated lazily through the shafts of light that came through the tall, wavy-paned windows on either side of the room.

The library was empty, although a lone figure stood behind the long circulation desk to the left of the door. It was a man, and he looked up as Burke entered, a somewhat startled expression on his face, as if Burke were the first person to pass through the doors in a century. Burke smiled and went over to him.

"Hi," he said. "I'm wondering if you can help me."

"I can try," the man answered. He was shorter than Burke and slight of build. His sandy brown hair was cut short but still managed to look as if it needed a trim. He had blue eyes, hidden behind wire-rim glasses, and a short-cropped beard. The sleeves of his white shirt were rolled to the elbow, exposing forearms covered in more sandy-colored hair. "What is it you're looking for?" he asked.

"I'm not entirely sure," Burke admitted. "I've kind of gotten into the history of Vermont soldiers in the Civil War. A friend of mine wrote a book about it."

"Jerry Grant?" the man asked.

"Yes," Burke replied. "You knew him?"

The man nodded. "He did some of his research here," he said. "He was a friend of yours?"

"Not him," Burke admitted. "His wife. She's kind of dating my father." He laughed. "That sounds weird. Dating my dad. Like he's fifteen."

"Wait until he asks to borrow the car," the man said. His voice was low; his tone, dry. At first Burke wasn't sure if he was joking or not.

"I'm Sam Guffrey, by the way," the man said. "Town librarian."

"Burke Crenshaw."

"All right, Burke Crenshaw, what is it you want to know?"

"Well, I'm a photographer," said Burke. "I'm stuck here for the summer, and while I'm here, I thought I might photograph some sites related to the war."

Sam pushed his glasses up his nose. "I assume you know there are no actual battle sites here," he said.

Burke nodded. "I'm thinking something more personal," he said. "Places where the soldiers lived. The other day I was photographing this pond by the ruins of an old house and—"

"The Wrathmore place," Sam said. "I know it."

"Is that what it's called?" said Burke. "All that's there is a foundation."

"And the pond beyond it, through the trees," Sam said. "That's the one."

"The friend who took me there said it dates from the Civil War," said Burke.

"A lot of things around here do," Sam said. "It very well could. I know the last family that lived there was the Wrathmores. That was around the turn of the century."

"Interesting," said Burke. He hesitated. "I don't suppose you know anything about a man named Amos Hague?"

Sam thought for a moment. "Doesn't ring any bells," he said. "Is he a relative of yours?"

Burke shook his head. "One of his letters is in Jerry's book."

"Oh, right," said Sam. "The sweet flag letter. That's an odd one, isn't it?"

"How do you mean?"

"'Take thou also unto thee principal spices, of pure myrrh five hundred shekels, and of sweet cinnamon half so much, even two hundred and fifty shekels, and of sweet calamus two hundred and fifty shekels,'" Sam said. "Exodus thirty, twenty-three," he explained when Burke looked at him blankly. "God is giving Moses the recipe for making anointing oil to consecrate the tabernacle and everything in it. Calamus is another name for sweet flag, although scholars argue about what the exact meaning of the original Hebrew is. But that's the generally accepted translation."

"Sorry," Burke said. "It's been a long time since I read the Bible."

"It's an interesting section," said Sam. "The instructions for building the tabernacle and making sacrifices are very explicit. The directions for putting together an IKEA bookcase should be so easy to follow."

Burke laughed. Sam Guffrey was an odd little man. Burke wondered what his story was. Out of habit he glanced at Sam's left hand, looking for a ring. It was something he did whenever he met someone new. Gregg teased him that he was looking to see if the guy was fair game, but Burke was just curious. He noted that Sam's hand was bare.

"That's why the letter stuck in my mind," Sam continued. "There's something almost ritualistic about how he crushes the sweet flag and inhales the scent. Well, it's not even *almost* ritualistic. It *is* ritualistic. You might already know this, but sweet flag ingested in high doses can act as a hallucinogen."

"No," said Burke, "I didn't know that."

Sam nodded and pushed his glasses up again. "It can," he said. "So now we have a plant that is used in anointing oil and can cause visions. The fact that Amos Hague was using it to invoke visions of Tess Beattie is fairly, well, provocative."

"Provocative," Burke repeated. "I suppose it is. So, do you know anything else about Amos and Tess?"

"Unfortunately, no," said Sam.

"Do you know where Jerry got the letter and photo?"

"Photo?" Sam said. "There's a photo?"

"Yes," Burke replied. "I didn't bring it, but next time I come in, I will."

"I didn't know about a photo," said Sam. "As for the letter, I think Jerry got it from the Sheldon Museum. I have a friend over there. I can give him a call if you like."

"I'd appreciate that," said Burke. "I don't know why this guy has piqued my interest, but he has."

"History has a way of doing that," Sam said. "That's why I became a librarian. Nobody cares if I spend all day looking up obscure information."

"They even pay you to do it," said Burke.

"I suppose they do," Sam agreed. "I hadn't thought of it like that."

How could you not? Burke wondered.

"Is there anything else I can help you with?" Sam asked him.

"We can start there," said Burke. "I think I'll pick up some novels while I'm here, though. I just finished *Watership Down,* and I think it's the only thing in my father's house I hadn't read."

"'If a rabbit gave advice and the advice wasn't accepted, he immediately forgot it and so did everyone else,'" said Sam. "That's my favorite line from *Watership Down.*"

"You remember a lot of what you read, don't you?" Burke commented.

"'Show me the books he loves and I shall know the man far better than through mortal friends,'" Sam replied. "Silas Weir Mitchell. Sorry," he added. "It's a bad habit. You're right. Things do stick in my head. Usually they just bang around in there, but every so often two of them collide and—boom. That quote, for instance. We were talking about the Civil War. Mitchell was a physician during the war. He was also a Poet and a novelist."

"Isn't he an actor?" said Burke, recalling hearing the name somewhere before.

"Different one," Sam said. "One was on *My Name Is Earl.* The other one is the inspiration for Charlotte Perkins Gilman's short story 'The Yellow Wallpaper.' Have you read it?"

"No," Burke said. "Should I?"

"Depends on whether or not you want to be depressed for a month," said Sam. "New fiction is over there, if you want something more or less current. Everything else is on the shelves. I'll leave you alone."

Sam went back to the desk, where he immediately started writing something down. As Burke looked through the books Sam had directed him to, he watched the librarian. *What is he writing?* he wondered as the man scribbled ferociously. He certainly was a character.

He turned his attention to the books, finding two or three that didn't look too bad. He was trying to figure out how to carry them to the counter to check them out when his father appeared in the doorway. "Ready to go?" he asked.

"Just a minute," Burke said. "Can you take these for me?"

"Let me," said Sam, coming over and picking the books up.

"I don't have a library card," Burke told him.

"Don't worry about it," Sam said, taking the checkout cards from each book. He wrote on each card. "Burke Crenshaw. You'll be back."

"You're very trusting," said Burke.

Sam wrote something on a piece of paper. "'To be trusted is a greater compliment than to be loved,'" he said. "George MacDonald. This is the number here. Call me in a few days."

Burke took the paper and put it in his pocket. "Thanks," he said. "I will." He looked at the books on the counter. "Dad," he called out, "I need your help."

His father came and picked up the books, nodding at Sam. When they left the library, Burke discovered that his father had parked right in front. "Didn't want you to have to walk too far," he said as he opened the door for his son.

"Did you find everything you were looking for?" his father asked a minute later, as they drove through town.

"Maybe," said Burke. "Sam is going to look up some things for me."

"Queer little fellow, isn't he?" said Ed.

"How do you know he's . . . ," Burke began. *He means it the old-fashioned way,* he realized. "I suppose he is a little . . . queer," he agreed. "He certainly knows a lot."

"Don't know why anyone would want to spend his life stuck in a room full of books," his father said.

"Some people just like knowing things," said Burke. "There's nothing wrong with that."

"I'd rather be *doing*," his father said.

"Did you find everything on Lucy's list?" Burke asked, changing the subject.

"Darn near," said his father.

Burke hesitated before asking his next question. *Just do it,* he urged himself. He took a breath. "I'm glad you found someone," he said.

His father said nothing, looking intently out at the road, as if at any moment someone might dash in front of the car.

"I know it was hard for you to watch Mom get sick," Burke tried. "I can't imagine what it must have been like for you having to take care of her."

"I managed," his father said.

Burke turned to him. "You know, it's okay to say it was painful," he said. "You don't have to pretend it wasn't."

"I didn't say it wasn't," his father said. "I just said I managed."

Burke shook his head. "You really can't talk about how you feel, can you?" he said.

"What's this about?" his father asked. "Don't you like Lucy?"

"Of course I do," Burke answered. "I told you, I'm happy for you."

"Then let's leave it at that," said his father.

"Why should we leave it at that?" Burke said. "Why can't we talk about anything?"

"There's nothing to talk about."

"There is, Dad," Burke said. "We can talk about your life and my life and Mom. We don't have to stick to Old Jack and the weather and the fact that Vermont doesn't have a professional baseball team."

"We've got the Lake Monsters," his father said. "They're good enough."

"Fuck the Lake Monsters!" Burke said.

His father's hands tightened on the wheel, and Burke saw the muscles in his jaw clench. *Just like when I was a kid,* he thought. He knew his father had clamped down tight, both on his words and on his feelings. *He's pretending this isn't happening.*

Burke had a choice. He could keep prodding his father, or he could let it go. His entire life he'd avoided prodding. One of his earliest memories was of standing in the doorway of the kitchen watching his parents fight. It was late at night, and he'd come downstairs for a drink of water. His mother's raised voice stopped him at the door, where neither of his parents noticed him.

He was four, maybe five, not old enough to know what the fight was about but more than able to recognize the frustration in his mother's voice. As she stood by the sink, her hands on her hips, Burke's father sat at the table, his hands folded in front of him and his eyes looking down at the red Formica tabletop as if he were searching for meaning in the gold flecks that speckled the surface. "Talk to me!" Burke's mother said over and over. "Say *something!*"

But he hadn't. Not a word. After several minutes Burke's mother began to wash the dishes in the sink. Burke's father, turning his head, stared silently at her back. Watching him, Burke found himself afraid. Something about his father's refusal to speak frightened him. It was as if he were storing up his anger, and Burke feared that at any moment it would explode, killing them all.

He'd turned and gone back to bed, his drink of water forgotten. And in the morning when he came down for breakfast his mother smiled as she set a plate of eggs and bacon in front of him, and they both pretended that everything was all right. But Burke had never looked at his father in quite the same way ever again.

Burke quickly learned that the answer to the question "How are things?" was always "Fine." Even if it was a lie. "Fine" apparently allowed his father to feel that he'd fulfilled his paternal responsibility by asking. Anything else resulted in uncomfortable silence. Similarly, saying, "I love you" to his father, which Burke had done on only a handful of occasions, was returned with a single nod of the head. Even hugging seemed to trigger something in him, some deep unease that caused his body to become rigid and his arms to turn into pieces of wood.

It wasn't until his first boyfriend, then the second, third, and fourth complained about his inability to communicate that Burke realized he had inherited—or at least learned to emulate—his father's reluctance to show emotion. And it had taken him a long time to overcome it to the extent that he had. But could his father do the same?

Maybe, he thought, *it was too much to ask.* Maybe after so many years it was simply too late. Maybe he just had to accept that his father was a closed book. Burke wondered if Lucy got anything out of him, or if she, too, just didn't bother trying. How many times could you bang on a closed door before you got tired of hurting your hand and went away?

He looked out the window. "Looks like it's going to rain," he said.

CHAPTER 15

"Don't you want to go somewhere else?" Will followed behind as Burke made his way clumsily through the grass. They had returned to the ruins of the Wrathmore farm.

"I want to try a different camera," Burke said. He had brought the little Brownie Hawkeye with him. It was the simplest of the cameras he'd found in the collection of his grandfather's things, essentially a box with a shutter, and the easiest for him to use with a broken arm. There was no focusing to be done, no lenses to manipulate or shutter speeds to consider. All he had to do was press a button and take the picture.

His plan had been to go back to the pond, but now that he was there, he found himself drawn to the field behind the house. The grass there was spotted with patches of brown-eyed Susans and Queen Anne's lace, and he thought they might make a nice background.

"Do you know why this is called Queen Anne's lace?" he asked Will.

"I'm sure you'll tell me," Will said, swatting at a bee that was flying around his head.

"After Queen Anne, wife of James the First," Burke said. "James was a big homo. Well, he was at least bi, but he certainly seemed to prefer men."

"Which has what to do with a flower?" asked Will.

"Nothing," Burke admitted. "It's just interesting. Anyway, the story goes that some of Anne's friends bet her that she couldn't make lace in the shape of a flower. She did, only she pricked her finger, and that's why there's a drop of red in the center of every flower."

Will picked the head from a nearby plant and looked at it. "Sure is," he said. "I suppose now you're going to tell me how the brown-eyed Susan got its name."

"That's an interesting story, too," Burke said, stopping to catch his breath. "According to legend, a girl named Susan was warned by her father not to run through the fields after the hay was harvested, because she might trip and hurt herself. She ignored him and did it, anyway. Sure enough, she tripped and fell. One of the stalks went right into her eye, and when she got up, her eye was stuck to it. It looked just like the flowers that grew in the field, so they named them after her."

"You just made that up," said Will.

"No," Burke said. "But my cousin Rhonda did. She told me that story when I was four, and I fell for it. She also told me the brown-eyed Susans could see me, and that if I did anything bad, Susan's ghost would come for me."

"Nice girl," said Will.

"Yeah, well, she's a proctologist now, so that will tell you something about her." He walked a little farther and found a spot where the grass thinned out a little and the flowers were denser. "Stand over there," he told Will. "You get to be my model."

"I thought you just wanted pictures of flowers," Will said.

"I'll get pictures of flowers," Burke assured him. "But this is a fixed-focus lens, and I can't bend my knee to get close. So I'm going to shoot the flowers *with* you. Now, get over there."

Will did as he was told. "How's this?" he asked, standing in front of a clump of Queen Anne's lace.

"Boring," Burke told him. "You're not posing for a yearbook photo. Try looking interesting."

Will grinned. "Some people think this *is* interesting," he said. "What do you want me to do? Stand on my head?"

"Can you?" Burke asked.

Will gave him the finger.

Burke snapped the photo. "That's better," he said as he advanced the film. "At least you did something."

"So that's what you want, is it?" said Will. "Then how's this?"

He unbuttoned the shirt he was wearing and pulled it off, revealing a white wifebeater underneath. He tossed the shirt aside and stood with his thumbs in the loops of his jeans, pulling them down a bit in front.

"Very Abercrombie," Burke teased. "You need to dirty it up somehow."

Will fumbled with the buttons on his fly, opening the top two. His jeans gaped, revealing a forest of dark hair. "Better?" he asked.

Burke didn't answer. He was busy framing Will in the shot. There was something both innocent and sexual about his pose, and having the flowers around him made the scene even more interesting. "Keep doing that," Burke said.

Will cocked an eyebrow. "You mean go lower?" he asked, reaching for his fly. Then his hand stopped. "Or maybe something like this." He pulled the wifebeater over his head, revealing a lean, well-muscled torso. His skin was pale where it was normally covered with a shirt, brown where it was exposed to the sun. His nipples were small, and when he lifted his arms, he exposed underarms furred with dark hair.

He's beautiful, Burke thought as he took another picture.

Will seemed to be settling into his role as model, turning one way and then another, looking directly into the camera and then away. Burke took shot after shot, until the roll ran out.

"I've got to change film," he told Will.

Will walked over to him. He took the camera from Burke's hand and set it on the ground. "I have a better idea," he said, taking Burke's hand and guiding it to his open fly. Burke felt rough hair beneath his fingertips and caught his breath. He hesitated a moment, then went farther. His hand touched Will's cock, which was already half hard. He wrapped his fingers around it and squeezed. Will moaned.

The sun suddenly felt too warm. Burke felt a bead of sweat run down his back. *You shouldn't do this,* he told himself.

Will shucked his jeans down, and his cock sprang free. He was now completely naked. Burke looked down at him and felt himself begin to stiffen.

"Come on," Will said. "Lie down."

He helped Burke onto the ground, where Burke lay on his back in the grass, looking up at the blue summer sky. He allowed Will to unbutton his shirt and pull it open. Then Will was undoing his belt and pulling his shorts and boxers down over his cast. The grass was scratchy against Burke's ass, but he ignored it as Will straddled him, his butt against Burke's thighs and their cocks touching. Will's smooth balls slid along Burke's belly as Will leaned forward and kissed him.

Burke moved his mouth down Will's neck, tasting his sweat. Will moved forward so that Burke could take one of his nipples into his mouth. He bit down gently and felt Will's dick twitch. He reached up and pinched the other one, and again Will's dick responded.

"Turn around," he told Will.

Will obeyed, swinging around so that his ass was on Burke's chest and he was facing Burke's cock.

"Suck me," Burke told him.

As Will bent and took the head of Burke's dick in his mouth, Burke parted Will's ass cheeks with his hands, exposing the rosy center. He leaned forward and tickled Will's asshole with his tongue. Will jumped, clearly unused to the sensation. This made Burke more excited, and he buried his face in Will's ass, holding him in place and moving his tongue, first in slow circles and then in longer, quicker thrusts.

Will worked on Burke's cock inexpertly but enthusiastically. He took as much of it into his throat as he could and used his hand to stroke the remaining length. His own prick leaked precum onto Burke's stomach, falling in thick drips the more Burke tongued his hole. His balls were nestled against Burke's chin, and every so often Burke took them into his mouth, sucking gently.

When Will was wet, Burke slid a finger inside of him. Will pushed back against the pressure, taking Burke to the knuckle. He continued to suck Burke's cock as Burke moved his finger in and out, and gradually Burke felt him relax. He pulled his finger out and pulled Will's face away from his cock. Will, understanding, turned again so that he was once more sitting on Burke's belly. He reached behind and grabbed Burke's cock. Then he lifted himself up, positioned the head of Burke's dick against his asshole, and lowered himself.

He moved slowly. Burke watched his face as his expression changed from one of discomfort to one of tentative pleasure. He resisted the urge to push up into Will's warm ass, letting him go at his own pace. Finally he was all the way in, and Will's ass was pressed against his stomach. Will put his hands on Burke's shoulders and lifted himself up until just the head of Burke's cock was inside of him. Will's ass and thighs were lightly haired, and Burke ran his fingertips gently over them, tracing the lines of muscle.

He kept his eyes open, looking up at Will's face. Behind Will's head the clouds passed slowly. All around them the grass formed a curtain, hiding them from view. A warm breeze caused it to rustle softly. Everything seemed to be happening in slow motion, and Burke had no idea how long their lovemaking had gone on. He felt only the sun and wind and Will's body against his.

He was getting close. His fingers gripped Will's thighs and he closed his eyes as the pressure rose to unbearable heights and exploded. As he came inside of Will, he cried out, his body shivering with the force of his orgasm. Will came right behind him. Thick ropes of cum exploded from his cock, covering Burke's neck and chest with their sticky heat. Will wrapped his fingers around his shaft and stroked, coaxing more from it. Burke felt him shake as he came repeatedly.

Will remained in place for a minute afterward, breathing heavily. Drops of sweat fell from his body onto Burke's. Burke felt the cum on his skin drying in the heat of the sun.

Finally Will slid off of Burke and rolled onto the grass beside him. "Fuck, that was hot," he said. Then he laughed. "You took my cherry," he said. "How's it feel to be a virgin killer?"

Burke wondered if this was true but said nothing. Instead, he picked up Will's wifebeater and wiped his chest with it. "As payment I get to keep this," he said.

Will slapped his leg. "Dirty old man," he said.

"You're the one who took advantage of my disability," Burke teased. "I couldn't have gotten away if I'd wanted to."

"If you'd *wanted* to," Will stressed. "But I don't think you did."

All of a sudden Burke realized something. "We shouldn't have done that," he said. "*I* shouldn't have done that."

Will turned his head. "Done what?" he said.

"I didn't use a condom," said Burke. "Fuck, what was I thinking?"

"Relax," Will said. "It was my first time. You've got nothing to worry about."

"I'm not worried about me," said Burke. "I'm worried about you."

"Why? You have something I should know about?" Will asked.

Burke shook his head. "No," he said. "But you don't know that. Promise me you won't ever do that again."

"With you, or with anyone else?" Will said.

Burke tried to sit up, wincing as pain shot through his leg. "With *anyone*," he said. "Guys my age didn't march and scream and convince themselves condoms are hot just so you guys can get sick all over again."

"Relax," Will said. "Message received. But I think since this is *your* fault, I should get to blow a load up your ass and we can call it even."

"Fucker," Burke said, reaching over and pinching Will's nipple.

"Seriously," Will said. "That was hot."

"Agreed," said Burke. "Not smart, but hot."

"You worry too much," said Will, sitting up. "I told you, it's okay."

He leaned down and kissed Burke, his tongue teasing Burke's. Burke resisted for a moment, then kissed him back. *What are you doing?* he asked himself. *You know this is a bad idea.*

"What is it about this place?" Will asked when they broke apart. "I feel like I'm dreaming."

"You too?" Burke said. "I was thinking the same thing."

"It's like time stopped or something," said Will. He grinned. "Or maybe you just fucked me silly."

"Keep it up and I'll do it again," Burke threatened.

"I'm ready when you are," Will countered, pointing to his cock, which was already hard again.

Burke groaned. "What are you trying to do, kill me?" he asked as he reached for Will's prick. "Come here."

CHAPTER 16

Will held the door open for Burke, then followed him into the library. Upon arriving home the previous afternoon, Burke had been surprised to hear that Sam Guffrey had left a message for him saying he'd found some information about Amos Hague. Will had once again offered to act as Burke's driver, for which Burke was both thankful and pleased. It not only meant not having to ask his father for a ride to the library, but it gave him some more alone time with Will. After their unexpected lovemaking, Burke found himself wondering if perhaps—despite Will's fears about accepting who he was—they might not be able to make something more out of their relationship.

As they approached the circulation desk, Burke saw Sam's gaze rest on Will for a moment before turning to him. He thought he caught in it a hint of appreciation of—or perhaps longing for?—the young man's beauty. Again, he found himself wondering what the librarian's story was.

"Hey, Sam," he said. "Will, Sam Guffrey. Sam, Will Janks."

"Nice to meet you," said Sam.

"Same here," Will replied.

Sam reached beneath the desk and pulled out a file folder, which he laid on the counter and opened. "After you left the other day, I started thinking about that letter," he said. "The one Amos Hague wrote to Tess Beattie. I don't know why I never made the connection before. I feel rather stupid about it now."

"What connection?" Burke asked.

"William Holburne," said Sam. "The young man Amos Hague writes about in the letter," he added when Burke didn't respond.

"Right," Burke said. "The one who died. What about him?"

Sam slid a photograph across the counter. It showed a young man wearing a soldier's uniform and carrying a rifle. "This is William Holburne," he said.

Burke picked the photo up and examined it more closely. William Holburne had a round, almost childlike face. His hair was on the longish side, and he was slight of frame. He looked weary but determined.

It was interesting to see the young man Amos Hague had written to his fiancée about, but Burke didn't understand what Sam had to feel foolish about.

"William Holburne's real name was Elizabeth Frances Walsh," said Sam.

"That dude's a girl?" Will asked, taking the picture from Burke.

Sam nodded. "It's not really as surprising as it may seem. There are quite a number of incidents of young women enlisting in the infantry under assumed names. For the past couple of years I've been doing research about it on and off. Mostly off, which is why I didn't immediately recognize William Holburne's name. But that's definitely him."

"Her," Will corrected.

Sam shook his head. "Technically, yes. But William Holburne is an unusual case. At least I believe he is."

He removed a handful of pages from the folder and spread them out. They were pages of what appeared to be a diary, written in a neat, compact hand.

"These are pages from the journal of Elizabeth Frances Walsh," he told Will and Burke. "Written when she was fifteen years old. What's fascinating about the journal is that in addition to containing the usual teenage complaints about parents and boredom and whatnot, much of it is taken up with stories about a young man named William Holburne. William is the same age as Elizabeth, and he has all kinds of adventures. Most scholars believe these stories are simply that—tales made up by Elizabeth to amuse herself and possibly some younger brothers."

"That makes sense," Burke said.

"It does," Sam agreed. "But when you read the William Holburne stories carefully, there's something about them. I can't quite explain it. It's as if Elizabeth isn't writing about someone else, but she's writing about herself."

"Holburne's not exactly an unusual name up here," said Will. "I went to school with three of them myself."

"That's true," Sam agreed. "Which might also explain why Elizabeth chose it for herself. Besides, there are other similarities in the lives of Elizabeth and William in addition to the coincidence of the name. Elizabeth is reported to have died when she was sixteen. Supposedly she came down with a fever, wandered outside in the night in the middle of a snowstorm, and was never seen again. William Holburne enlisted in the Third Vermont Infantry the following spring."

"Are there records of William Holburne's birth?" Burke asked.

"No," Sam answered. "But that isn't at all unusual. As Will points out, there are a lot of Holburnes in Vermont. And a lot of enlistees falsified their papers. This is almost entirely speculation on my part."

"You sound pretty convinced," Burke remarked.

Sam nodded. "I am," he said.

"I don't get the connection to Amos Hague, though," Burke said. "Apart from William Holburne being mentioned in the letter to Tess, I mean."

"That's where it gets interesting," Sam said. "Well, *more* interesting. There's no official record of William Holburne's death."

"Is that unusual?" asked Burke.

"Fairly," Sam said. "They may have been disorganized about a lot of things during that time, but identifying the dead was of great importance, not only out of respect, but to ensure the proper administration of death benefits to the soldier's surviving family. If William Holburne was killed in action, somebody would have recorded it."

"I'm still lost," said Burke.

"I think Amos Hague helped William Holburne disappear," Sam told him.

"Why would he do that?" asked Will.

Sam shrugged. "Maybe he knew Elizabeth's secret," he suggested. "Or maybe he just wanted to help out a young man he thought didn't belong fighting in a war. Again, this is all hypothetical."

"Where did the photograph of William Holburne come from?" asked Burke.

"A woman named Tanya Redmond," Sam said. "She had a box full of documents and photos that she found in her mother's house when the old woman died last year. She didn't know what they were, but she knew enough to bring them to me."

"And what's her connection to Holburne?"

"I'm not sure," Sam said. "I haven't had time to speak with her about that. The picture was one of maybe fifty or so, all of different people and places."

Burke asked, "Is she a local?"

"She lives out on Parker Road," Sam said. "Has a trailer set back about a quarter of a mile, near the creek."

"A trailer by the creek," Burke said. "That's a real white-trash mansion."

Will laughed, but Sam didn't. "Tanya's a nice woman," he said. "She does the best she can."

Burke, chastened, cleared his throat. "Maybe I should pay her a little visit," he said. "See if she knows anything about Amos Hague."

"I doubt it," said Sam. "She didn't seem to know anything about the papers and photographs when she brought them in. But I've been meaning to ask her about them myself. Mind if I come along?"

Burke looked at Will, who said, "I've actually got to be getting back to help my dad. Any chance we can do this another day?"

"I've got my car here," said Sam. He looked at Burke. "If you like, I can drive us over to Tanya's and then take you home."

"What about the library?" Burke asked.

Sam snorted. "You're the first ones to come in here since, well, the last time you came in here," he said. "I think I can close for a couple of hours without the reading public of Sandberg being inconvenienced."

"What about your leg?" Will said suddenly.

Burke looked at him. The young man had an expression of concern on his face. Burke, surprised and touched, laid a hand on Will's arm. "I think I'll be okay," he said gently.

"All right," said Will. "But be careful. You know what the doctor said. I'll call you tomorrow."

Burke almost expected Will to kiss him on the cheek before leaving, but he didn't. He did, however, turn at the door and give Burke a good-bye wave.

"He seems like a nice guy," Sam remarked.

Burke nodded. "His father and I grew up together." Immediately he regretted sharing this information with Sam. But if Sam thought anything was strange about the situation, he kept it to himself.

"My car's out front," he said, taking some keys from the counter. "I think we'll be able to squeeze you in."

Burke followed him through the front door, which Sam left un-locked. "I'm expecting Ellie Peterbaugh to come in for her biweekly pickup of romance novels," he explained. "She'll just leave the old ones on the counter with the slips from whatever she takes this time. Besides, anyone who would break in is probably too stoned to notice the place is empty."

"Oh, the joys of small-town life," Burke remarked as Sam opened the door of a Subaru wagon that had seen better days.

Sam helped him to sit, putting his hand under Burke's arm and supporting him. Burke was surprised at how strong his grip was. For a small man, he held Burke steady with very little effort. "Everything in?" Sam asked, shutting the door after Burke nodded.

"It was a car accident," Burke said when Sam got behind the wheel.

"Sorry?" said Sam.

"A car accident," Burke repeated. "That's what banged me up. I swerved to avoid hitting a dog or something and ran off the road. I could tell you were wondering but didn't want to ask."

"Actually, I wasn't," said Sam, "but I'm pleased to hear the dog is all right."

Burke didn't know how to respond, so he stayed quiet as Sam started the car and pulled away from the curb. What made you think he wanted to know anything? he asked himself.

"I shouldn't have said that," Sam remarked after they'd driven a mile or so. "I *did* wonder what happened to you. I just wasn't won-dering it when you said you could tell that I was. That's what I meant when I said I wasn't." He paused. "But I am pleased about the dog. I assume it's all right."

"It might not have been a dog," said Burke. "I honestly don't re-member. But I'm told I didn't hit anything."

Sam nodded. "That's good," he said. "So you grew up around here?"

"Yes," said Burke, relieved to have something else to talk about. "I assume you didn't."

"Why's that?" Sam asked.

"For one thing, you don't have the accent," Burke replied. "For another, we're about the same age, and I probably would have heard of you if you'd grown up here."

"Both reasonable assumptions," said Sam. "No, I didn't grow up here. I'm from Montana."

"I don't think I've ever met anyone who was actually from Montana," Burke said.

"That's because both of us left as soon as we could," said Sam. "And we tell everyone we're from other places."

Burke laughed. "I take it you weren't exactly excited about living there."

"It wasn't a great place, no," said Sam. "At least not for me. Conrad Burns, one of our former senators, once described Montana as 'a lot of dirt between lightbulbs.' Of course, he was also one of only two Republicans ever elected to the office, so he might have been a little bitter."

Burke laughed. "How did you get from there to Vermont?"

"Mostly by accident," Sam replied. "I went to college in Ohio and taught third grade for a couple of years. Then I realized that teaching eight-year-olds how to add and subtract wasn't what I wanted to do for the rest of my life, so I went back to college, got my degree in library science, and answered an ad for this position. I've been here for almost fifteen years."

"That's a long time," Burke remarked. "Don't you find it a little boring?"

"No more and no less than anywhere else," said Sam. "Every place has its interesting aspects. Sometimes you just have to look harder to find them."

"True," Burke agreed. "But what about culture? What about friends?"

"You might be surprised at how much of both are available here," said Sam.

Burke shook his head. "I'd go nuts up here," he said. "It was bad enough when I was a kid."

"You seem to have at least one friend here," Sam remarked.

Burke thought for a moment, trying to figure out to whom Sam was referring. "Will?" he said. "He's not exactly a friend. Like I said, I know his father."

"I'm sorry," Sam said. "The two of you seem to . . ." He stopped speaking. "Tanya's place is right up here," he continued. "Just past the church."

Burke wanted to ask him what he and Will seemed. Had Sam

picked up on something? He wondered if Sam had seen the same thing in Will's gesture that Burke had seen. *Do we look like lovers?* he wondered, not without some sense of satisfaction. *Is that what Sam meant?*

Sam turned the car onto a rutted dirt road, ignoring a NO TRESPASS- ING sign written in faded red paint on a piece of rotting plywood nailed to a tree. He said nothing else, and despite very badly wanting to, Burke didn't ask him to elaborate on his earlier statement.

A minute later the trailer came into view, a rectangle of metal sit- ting on cinder blocks. As the Subaru approached, two large brown dogs of dubious ancestry scurried out from under the trailer and ran toward them, barking madly. They were followed by a skinny boy wearing nothing but a pair of cutoff shorts, who came running from around the side of the trailer and called after the dogs.

"Smith! Wesson! Get back here!" he shouted in a high-pitched voice. "Mom! Smith and Wesson are raising hell!"

The trailer door flew open, and a woman stepped out. She was skinnier than the boy, and her long hair was bleached an unnatural lemon color. She, too, wore shorts, although she also sported a too- small T-shirt with a Mötley Crüe logo on it. She said nothing, stand- ing with a cigarette held inches from her mouth as she watched the dogs gallop toward the car, which had come to a stop. Each dog took up position on one side of the car, peering into the window and barking loudly.

"They seem friendly," said Burke doubtfully, staring at either Smith or Wesson, he didn't know which, joyfully covering the win- dow with slobber.

"'Let dogs delight to bark and bite, for God hath made them so,'" Sam replied. "Isaac Watts," he added as he unlocked the doors. "He wrote 'Joy to the World.' Interesting guy."

"Smith. Wesson. Get back here." The woman's voice was loud, but not frantic. The dogs, hearing it, turned and trotted back to her. They sat at the foot of the three makeshift stairs leading up to the trailer's front door, as if they were guarding the entrance to Buckingham Palace.

Sam got out and waved to the woman. "Afternoon, Tanya," he said. "Freddie," he added, waving to the boy. "I brought someone who wants to meet you."

CHAPTER 17

"Here you go," Tanya said as she handed Burke a glass. The Burger King logo was on one side, and a picture of a Transformer on the other. Burke looked at the drink, which was bright red in color. He took a hesitant sip and discovered that it was fruit punch.

He looked over at Sam, who had taken a drink and set his glass down on a coffee table covered in issues of *Field & Stream* and *NASCAR Scene* magazines. Sam didn't seem at all bothered by being served Kool-Aid in a fast-food restaurant glass. Burke, recalling his earlier assumptions about Tanya's life, felt a little guilty about judging her hostessing skills.

The inside of Tanya's trailer was not quite what he had expected. It was most definitely small, and the furniture was outdated and badly used, but it was also clean and homey in an odd kind of way. A crocheted afghan covered the back of the sofa, and a collection of ceramic chickens congregated beneath a table lamp made out of a much larger ceramic rooster.

On one wall pictures of Freddie provided a kind of timeline of his growth from infancy to the present. There were also pictures of Tanya in a wedding dress, standing beside a man, who Burke assumed was her husband. The man was large in all directions and sported an impressive beard and sideburns. He smiled uneasily, as if unused to exercising those particular facial muscles, and wore the bemused expression of one who very much hoped his suffering would soon be over.

"I hope we're not interrupting anything," Sam told Tanya.

The woman shook her head. "I was just doing my homework,"

she said. "I'm getting my degree in medical billing. You know, from that place they advertise on the TV. You do it all on the computer. Carl wasn't crazy about the idea, but I told him he could play video games on the computer if we got one, and that did the trick. Problem is, I have to do all my schoolwork when he ain't home."

"We won't keep you long, then," Sam said politely. "I appreciate you making time for us."

Tanya smiled. *She's not used to people treating her kindly,* Burke thought.

"You remember that box of papers and photographs you brought me a while back?" Sam continued.

Tanya nodded. "Sure," she said. "Carl wanted to throw all that out, but I told him it might be important."

"It very well could be," said Sam.

Tanya's face lit up. "You think maybe we can make some money from it? I'll tell you, Mama didn't leave much, and what with her not payin' taxes for a bunch of years, we had to sell the house to cover that. It sure would make Carl happy if I could tell him we might be seeing something from it all."

"I can't promise anything," Sam told her. "But I'll see what I can do. Might be there's a library or museum that will be interested."

Burke didn't know if this was true or not, but he suspected that at some point not too far off Sam would be returning to the Redmond house with a check.

"This is one of the pictures that was in that box," Sam said, showing Tanya the photograph they had been discussing at the library. "The soldier's name is William Holburne. Does that name mean anything to you?"

Tanya shook her head. "Nope," she said. Then she took the picture from Sam and stared at it for a minute. "You know, there is something kinda familiar about that face. Hold on a minute. Let me get something."

She got up from the sofa and disappeared into another room, where Burke heard her moving things around. She did this for several minutes, during which time she twice goddamned an unseen cat for getting in her way and once referred to "that dumb shit Carl" while apparently speaking to herself. Then she emerged from the room, carrying a battered photo album.

"This is one of the only things I kept from Mom's house," she said as she set the album on the coffee table. "You know, besides the Precious Moments." She opened the album to the first page. "When she got sick and couldn't get around much, Mom got all into researching the family history. She tried to talk to me about it, but to me it's just a bunch of old people I never met. But some of the pictures were interesting. I don't even know where she got most of them. She wrote to relatives all over the place, asking for what they had. I guess that's where they came from."

She removed a piece of lined notebook paper and handed it to Sam, who unfolded it and smoothed it out. "It's a family tree," he said, looking at the scrawled names with lines running between them.

"That's right," Tanya said. "Mom was trying to work back as far as she could." She had reached the back of the album. "Here's what I wanted to show you," she said.

The photograph was very old, and at some point it had been torn in two horizontally and taped back together. It depicted a beautiful woman standing beside a small, wiry man wearing a dark suit.

"Look there," said Tanya, pointing to the man. "His face. Don't it look like the soldier in the other picture?" She took the photo of William Holburne and placed it beside the one in the album.

"It does," said Sam. "It looks very much like him."

Burke nodded. "It's got to be the same guy."

"Who is this?" Sam asked Tanya.

Tanya removed the picture from the album and turned it over. "Mom wrote on the back of some of these," she said. She pointed to a note at the bottom of the page. "Peter Woode and Tess Hague," she said. She frowned. "I guess it ain't the same guy, after all. They sure do look alike, though."

"Tess Hague?" said Burke. "As in Amos Hague?"

Sam nodded. "That's what I was wondering myself," he said.

Tanya was looking at the sheet of paper on which her mother had written her genealogical notes. "Here," she said. "Peter Woode and Tess Hague. They were married in 1884. That means they're my . . ." She began counting silently, moving her lips and touching her thumb to each of her fingers in turn.

"Great-great-great-great-grandparents," Sam said, helping her out. "At least if this chart is right."

He followed the lines that Tanya's mother had drawn, reading the names. "Tess and Peter had a daughter, Grace. She married John Black-burne, and they had a son, Peter. Peter married Sarah Harper and produced Stephen, who married Francis Williams and had Agnes."

"Agnes Blackburne was my grandmother," Tanya said. "My grand-father was Finnegan McCready. My mother was Caroline McCready, and my father was Robert Ayres. That was my name before I married Carl. Tanya Ayres. I never liked it, because of the two *a*'s. Everyone said it like it was Tanyairs. I like Redmond a lot better."

"Let's assume Tess and Amos Hague did get married," said Sam. "He could have died, and she could have remarried."

"Those two sure do look alike," Tanya remarked. She was once again looking at the pictures of William Holburne and Peter Woode. "I'd swear they were brothers."

Sam looked at Burke. "They certainly do," he said.

He thinks Peter Woode is William Holburne, Burke thought. *Who was really Elizabeth Frances Walsh.* It was getting more and more complicated with every new discovery. If, for instance, Elizabeth was William, who was Peter? How could he have married Tess Hague and have had at least one child? It didn't make any sense.

"I wonder if Amos and Tess had any children," he said.

"The tree lists only Tess and Peter Woode," Sam said. "Tanya, did your mother or grandmother ever mention someone named Amos Hague?"

"There's the Hague farm," Tanya said. She picked up a pack of Camels, tapped one out, and lit it. She inhaled and blew out a cloud of smoke before continuing. "There was bad blood about it way back, but I don't know anything about that. Gran just used to say the Wrathmores took what ought to have been ours."

"Wrathmores?" said Sam. "You mean the old Wrathmore place?"

Tanya shrugged as she took another drag on her cigarette. "All I know is there's some old farm that was supposed to get passed on to my great-great-great or whatever grandfather. But some Wrathmore guy stole it out from under him." She took a swig of Kool-Aid.

"Wrathmore," Burke said to Sam. "That's what you called the farm Will took me to."

Sam nodded. "I assume it's the same one," he said. "I've never heard anyone call it the Hague farm before, though."

"Gran seemed to think our lives would be different if we hadn't of lost the farm," said Tanya. "Me, I think she was just an angry old bitch." She puffed on her cigarette. "Don't get me wrong. I loved her and all, but she was a major pain in the ass."

"That's all you remember her saying, that the Wrathmores somehow stole the Hague farm from your family?" asked Sam.

Tanya gestured with her cigarette. "She said all kinds of weird shit at the end," she said. "Who knows what was true? But yeah, that's all I remember her saying."

"And your mother never said anything about it?" asked Burke.

"Never talked to her about it," said Tanya. "Truth be told, we didn't speak much the last four or five years. She didn't like Carl. Loved Freddie, though. She never took it out on him. Always remembered him on birthdays and Christmas and such. Sometimes he stayed over with her."

"Would you mind if I asked Freddie if she ever said anything to him?" said Sam.

Tanya shrugged. "If you want," she said. "He's kinda slow, though. Don't expect much."

She got up, went to the door, and called out for her son. A minute later he ran in, his face red from exertion. "What you want?" he asked.

"Mr. Guffrey wants to ask you something," said Tanya.

Freddie looked over at Burke and Sam and grinned, revealing a mouth missing a tooth or two where the baby ones had recently fallen out. "Sure," he said.

"Your mom says you spent a lot of time with your grandmother," Sam began. "I'm just wondering if you remember her ever telling you stories about a place called the Hague farm."

Freddie laughed. "Yeah," he said. "I used to think she was sayin' something about a hog farm. Didn't know it was someone's name."

Sam laughed gently. "It does sound like *hog farm,*" he agreed. "So she did tell you about it?"

Freddie nodded and wiped his nose on the back of his hand. "Took me there once," he said. "There's a pond and everything. But Gran said never to go there again. Said it was haunted."

Tanya sighed. "She was always filling his head with crap like that," she said to Burke and Sam. To Freddie, she said, "You know that's all bullshit."

Freddie shook his head. "She *said* so," he insisted. "Said it was haunted. Said never to go there, ever."

"Did she say why it was haunted?" asked Sam.

Freddie shrugged. "Just said it was," he answered, as if that was all the reason required. He looked at his mother. "Can I go? Andy's waitin' for me to go fishing."

Tanya glanced at Sam, who nodded. "Go on," she told her son. "Be back for dinner. Ask Andy if he wants to stay over."

Freddie took off, banging through the trailer's front door. Smith and Wesson barked happily, the sound fading as they apparently ran after him.

"It's just like Ma to tell him ghost stories," Tanya said, stubbing out her cigarette.

"She never said anything like that to you?" Sam asked.

Tanya shook her head. "Probably knew I wouldn't buy it. Freddie, though, he believes anything you tell him. Like I said, he's a little slow. He's repeating fourth this year cuz he can't read good."

"Bring him into the library," said Sam. "He probably just needs a little help. I can probably get him up to speed before school starts."

"Yeah?" said Tanya.

"How about Wednesday at one?" Sam suggested. "I can see what level he's at and go from there."

Tanya smiled. "Okay," she said. "We'll come by then."

Sam stood. Burke, following his cue, reached for his crutch. Sam took his arm and helped, making sure Burke was steady before letting go.

"Thank you for talking to us, Tanya," Sam said. "And thanks for the drinks. I'll look for you and Freddie on Wednesday." He held out his hand. Tanya looked at it for a moment, then shook it.

"Yes, thank you," Burke said, feeling awkward in the face of Sam's politeness.

"Anytime," Tanya said.

Sam opened the door and helped Burke down the stairs. When they were in the car and pulling away from the trailer, Burke said, "That was nice of you to offer to help her kid."

"I'm not doing anything else with my teaching degree," Sam replied. "Might as well help him out, right?"

Burke laughed. "It's more than that. You want to help him. I can tell."

Sam shrugged. "There's not much point to being alive if you don't do what you can to make life better for someone else, is there?" he said. "'A life is not important except in the impact it has on other lives.' Jackie Robinson."

Burke thought about it. If he was honest, he had to admit that he'd never really done much for anyone else. Sure, he'd helped a few friends move, fed some cats and watered some plants while their owners were away on vacation. But he'd never really *helped* anyone. It had always been about him.

"I guess I really wouldn't know," he said.

CHAPTER 18

"Damn it. These are messed up, too."

Burke set the photos on the dining room table. They had arrived from the printer twenty minutes earlier. Because he had shot in color and couldn't easily develop the film himself, he had sent it to his favorite processing lab in Boston, the one that always did a stellar job. The prints had arrived with a note from the lab technician saying that they'd done the best that they could.

Not that the images were bad. They were beautiful. But in each one there was not one but two areas of blur. Oblong in shape, they disrupted the landscape of the photos like twin pillars of cloud. In one of Burke's favorite photos, a shirtless Will was standing in front of the low stone wall, his face turned toward the camera. But behind him and to the left, as if looking over his shoulder, were the two smudges of gray.

The rest of the shots were equally marred. Unusable. Burke thumbed through them again, annoyed at the results. He had to remind himself that he was shooting with old cameras, and that if he wanted flawless pictures, he would have to either clean them or use more modern technology. Perhaps he would go back to the site and take some shots with one of his digital cameras. It was such a beautiful place that it was a shame to have wasted so much time and film on imperfect pictures.

It occurred to him that he might be able to fix some of the images using photo-correction software. Along with the prints and developed negatives, the lab had sent him the pictures on a CD. He took this and put it into his computer. Opening the software, he selected the image of Will and imported it into the program. It appeared on the screen, much reduced in size. Burke focused on the cloudy areas and enlarged that area of the photo in order to better see what might be done. He didn't like manipulating his work this way, but if he could salvage the pictures, it might be worth it.

He increased the overall size of the image to twenty-four by twenty-four inches. On his laptop screen he was able to see only a small portion of the photo, so that the picture appeared as a mosaic of colored blocks. He wished he had the large monitor on his computer at home, which would have made things much easier. As it was, he had to move the image around until the cloudy areas were in the frame.

When he found them, his fingers froze over the keyboard. There was Will's shoulder, the freckles on his skin clearly visible in their magnified state. And behind his shoulder two faces looked directly into the camera. Indistinct, as if shot through water, they were nonetheless faces. Burke could make out eyes and mouths, although they were mostly shadow, and within the blur of gray the outlines of two bodies were visible.

With a few more clicks, he called up the black-and-white images he had taken with the Yashica-Mat. He selected the one of Will looking into the pond and increased it to the same size as the newer photo, again focusing on the blurred area. Placing the two images side by side, he compared them. Although in many ways it was like comparing a cloud to a cloud, there was something about both photos that was undeniably similar. Looking at them, Burke couldn't escape the feeling that the unidentified face in the pond was one of the same ones looking over Will's shoulder in the more recent shot.

A chill passed over him. *Don't be ridiculous,* he immediately told himself. *They're just lens aberrations.* But even as he thought it, he knew that he didn't believe it. There was something too—he searched for the right word and could come up only with *real*—about the images.

The box of research materials Lucy had brought over earlier in the week was sitting on the dining room table. Burke found himself pulling it toward him and looking through it for the smaller box of photographs. He found it and removed the picture of Amos Hague, Tess Beattie, and the unidentified man. Holding the photo beside the images on the computer screen, he compared them.

Again, he felt a tingle of fear. The face in the photo taken at the pond bore an eerie resemblance to that of the unidentified man standing with Amos Hague and Tess Beattie. And it was there again in the second photograph. And the other face in the second photo looked remarkably like that of Amos Hague.

Burke set the photograph down. He couldn't help but think about what Freddie Redmond had said about the Hague farm being haunted. Had that story gotten into his head and made him see ghosts wherever he looked? But you thought something was strange even before you heard that, he reminded himself.

Ever since he was a child, he'd loved haunted-house stories. But did he believe in ghosts? He found it difficult to say. He'd always said that he'd believe in them when he saw one for himself. Had that moment come?

He opened another of the photographs he'd taken on the second visit to the farm, then applied a grid overlay to the photo to mark it off in equal sections. The same two blurs appeared there, but they were positioned slightly to the right of where they'd appeared in the first photo. As he opened the remaining files to compare them, he discovered that in each one the pair of figures appeared in a different place, all within a limited range, so that without looking at them using the grid overlay, it would be easy to overlook the fact that they traveled. But travel they did.

He'd felt better when he'd thought the blurs were the fault of the lenses. But if that were true, the position of the blurs would remain constant. Now he had to accept that they likely weren't caused by the camera. He could always test the cameras again with different film—and probably would just to satisfy his curiosity—but he suspected he would get the same results. And even if he got nothing, it was still impossible to ignore the faces within the distortions.

Burke had seen numerous examples of photos that supposedly showed spectral bodies or faces. But he'd always assumed these photographs to be either fakes or defects that could be explained by shadows, light flares, or issues with the camera lenses. Now, faced with evidence of his own making, he wondered if anyone else would see what he saw.

Lucy was in the kitchen, making lunch. Burke was about to ask her to come look at the photos when he heard his father come in from outside. *He'll be less likely to see things,* he told himself. *He has no imagination.*

"Dad!" he called out. "Come in here a second. I want to show you something."

Ed entered the dining room, wiping his just-washed hands on a dish towel. "What's the emergency?" he asked.

"Just look at this photo," said Burke, handing him the shot of Will against the stone wall.

His father took the photograph and peered at it over his glasses, his eyebrows arched. "The Janks boy seems to have lost his shirt," he remarked after a moment.

"Do you notice anything else?" Burke asked him.

"Looks like you smudged it right here," said his father, indicating the cloudy areas. "Get your thumb on the negative, did you?"

"I didn't develop these," Burke told him. "I sent them to a lab."

"Might want to ask for your money back, then," said Ed.

"Maybe I should, Dad," Burke replied. "Thanks."

"They almost look like ghosts," his father said as he handed Burke back the photo. "I suppose you could tell people you got yourself some dead folks on film. Probably make a lot of money with that." He chuckled. "Some folks will believe anything if you tell them you've got a picture of it."

Burke said nothing. *Got yourself some dead folks on film,* he thought to himself.

"I'm going over to Sandberg after lunch," said Ed. "You're welcome to come along, if you want to get out. No bother."

Burke could tell that his father wanted him to say no. They both continued to pretend that their awkward discussion the last time they'd ridden together hadn't happened. Burke was only too happy to avoid the possibility of another confrontation, but he wanted to see Sam. He needed to discuss the photographs with someone who wouldn't think he was crazy, or who at least might listen with an open mind.

"That would be great," Burke said, turning away so that he wouldn't see any look of disappointment that might appear on his father's face. "I'd like to go to the library, if it's not too much trouble."

"That'll be just fine," said his father. "I'll drop you off and come back for you when I'm done with what I need to do."

Burke nodded. He didn't ask what his father needed to do. Not inquiring about one another's lives was a familiar approach to their relationship. It had worked well for many years, and after seeing his father's reaction to the suggestion that they have an actual conversation, Burke wasn't eager to try to change things.

Lucy called them into the kitchen, where she fed them grilled cheese sandwiches and tomato soup. "Firing up that toaster oven and opening that can of soup is as close to cooking as I'm getting," she declared. "I don't know what's for dinner, but I'm not making it."

Burke and his father left as soon as they finished eating. They rode in silence, although this time Burke wasn't thinking about their relationship. He was thinking about the pictures in the envelope he'd brought, and about the ones on his laptop, which sat on the seat beside him. And he thought about how to tell Sam what he thought was in them.

His father dropped him at the library, pausing only long enough to help Burke down from the truck and hand him the laptop and envelope. Burke held these awkwardly with his one good hand and made his way slowly up the steps to the front door. As he stood trying to figure out how to open it, he was nearly knocked down by Freddie Redmond, who ran out holding a book in his hands.

Looking up, Freddie faced Burke and read in a slow but firm voice: "'Weasels—and stoats—and foxes—and so on. They're all right in a way—I'm very good friends with them—pass the time of day when we meet, and all that—but they break out sometimes, there's no denying it, and then—well, you can't really trust them, and that's the fact.'"

Beaming, Freddie raced down the steps, the copy of *The Wind in the Willows* flapping in his hands like an excited bird.

Burke caught the door with his foot and went inside, again almost getting knocked down, this time by Tanya. She had been walking toward the door and had stopped to say something to Sam, who was standing behind the desk. When she'd turned around, she'd nearly smacked into Burke.

"Shit!" she said, laughing. "Don't sneak up on a girl like that. You're lucky I don't have my pistol on me."

"The Redmond family seems to be in a good mood this afternoon," Burke remarked as he made his way to the desk and Tanya made her way outside.

"Turns out Freddie isn't as dumb as some people seem to think," Sam said.

"Hey," Burke objected, "I never—"

"I meant his teachers," Sam interrupted.

"Right," Burke said, trying to salvage his dignity. "So, I have something to show you."

"Great," Sam said. "Because I have something to show *you*. Well, to tell you, anyway."

"You go first," Burke told him. Now that he was there, he felt foolish about the whole ghost thing, and suddenly he didn't want to say anything about it to Sam.

"Okay," said Sam. "Well, I did some digging around, and I found out some interesting stuff about our friend Amos Hague."

"How interesting?" Burke asked.

Sam seemed to think about this for a moment. "I'd rate it a firm B plus," he said. "Do you remember Tanya mentioning that her grandmother said the Wrathmore place was stolen from their family?"

Burke nodded.

"Turns out she was right," Sam said. "Well, I don't know that it was stolen, but it certainly was taken. I found a couple of old newspaper articles about it."

"What are they written on, parchment?" Burke joked.

"Close," said Sam. "Fortunately, the *Sandberg Crier* was one of half a dozen newspapers in the state selected for preservation by the Vermont Historical Society. The fellow who printed it kept several copies of each issue and stored them in his cellar. It apparently was a remarkably well-built cellar, as it provided the perfect levels of temperature and humidity for keeping the papers from deteriorating."

"Thank goodness for that Yankee know-how," Burke said.

"Indeed," Sam agreed, smiling. "At any rate, the papers were found in remarkably good condition, which made them perfect for digital transfer. You can look up the daily news for any date from September 17, 1902 to December 31, 1936."

"Exciting reading, is it?"

"If you want to write a history of the Sandberg Ladies' Society annual cakewalk, it's riveting," Sam said. "Also, if you want to find out a couple of things about Amos Hague and his farm."

"Which we do," said Burke.

"First things first," Sam said. "Tess Woode—formerly Hague—died on February 2, 1903. Cause of death unknown. A year later, on June 21, 1904, her daughter, Grace Woode, married a Mr. John Blackburne."

"Just like Caroline Ayres wrote on the tree," said Burke.

"It should be noted that the bride was given away by her father, Mr. Peter Woode," Sam added. "We'll get back to that. For now skip ahead to 1911, when the same Mr. Peter Woode dies on December 23. Again, no cause given."

"Christmas was a grim affair that year," said Burke.

Sam nodded. "It gets worse," he said. "On December 24, a Mr. Calvin Wrathmore presented a claim of property ownership for the Hague farm to the town clerk, a Mr. Jackson Paltry. I found that little tidbit buried in the legal notices section."

"Did it say on what grounds he claimed ownership?"

Sam shook his head. "No. But apparently he was successful."

"How do you know?" asked Burke. "Because of Grandma Mc-Cready's spirited condemnation of the Wrathmore clan?"

"That and the fact that in 1920 the place burned down, killing Calvin Wrathmore and his wife, Edna. And guess who was fingered for starting the fire?"

"Freddie Redmond?" Burke joked.

"Peter Blackburne," said Sam. "Son of Grace Woode and John Blackburne."

"He was, what, all of twelve years old?" Burke said, surprised.

"Sixteen," said Sam. "Apparently, the trial was the talk of the town for the week that it lasted."

"And then they hanged him from the oak tree in the town square," Burke said.

"They found him innocent," said Sam. "He's Tanya Redmond's great-great-grandfather."

"So he got the farm back, then."

"No," Sam said. "The farm passed to Olivia Wrathmore, Calvin and Edna's seven-year-old daughter. She survived the fire. It was Olivia who first accused Peter Blackburne of starting the fire. She said she saw him running away from the house."

"The little liar," Burke remarked.

"Maybe," said Sam. "Maybe not. At any rate, she got the farm."

"But apparently let it sit there," Burke said. "I wonder what happened to her?"

"I can tell you what happened to her," said Sam. "She left town, got married, and had a baby. His name is Gaither Lucas."

"Is?" Burke asked. "You mean he's still alive? He must be a hundred."

"He's seventy-seven," said Sam. "And he lives less than an hour from here."

Burke whistled. "Good detective work," he said.

Sam gave a little bow. "Thank you. Now, what is it you have to share?"

Burke, who had forgotten about the photos, suddenly felt very self-conscious. Sam had unearthed actual information, while all he had was a wild idea based on some blurry pictures. But Sam was expecting him to say something, so Burke took a deep breath. "Do you believe in ghosts?" he began.

CHAPTER 19

The cemetery was remarkably well maintained. The grass was mowed, the headstones were mostly free of moss, and best of all, there were none of the tacky plastic flowers that so often litter such places. Even the oldest graves—the ones farthest from the front—were neat and orderly. The markers, worn from years of rain and bitter Vermont winters, nonetheless retained an air of dignity, which Burke found comforting. He tried not to think about the bodies that lay beneath their feet.

"Somebody sure takes care of this place," he remarked as he and Sam wound their way through the rows, looking at the names on the gravestones.

"Remember the Ladies' Society that liked to throw those cakewalks?" Sam said. "They're still around, only now they tend the garden of the dead."

"Cheery," said Burke.

Sam smiled. "You like that? It's from a poem by Ruth Downing, Vermont's own Emily Dickinson. 'Through hidden doors the darklings pass the living slumb'ring in our beds. They come at night the faceless ones who tend the gardens of the dead.'"

"Sounds more like Vermont's Stephen King," Burke said.

"She supposedly held séances in her house," said Sam.

"Can we not talk about ghosts right now?" Burke said.

"You're the one who brought them up," Sam reminded him. "That's why we're here."

Burke didn't reply. Sam was right. It was because he had told Sam about the ghost images in his photos that Sam had suggested making a visit to the cemetery.

"You still haven't said whether or not you believe in them," Burke said.

Sam was quiet as they walked deeper into the area of the older graves. "I don't *not* believe in them," he said.

Burke snorted. "Fence-sitter," he accused.

"So you *do* believe in them?" Sam countered.

Before Burke could answer, the end of his crutch sank into soft ground and he stumbled. Sam reached out and grabbed him, but not before Burke had lost his grip on the crutch, which now lay on the ground while he balanced flamingo-like on one leg. Sam made sure Burke was steady before he knelt down to retrieve the fallen crutch.

"Well, this is spooky," Burke said. "Look who we have here."

Burke peered at the gravestone in front of which Sam was kneeling. He couldn't quite read the faded lettering. "Who is it?"

"Amos Hague," Sam replied. "Born October 3, 1843 and died August 9, 1883."

"He was almost forty," Burke observed. "The same age I am."

Sam was looking at the gravestone to the right of Amos's. "This is odd," he said. "Thomas Beattie. Born March 11, 1850 and died August 9, 1882."

"Beattie," Burke said. "As in Tess Beattie?"

"I don't know," said Sam. "Could be. And how weird is it that he and Amos died on the same day a year apart?"

"Is Tess here, too?"

Sam searched the headstones in the surrounding area. "Not that I can tell," he said. "No Peter Woode, either."

Burke was examining the headstones more carefully. Amos's was decorated at the top with a carving of a grinning skull that had wings on either side. Thomas's was marked with a simple row of three *X*s.

"Could you get the camera from my backpack?" Burke asked Sam. "I want to get some shots of these."

Sam stood and unzipped the backpack Burke had slung over his shoulders. "Which one?" he asked.

"The digital one first," said Burke.

Sam removed the camera and handed it to Burke. "Do you need me to do anything for you?"

Burke shook his head. "I've been practicing my one-handed

method," he joked. "But if you wouldn't mind standing by in case I decide to fall over, that would be great."

Sam took up a position to Burke's right as Burke fussed with the settings on the camera. "This would be so much easier without these damn casts," Burke complained.

"'Nothing in this world is worth having or worth doing unless it means effort, pain, difficult—'"

"Thank you, Mr. Bartlett," Burke interrupted testily.

"Actually, it was Mr. Roosevelt who said that," Sam replied. "Teddy, not FDR."

"Just keep me steady," said Burke.

He bent down as far as he could without losing his balance. He felt Sam's hand on the small of his back and relaxed a little. He knew he could trust Sam to catch him if he started to fall. With that worry gone, he began taking pictures.

"That should do it," he said after shooting a dozen images. "Now I want to try it with the Hawkeye and the Yashica-Mat."

Again, Sam assisted him, taking the cameras out and acting as Burke's bodyguard during the shooting. Burke was done within fifteen minutes, but even that amount of effort had tired him. "Do you mind if we leave?" he asked Sam.

"Not at all. I don't see Tess or Peter anywhere around here, anyway. Just the two boys."

"Now we have another mystery to solve," Burke said. "Who was Thomas Beattie, and why is he here?"

They made their way back through the cemetery to Sam's car. Once he was sitting down, Burke felt better. He couldn't wait to get his casts off and tried not to think about how much longer he had to have them on. He distracted himself by trying to puzzle out who Thomas Beattie might be.

Then he remembered the picture he'd found in Jerry's collection, the one that was labeled as possibly being of Amos Hague and Tess Beattie. There had been that second, unidentified man. "Maybe it's Thomas Beattie," he said aloud.

"Maybe who is?" said Sam as he started the car.

Burke told him about the photograph. "Now that I think about it, the guy and Tess do sort of look alike."

"We can look him up back at the library," said Sam.

As they drove, Burke took the digital camera and reviewed the pictures he'd taken. Not a single one showed any ghostly figures. He wondered what would appear on the film in the cameras. He was anxious to develop it.

"I need to shoot at the farm again," he told Sam.

Sam nodded. "By the way," he said, "I think you should do something with these photographs."

"Like what?"

"Show them," Sam elaborated. "They're really beautiful. I think they'd make a great show. You can call it the Ghosts of War, or something like that."

Burke laughed. "Yeah. They'd just *love* that in New York."

"Who said anything about New York?" said Sam. "I'm talking about here."

"Here? Where would I do a show here?" Burke said.

"I can think of half a dozen places," said Sam. "The library, for one. It would be a great local interest thing. But what I'm really thinking is that you should do it at my friend Colton's gallery in Montpelier."

"Gallery?" Burke said. "What kind of gallery?"

"*Art,*" Sam said. "What kind do you think?"

"I don't know. It just never occurred to me that there would be a real gallery up here."

"Oh, it isn't a real one," said Sam. "He just sells cross-stitch samplers and finger paintings of maple trees. But they're *really* good."

"You know what I mean," Burke said.

"Sure I do," said Sam. "You mean that we can't possibly have any real culture up here in the sticks. Your big cities have the monopoly on real art."

Burke shrugged. "Well, we do."

"We?" said Sam.

"I'm just saying, I don't see myself doing a photography show here," Burke said testily. "I'm sorry if I insulted the artistic community of Vermont."

Sam looked at him. "You're a real snob, you know that?"

Burke, taken aback, objected. "I am not."

"Yes, you are," Sam insisted. "You really think things are only worthwhile if people in New York or Boston or wherever say that they are. Isn't it enough if *you* think they're worthwhile, or if someone like me thinks they're worthwhile?"

"It's not the same thing," Burke argued. "If your mother likes your drawing of a duck and hangs it on the refrigerator, that doesn't mean it's good."

"Snob," Sam said.

"Stop saying that!"

"I will," said Sam, "when you stop being a snob."

Burke, annoyed, settled into a resentful silence. He hadn't expected such an attack from Sam. He'd thought they were friends. But now Sam was lecturing him as if he were a child. *Where does he get off being so high and mighty?* he thought.

Unexpectedly, it began to rain. As the first drops hit the windshield, Sam turned on the wipers. Within a minute they were working overtime, sweeping the water from the glass as it relentlessly battered the car. Burke watched it running down the window beside him.

"I'm sorry," Sam said after a few minutes.

Burke grunted.

"I'll take that as an acceptance of my apology," said Sam.

Burke nodded. "Don't worry about it," he said.

"It's just that I think you're overlooking a great opportunity," Sam continued. "Think about it?"

"Sure," Burke said. He had no intention of considering doing a show, but he feared Sam wouldn't shut up about it if he didn't at least pretend he would.

"I'll mention it to Colton," said Sam.

Please don't, Burke thought.

"Actually, let's have dinner," Sam said brightly. "I'll invite a couple of people. Would you want to do that?"

Burke absolutely did not want to do that. The idea of talking about his work with people who probably wouldn't know an Arbus from an Ansel Adams was not his idea of a pleasant evening. But he found himself nodding and saying, "That would be nice."

"By 'nice' I assume you mean 'excruciating,'" Sam replied. "But I'm holding you to it. How about this Friday?"

"I'll check my appointment book," Burke said.

Sam coughed, and for a minute Burke thought he heard him utter "Snob" under his breath, but when he looked over, Sam was only watching the road.

"You know, there's nothing inherently virtuous about living in the country," Burke said. "Some people might even say your attitude about cities is reverse snobbery."

"True," Sam admitted. "But I would argue that there's a difference. People who look down on us poor country folk usually won't admit that anything worthwhile can come out of here. We, on the other hand, admit that occasionally something good can come out of a city."

"What's wrong with cities?" Burke asked.

"Nothing," said Sam. "If you like crowded, noisy, dirty places that cost way too much to live in. How did Thoreau describe them? Right. 'Millions of people being lonesome together.'"

"Snob," Burke said.

Sam laughed. "I'm just playing with you. Cities are fine. I'm happy to visit them. I just don't want to live in one."

"Because they're crowded, noisy, and dirty," Burke said.

"Well, yes," Sam said. "At least to me they are. I'm sure other people find them beautiful and stimulating."

"I do," said Burke. "They're alive."

"Meaning places like Wellston and Sandberg are dead?"

"More like asleep," Burke said. "Or afraid."

"Afraid of what?" said Sam.

"Changing," Burke replied. "Anything new. I don't know. Don't you ever feel like you're just standing still?"

As Sam seemed to consider the question, Burke listened to the sound of rain pounding on the roof. It was pleasant being inside the car, racing through the storm, as if they were in a protective bubble. For some reason it made him sleepy, and he closed his eyes.

"I don't know about standing still," Sam said, his voice quiet beneath the drumming of the rain. "Sometimes I think it makes it easier to make excuses for why you haven't done certain things."

Burke started to respond but found that he couldn't. The rain was lulling him to sleep. Sam's voice seemed to be coming from far away, and the rhythmic *wush-wush-wush* of the wipers drowned it out until it became just a whisper.

CHAPTER 20

"What was my dad like in high school?"

Will looked up from between Burke's legs, where he was teasing the head of Burke's cock by running his tongue slowly around the edge. They were in Will's bed, in his room above his parents' garage. Burke, already nervous about being there, felt his excitement wane even more.

Will tugged on his dick. "Well?" He shifted position on the bed, nuzzling Burke's balls with his nose. He was lying on his side, his back and ass pressed against the length of Burke's cast. His own cock jutted out, resting against his thigh.

Burke stared at it, trying not to picture Mars's dick. *It looks just like his,* he thought. "I don't know," Burke said. "He was like most guys that age. Thought he knew everything."

Will snorted. "He still does," he said, running a hand up Burke's stomach. "Did the two of you ever get it on?"

Burke flinched. "No!" he said. "Why would you think that?"

Will grinned. "You wanted to, though, didn't you?"

"I never really thought about it."

"Like hell you didn't," said Will. "I've seen his yearbook pictures. He was hot."

"Can we not talk about your father while we're . . . you know?"

Will pushed his nose beneath Burke's balls and flicked his tongue against Burke's asshole. Burke closed his eyes and groaned. For a guy who was new to man-on-man sex, Will had taken to it with a vengeance. When he placed a hand beneath the knee of Burke's good leg, Burke let him push the leg back. Will probed deeper into Burke's exposed ass.

"I want to fuck you," he said when he came up for air.

"Uh-uh," Burke said. "I don't get fucked."

Will laughed. "What do you mean, you don't get fucked?" he said.

"I'm a top," Burke told him. "I do the fucking."

Will looked at him with a puzzled expression. "That's fucked up," he said. "What difference does it make who does what?"

Burke shrugged. "It just does," he said.

"Have you ever *been* fucked?" asked Will.

"A couple of times, I guess," Burke answered.

"Then what's one more time?" said Will. He tickled Burke's asshole with his finger, pressing against it.

Burke tensed up. "Not with my leg and everything," he said nervously.

Will lay beside him. "You took my cherry," he said. "I think it's only fair you be *my* first, too." He pressed his hard cock against Burke's leg. "I'll be gentle," he said.

Again, an image of Mars, his dick sticking out of his pants, came to Burke's mind. *Pretend it's Mars,* he told himself. A moment later he rolled onto his side. Will pressed against his back. Burke heard him spit into his hand. Then the head of his cock was thrust between the cheeks of Burke's ass.

He's not wearing a condom, Burke thought vaguely, but he said nothing.

Will fumbled with his dick as he located Burke's asshole. When the head was in position, he pushed forward, sliding inside. Burke gritted his teeth at the pain.

"Holy shit," Will whispered, his breath hot against Burke's ear. "It's so tight."

Burke closed his eyes. His thoughts went back to that night at the lake, and to what he would have liked to have happened. He and Mars were in the backseat, making out. Their clothes were on the floor, and Mars was on top of him. "I want to fuck your ass," he said, his breath smelling of beer.

Burke felt Will moving in and out of him. Will had one arm around Burke's stomach, his fingers wrapped around the base of Burke's cock. As he pumped himself in and out of Burke, his hand matched the strokes.

"Oh, fuck," he gasped. "Oh, fuck, I love your ass." But it was Mars's voice Burke heard.

Will came with a groan. He pulled Burke to his belly and held him tight as he unloaded in Burke's ass. When he was done, he pulled out slowly and rolled onto his back. A moment later he laughed. "That was fucking *hot*," he said. He looked over at Burke. "You didn't come."

Burke was stroking himself, still thinking about Mars. When Will reached over and took over, Burke put his arm behind his head and thought about the taste of Mars's cock in his mouth. He came not long after, covering his chest with cum. Will milked the last drops from him, then bent down and licked some of the cum from his belly.

"Now, don't tell me you didn't like that," he teased Burke.

Burke didn't reply. He was looking for tissues with which to wipe himself clean.

Will tossed him his T-shirt. "Use that," he said. "I'll keep it as a souvenir of my first time."

Burke wiped the cum from his chest and dropped the shirt on the floor.

Will lay on his back beside him, his leg tossed casually over Burke's. "I could do that fifty times a day," he said.

Burke remembered a time when he felt the same way himself. When you were his age, he reminded himself. When had the thrill gone away? He recalled those early nights in the bars, looking for someone to go home with. Every man had been a potential lover; every encounter, another opportunity to experience the dizzying thrill of touching another man's body, tasting his cock, fucking his ass. Just a glance on the street could send him reeling as he imagined the possibilities. Often he'd run home and beat off, thinking about what might have been.

Now here he was, in bed with a man half his age. A very attractive man who enjoyed making love with him. And it wasn't nearly as fulfilling as he thought it should be. *He's just excited because I'm his first,* he thought. *It's not as if there are a lot of options for him. In the real world he'd never look at me twice.*

"Why do you think guys suck cock better than girls do?" Will asked.

"I guess because we know what we like to have done," said Burke.

"If I were a girl, I'd be sucking every cock I could get my mouth on," said Will. "Fuck, I'd take on the whole football team at one time."

Burke ran his hand through Will's hair. "Careful," he said. "You don't want to get a reputation as a bad girl. No one will marry you, then."

He imagined Will with a lover. It would probably be someone as young and handsome as he was. Gay twins, Gregg called them, men who so similarly resembled one another that they might as well be making love to their own reflections. They usually managed five or even ten years together before they looked at one another and, frightened by the signs of aging they saw mirrored in one another's faces, they split up.

Sometimes seeing the changes in one another had the opposite effect and actually comforted them. Seeing that they weren't alone in growing older, they stopped caring, or at least caring so much. But often this seemed to be accompanied by a kind of neutering, a gradual disappearance of anything remotely resembling sexuality, until finally the men in question were more like kindly old aunties than men who liked to fuck other men.

Burke sometimes feared he was heading for something in between. He'd never been particularly interested in men like himself, and he had no partner with whom to grow older. Like many men his age, he occupied a kind of limbo, not young enough to be the new face in the bars that everyone wanted and not old enough to be—and didn't want to be—the funny old queen whose jokes everyone laughed at. Instead, he was just middle aged and alone.

"Hey, maybe I'll come visit you in Boston," said Will, interrupting Burke's dreary thoughts. "That would be fun."

Big fun, Burke thought. *Especially when you go home with some hot young guy and I spend all night wondering what you're doing with him.*

"Sure," he told Will.

Will glanced at the clock on his dresser. "Shit, I've got to be somewhere in an hour. We've got to go."

Burke dressed as quickly as his casts would allow. After checking to make sure Will's parents weren't around—Burke felt like a teenage boy slipping out of his girlfriend's bedroom window in the middle of the night—they got into Will's truck. Ten minutes later Burke was standing on his father's porch, watching Will drive off.

"There you are," Lucy said as he walked into the kitchen. "Did you have a good afternoon?"

"It was pretty good," said Burke. "I took some pictures. Nothing amazing."

"Well, your friend Gregg called," Lucy told him. "Maybe that will cheer you up. He said he'll be home all evening if you want to call back."

"I will," said Burke. The thought of talking to Gregg really did make him feel better. Finally, he could talk to someone from his real life. Then he remembered that his cell phone didn't get reception there and that he would have to use the phone in the kitchen.

"I've got to run out to the store," Lucy said, as if on cue. "I'll be gone about forty-five minutes or so. Is there anything I can pick up for you?"

"Thanks," Burke said. "No, I don't need anything."

"Your father is off doing God knows what," said Lucy. "You sure you'll be okay on your own?" She winked at Burke as she picked up the car keys.

"I think I can manage," he said, thankful for her kindness.

When she was gone, he dialed Gregg's number and waited for him to pick up. On the fourth ring he almost hung up, as he expected Gregg's machine to pick up and he didn't feel like leaving a message. At the last second, though, Gregg's voice came through the phone. "I break the door down to get to the phone and it's *you?*" he said.

Burke heard mumbling in the background.

"Rick says to tell you hello," said Gregg.

"Right. Tell him to fuck off himself."

"Burke says hi back!" Gregg yelled. "I see that country charm has worn off on you," he said to Burke.

"I'm thinking of opening a B and B," said Burke. "What's going on in the real world?"

Gregg sighed. "Let's see," he began. "Tony met some guy in P-town and was in love for two weeks, but then he decided he couldn't overlook the back hair anymore and called it off. Dylan found e-mails on Lee's computer that had pictures of some guy's cock attached to them and threw a fit, although I'm not sure why, since he's been blowing that delivery guy at his office for six months. Anyway, they're taking a break. Abe is still single and complaining that there are no tops left in Boston, John is still single and complaining that there are no bottoms left in Boston, and a certain former male model we know and love had an eye lift and now looks like he could star in *The Mikado.* Oh, and Peter painted his apartment a hideous shade of brown that makes it look like he's living inside a colon. And everyone misses you and wants you home."

"Naturally," Burke said.

He was surprised to find that while listening to Gregg, he didn't feel homesick. Nor did he find the gossip particularly interesting, or even interesting at all. All the supposed news was nothing more than the usual antics of his circle of friends. They were always hooking up and breaking up, falling in love and out of love, changing their lovers and the colors of their apartments. Normally, he didn't notice, as it was part of his everyday life. But having been away from it for a while, he now saw it from a distance, and he was finding the view less than breathtaking.

"Hasn't anyone *done* anything?" he asked Gregg.

"Well, if you mean, has anyone written a novel, or built a bridge, or landed a job as Michelle Obama's personal stylist, then no. What were you expecting?"

Burke sighed. "I don't know," he said. "I guess I was just hoping life there was more interesting than it is here."

"You mean it's not?" asked Gregg.

"Apparently," Burke replied.

"Well, what have *you* been doing?" Gregg said.

"Taking some pictures," said Burke. "Not much else. I still have the casts on, so I can't do a whole lot."

Originally, he'd thought about telling Gregg about Will. He knew Gregg would love that story. But now he didn't want to share it. Nor did he want to tell Gregg about Sam and the mystery of Amos Hague. He wasn't sure why, but he wanted to keep that to himself. Thinking about Gregg telling all their friends about how Burke was occupying his time out in the boonies made him irritable. He pictured them laughing over their eggs Benedict at brunch, saying how sorry they felt for poor Burke, all alone in Vermont.

"Have you at least met some hunky maple-syrup farmer, or whatever they have there?" Gregg's question brought him back to the conversation.

"Not so far," he answered. "But the big lumberjack competition is this weekend, so I might luck out."

Gregg laughed. "Sweetie, I'd love to chitty-chat some more, but I have to go."

"Lucy said you were going to be in all night," said Burke.

"I was," said Gregg. "Then Lee called and asked if I wanted to go see *Wicked* with him. He got tickets for Dylan's birthday, but what with the whole dirty e-mail thing, he doesn't want to go with him, so yea for me."

"You've seen that show at least half a dozen times," said Burke.

"As if you could ever see it enough," Gregg said. "I'll give Glinda and Elphaba your love. Call me in a few days."

"Sure," Burke assured him. "Bye."

After he hung up, he sat in the kitchen, thinking. Gregg was his best friend. They had been lovers. But now he almost felt like a stranger. And the familiar world Burke thought he missed now felt cold and empty. Did I really used to think all that shit was real life? he wondered.

An hour before, he had been in bed with Will, thinking about how different they were. Now he was thinking the same thing about his friends, his city, his life. Nothing felt familiar anymore, or comforting. But what had changed? He was the same man he'd been the night of his accident, the same man who had come into his father's house a month before. And yet he wasn't. But who was he? More important, where did he belong?

He got up and went upstairs. Standing in the doorway of his room, he looked at what was left of his childhood. He'd left all of that behind to go into the world and find out who he was. Now he wondered if he'd ever really figured it out.

CHAPTER 21

"So then Luke decides he's going to 'accidentally' fall into the canal, like Katharine Hepburn in *Summertime*."

Luke held up his hand, interrupting Colton's story. "In my defense, nobody ever bothered to tell me that Hepburn contracted an eye infection from the water and had problems with it the rest of her life."

"Yes, well," said Colton, suppressing a smile, "the gondolier was nice enough to catch him before he went overboard."

The rest of the table laughed, Burke included. They were seated around the table in Sam's dining room. There were six of them: Colton and Luke, Sam, Burke, and Nan and Sophie. The latter were a lesbian couple in their forties. Nan, Burke had learned, taught English literature at a high school, and Sophie was a chef. She had a small restaurant specializing in French food.

"It was a perfect honeymoon," Luke said.

"Fifteen years late, but worth waiting for," Colton agreed. He looked at Nan and Sophie. "So when are you two going to tie the knot?"

"Nan doesn't want to," said Sophie, sipping from her glass of wine. "She says it's buying into the heterosexual-relationship model."

Nan rolled her eyes and shook her head. "That's not it," she said. "I want to wait until *everyone* can get married, in every state. Besides, I still believe polyamory is the way to go."

"Polyamory?" said Sam. "Since when?"

"Just because I don't *practice* it doesn't mean I don't believe it works," Nan replied.

Sophie said, "She just doesn't want you to know about the three other women she's sleeping with." As everyone laughed, she leaned over and gave her partner a kiss on the cheek. "My little tramp," she joked.

Luke looked across the table at Burke. "Do you have a boyfriend back home?" he asked.

Burke shook his head. "Nope," he said. "I don't seem to do relationships very well."

"You sound like Sam," said Luke. "I can't remember the last time he had a date." He thought for a moment. "Yes, I can. It was with that Radical Faerie you met at Camp Destiny. The Midsummer gathering."

"That was a *year* ago," Colton said. "And I wouldn't exactly call it a date. What did you do? Paint each other with mud and do a spiral dance or something?"

Sam, looking uncomfortable, glared at his friends. "No, we did not paint each other with mud."

"Did you know Sam is a pagan?" Luke asked Burke.

Burke shook his head. "It hasn't come up." He glanced at Sam, who appeared to be doing his best to disappear. *At least now I know for sure that he's gay.*

"I suppose he hasn't shown you his book, either," Sophie said.

"Book?" Burke said, interested. "No, he hasn't."

"Sam published a book of short stories with pagan themes," Nan explained. "It's called *In the Wood of the Holly King.*"

"I'd like to read that," Burke said to Sam.

"It's not a big deal," Sam said, looking at his plate. "Just a small press."

"In case you haven't noticed, Sam doesn't like to talk about himself," Colton said.

"'We have two ears and one mouth so that we can listen twice as much as we speak,'" Sam quoted. "Besides, I invited Burke here to meet all of *you.* He already knows me."

"Apparently not as well as he should," said Sophie. She shot Burke a smile.

She's trying to set us up, Burke thought. But that wasn't going to happen. Sam Guffrey was definitely not his type. He was a great guy, but he was so odd. Burke didn't know what to make of him.

"Sam showed me some of your photos," said Colton. "I really like them. He said you might want to do a show."

"I don't know," Burke told him. "I don't really have enough pieces, and I'm not sure this is the right place for—"

He was cut off by a collective "Oooooh" from the two couples at the table. Surprised, he looked around.

"You think we're not cosmopolitan enough," said Sophie.

"No," Burke said quickly. "It's not that. I just—"

Sophie raised her hand, stopping him. "It's okay," she said. "I thought the exact same thing when I moved here."

"Sophie lived in Chicago," Nan explained. "She and I met when I was there for a teaching conference. We dated long distance for a year, then decided one of us needed to move."

"I thought it would be *her*," said Sophie. "I mean, I thought it was beautiful here and everything, but *move* here? I couldn't imagine it."

"How did you convince her?" Burke asked Nan.

"I told her it was move here or else," she said.

"Actually, I agreed to try it for six months," Sophie told him. "I kept my apartment in Chicago, got the owner of the restaurant I worked at to give me the time off, and came here, fully expecting I'd be able to convince this one to come back to Chicago with me."

"What made you change your mind?"

Sophie pushed her hair behind her ear. "I fell in love," she said.

"Awwwwww," said Nan, rubbing her shoulders.

"Not with you, with the place," Sophie joked. "Really, it was that simple. One day I woke up. It was February, I think. I'd moved here in October, and I think it started snowing about five minutes after Nan picked me up at the airport."

"Lies," Nan said. "It was at least a week later."

"It snowed pretty much every day," Sophie continued. "I grew up in Chicago. I thought I knew winter. But this was winter. I was literally counting the days until my six months were up. Then one morning I woke up, looked out the bedroom window at the seventeen feet of snow, and thought, 'This is the most beautiful place in the world, and I can be completely happy here.'"

"It was cabin fever," said Luke.

"I'm serious," Sophie objected. "I knew that although this was never the place I'd imagined when I'd thought about where my life would take me, it was the right place all along. I just needed to see that."

"I had a similar experience," Colton chimed in. "I used to have a gallery in New York. In fact, this isn't the first time I've seen your work," he told Burke. "Years ago I worked at Charles Geary's gallery in SoHo. I remember you had two pieces in a show we did."

"That's right," Burke said. "I'd forgotten about that. It was something about faces of the city, I think."

Colton nodded. "Yours were two of the best. Anyway, a year or two later I was dating this guy who loved to ski."

"Philip," Luke said. "And he didn't like to ski. He liked to go antiquing and say he was going skiing."

"True," Colton agreed. "Anyway, one weekend we came here to ski. We had a miserable time. I didn't like skiing, didn't like antiquing, and, I discovered, *really* didn't like Philip. I was so glad to get back to New York and civilization. I dumped Philip, and Luke and I started dating that summer. Fourth of July weekend was coming up. It had been unbearably hot for days and days, and New York smelled like the Dumpster behind a fast-food restaurant."

"It was vile," Luke agreed. "I couldn't wait to get out of there. My friends had invited us to their place on Fire Island."

"And mine had invited us to their place in Provincetown," said Colton, taking back control of the story. "We couldn't decide where we wanted to go. Then I realized I didn't want to go to either place. I was considering it only because it was *what you did.* If you lived in New York and were gay, on the weekend of the Fourth you went to Fire Island or Provincetown. I just couldn't do it. Out of the blue I suggested Vermont."

"At which point I felt certain I would have to break up with him," Luke said.

Colton nodded. "But I talked him into it. I found a little inn that still had rooms, we rented a car and drove up, and we had an amazing time."

"Didn't think about P-town or the Pines once," said Luke.

"This time when we drove back to the city, I didn't feel like I was getting back to civilization," Colton said. "I felt like I was going back into a cage."

"I felt the same way," Luke agreed. "But I didn't want to say anything, because I thought Colton would think I'd gone mad. After all, New York is the most important city in the world, right? People would kill to live there, and once you're in, you don't think about leaving. Ever."

"Only I couldn't stop thinking about the place," Colton continued. "We had found some great little restaurants here, and two not bad galleries showing local artists. We saw a great production of *Twelfth Night,* put on by a local company. I kept thinking that it would be nice to open a gallery myself, something that would encourage an artistic community, instead of just preying on it. Still, I couldn't let go of the whole New York thing."

"At some point you did, though," Burke said.

"Labor Day weekend," said Luke. "I'd been thinking about coming back, too. When the whole 'where should we go' conversation started, I said, 'What about Vermont?' Colton pretended to think it was a compromise, but on the drive up here he started talking, and before we'd hit the border, he'd admitted that he'd been thinking about what it would be like to live here."

"It took a year to actually do it," Colton said. "I had to find a space, we had to find a house, and Luke had to convince his boss to let him work from here."

"I was doing financial bullshit," Luke explained. "Making money for people who already had too much of it. After six months here I quit and opened a pet boutique. High-end bowls and toys, organic food, hideous sweaters. That kind of thing. I thought it would last a month. It's been almost fifteen years."

"Paws to Consider," said Colton. "Your one-stop shop for the discerning doggy."

"And persnickety pussy," Luke added.

"Their point," said Nan, "is that they all came here with ideas about what it's like. And they were wrong."

"What about you?" Burke asked her.

"I've never lived in a big city," she answered. "So this felt like home to me from the beginning."

"Well, I did grow up here," Burke said. "And I couldn't wait to get out. I have a hard time seeing it the way you all do."

"Maybe you need to see yourself differently," Luke suggested. "Not this place."

"Thank you, Mr. Armchair Psychiatrist," said Colton, patting Luke's hand.

"Who wants dessert?" Sam asked, standing up. He began picking up plates. Sophie joined him, as did Luke.

"Ignore Luke," Colton said to Burke as the trio went into the kitchen. "But do think about doing a show. I can't promise you a write up in the *Times* and collectors snapping you up because someone else tells them to, but I can promise you an appreciative audience and a wine-and-cheese opening night."

"Wine *and* cheese?" said Burke. "I may just have to think about it, after all."

"Please do," Colton said.

Sam returned, carrying two plates, one of which he set in front of Burke. On it was a beautiful little pie in a ceramic dish. On top of the pie was a scoop of ice cream.

"Sophie made the pies," Sam said as Luke and Sophie emerged from the kitchen with two plates each.

"Three are peach and three are apple," Sophie said. "Enjoy."

Burke pushed his fork into the pie, breaking the crust and releasing the smell of peaches. He took a forkful, added some ice cream, and put it in his mouth. It was delicious. Around the table the others made moans of pleasure as well.

"Who got peach?" Sophie asked.

Nan, Burke, and Colton lifted their forks. "I bet the apple is just as fantastic," Colton said.

"See for yourself," said Luke, holding out a forkful of his pie.

Colton accepted it, closing his eyes while he chewed. "I think I'm in love," he said after swallowing. "I could marry that pie."

"According to the anti-gay marriage crowd, that'll be next," said Nan. "Pies and sheep."

Burke looked at Sam. He had eaten half of his pie. "You should try the peach," Burke said.

Sam picked up his plate and exchanged it with Burke's. "There," he said. "The best of both worlds."

As Burke took a bite of the apple pie, he noticed Luke looking at him. Then Luke switched his gaze to Sam. A smile played across his lips, but he didn't say anything.

After dinner they moved from the dining room to the living room, where talk turned to everything from current movies to politics to their favorite childhood games. A lively debate ensued between Luke and Nan over the merits of Chutes and Ladders versus Candy Land, and Burke used the opportunity to make a trip to the bathroom. On the way back he looked into the kitchen, where Sam was rinsing dishes.

"I'd offer to help, but I'm more likely to break something," Burke said. "Shouldn't you be out there, anyway?"

"I stay out of the board-game controversy," Sam said. "Besides, I'm just rinsing these off. If they dry, they're impossible to wash."

Burke leaned against the counter, taking the weight of his leg off his crutch. "So, when were you going to tell me that you're a celebrated author?" he asked.

Sam chuckled. "It's really not a big deal," he said. "But if you want to read the book, I'll find you a copy. I have a box of them somewhere around here."

"I do," Burke said. "I don't know any authors personally. Wait. I take that back. I do know one, but nobody likes him *or* his books."

"You don't know that you'll like my book, either," Sam said.

"If I don't, I won't say a word," said Burke.

Sam rinsed the last dish. "Then I'll never know if you're telling the truth or just being nice."

"You'll just have to trust me," Burke told him. He paused a moment. "I really like your friends," he said. "I'm envious."

"I'm sure you have a lot of friends," said Sam.

Burke shook his head. "I have a lot of people that I *know*," he said. "I'm not sure I'd call them friends."

"'Your friend is the man who knows all about you, and still likes you,'" Sam said quietly. "Elbert Hubbard."

"Who?"

"American writer, after a fashion," Sam explained. "My favorite quote of his is, 'There are just two respectable ways to die. One is of old age, and the other is by accident.'" He laughed nervously, putting his fist to his mouth as he choked.

They looked at one another, neither speaking. Burke suddenly felt awkward and searched for something to say. His heart beat loudly in his ears. Sam seemed not to know what to do with his hands. Finally, he shoved them into his pockets.

"Sam!" Colton's voice seemed to echo like canon fire in Burke's ears, startling him. "Nan just said tiddleywinks sucks. Get in here before it gets ugly!"

"We should go," Sam said quickly.

Burke nodded. "Yeah," he agreed. "We should. Before something happens."

CHAPTER 22

Gaither Lucas lived in a Victorian house as stately and well preserved as the queen herself. As Will pulled the truck up to the curb in front of it, he whistled. "That paint job cost him a bundle," he said. "There must be five different colors on there."

Burke would rather have paid Gaither Lucas a visit with Sam accompanying him. But fifteen minutes before they were to leave to make the journey to Burlington, a water line in the library's seldom-used men's room had decided to burst, flooding the bathroom and threatening to dampen the carpeting in the main room. Sam had been able to turn the water off but had to stay there to await the arrival of the local plumber. Burke would have canceled, but Gaither Lucas had been very insistent that Tuesday afternoon was the only time he could meet with them. And so Burke had called Will, who had been only too happy to offer a ride.

"Only *one* old guy lives here?" Will asked as he helped Burke out of the truck.

"As far as I know," Burke answered, starting up the manicured walk to the front porch. His leg was hurting him after the long ride, and this only added to his bad mood. Also, Will had resumed the discussion about possibly visiting Burke in Boston, and for some reason he couldn't pinpoint, it annoyed Burke that Will was speaking as if the two of them were developing an actual relationship. He wished he could ask the boy to wait in the truck.

Will knocked on the door before Burke could point out the button for the doorbell. "Oops," Will said when Burke nodded at it. He reached out and pressed the button, and a soft clanging came from within the house.

The door opened almost immediately. A very tall, very thin man with snow-white hair peered out at them. "No need to do it twice," he announced in a firm voice. "My hearing's as good as my sight is. I'm Gaither Lucas, and I'm guessing you're Burke," he said, correctly identifying one of his visitors. "Which means you must be Sam Guffrey," he said to Will.

"Sam couldn't come," Burke said quickly. "An emergency at the library."

"Emergency?" Gaither said. "At a library? What happened? Someone keep a book out too long and the law had to be called in? I've never known books to raise a ruckus. Mostly, they just sit there."

Burke suppressed a smile. "A water line broke," he explained. "This is Will Janks, my . . . friend."

Gaither looked at Will for a moment, then moved his small, dark eyes back to Burke. "I see," he said. "Well, come on in before Antoinette breaks her neck."

"Antoinette?" said Burke, not understanding.

"Antoinette Couteau," Gaither replied as Will and Burke came inside. "My neighbor. Has to know everything that goes on. She's too short to get a good look out the window, so she stands on a stool. And she's got cats. One of these days one of them is going to get between her feet, and she's going to fall over and do herself a mischief." Stepping outside, he waved at the house next door and called out loudly, "Watch those damn cats, Annie!" He chuckled as he shut the door. "Let's go into the parlor," he said.

The inside of the house was as beautiful as the outside. Burke wondered if Gaither Lucas had had the place renovated or if it simply had never fallen into disrepair. Looking at dark wood floors polished by years of feet passing over them, walls plastered and smoothed by hand and not simply drywalled, and moldings featuring minor damage that could be caused only by a lifetime of use, he suspected it was the latter. Even the paintings and photographs decorating the walls had an air about them that suggested they'd been there long before Gaither had first passed through the front door.

The parlor was large and surprisingly airy. Although definitely of a different time, the furniture was not as overstuffed as Burke would have expected in such a house. Rather than having the claustrophobic aura of a dowager's sitting room, the parlor was inviting. Burke sat down on a Directoire-style sofa, which he was almost certain was a Phyfe. Across from it were two Sheraton armchairs, and between those was a lovely table, upon which stood an unusual lamp featuring three nude female figures holding up a large glass globe shade.

"Is that a Nuart?" Burke asked Gaither.

The older man glanced at the lamp. "Indeed it is," he said. "It was given to my mother as a wedding present. She was a bit scandalized by the nudity, but not so much that she wouldn't display it. She did, however, forbid me to turn it on or off. I think she feared brushing my fingertips against one of the ladies' breasts might corrupt me."

Burke laughed. He liked Gaither Lucas. The old man had a fine sense of humor. *He's what I want to be when I grow up,* Burke thought as he watched Gaither move around the room.

"Would you gentlemen like something to drink?" Gaither asked. "I'd suggest cocktails, but as it's only just ten o'clock, I think that would be in poor taste. Perhaps some iced tea?"

"That sounds perfect," said Burke.

Gaither nodded and left the room. Will, seated in one of the chairs, looked around the room. "How do you know what all this stuff is?" he asked Burke. "And what's a Nuart? Sounds like a porn theater I saw once, driving through Rhode Island."

"They made Art Deco lamps," Burke said. "And I know about this 'stuff' because I'm interested in the history of design."

"Why?" said Will, looking genuinely confused by the idea.

Burke pointed at the wall behind Will, which was covered by a wallpaper adorned with pale green vines with yellow flowers and small birds. "Do you know who designed that?" he asked.

Will shook his head.

"William Morris," Burke informed him. "An English designer. He was part of the Arts and Crafts movement."

Will shrugged. "It just looks like some birds and flowers."

"That pattern is called 'Tom Tit,'" Burke said. "A tit is a kind of bird," he added quickly, seeing the grin that had started to cross Will's face.

"So the guy made some freaky wallpaper," said Will. "What's the big deal?"

"It's the *idea* behind the wallpaper," Burke explained. "Morris and his contemporaries wanted to make interior design—architecture, textiles, furnishings, art, everything—more in line with the natural world. It was a major shift in the way people thought about design."

"So what you're saying is that we're sitting in a museum," Will remarked.

"It does sometimes feel that way," agreed Gaither Lucas as he entered with a tray carrying three glasses and a pitcher of tea. "And occasionally I feel like one of the antiquities housed in it." He set the tray on a table and poured tea into the glasses.

"I don't really know anything about this kind of stuff," Will admitted as he accepted the glass Gaither handed him. "I'm more into things that move—cars, engines, that sort of thing. I guess I don't have the artistic gene or whatever." Before either Burke or Gaither could reply, Will's cell phone trilled. He took it from his pocket and looked at it. "It's my dad," he said. "I'll take it outside."

He went into the hall and out the front door, leaving Burke and Gaither alone. Gaither handed Burke a glass of iced tea and resumed his seat. "He seems like a nice boy," he said, taking a sip from his glass.

"His father and I went to school together," said Burke. "He drives me around." He nodded at his leg cast for emphasis.

"Yes," Gaither said, "I noticed that you're a bit . . . impaired at the moment. May I ask what happened?"

"Car accident," said Burke. "On my fortieth birthday."

Gaither raised an eyebrow. "Forty?" he said. "I think I remember forty. It was a *very* long time ago."

Burke already knew that Gaither Lucas was seventy-seven. Sam had found the birth announcement from 1933. *He's almost twice my age,* he thought. *And I'm twice Will's age.* Will could be his son, and Gaither could be his grandfather. For some reason he found this unnerving.

The front door opened, and Will returned to the parlor. "I've got to go," he said. "Dad needs my help with a calving. I'm sorry."

"Oh," Burke said, taken aback. "Okay. Well, maybe we can do this another time?" he asked Gaither.

"Why don't you stay?" Gaither said. "Will here can go help his father and come back for you later."

"It's an hour back," Burke said.

"And this could take a while," said Will.

Gaither shook his head. "You can stay here tonight," he told Burke. "I assume you don't need any particular looking after, other than perhaps some help up the stairs?"

Burke shook his head.

"And I'm sure I can scare up the necessary toiletries and such," said Gaither. "It will give us more time to talk, and I'd be happy for the company."

Burke looked at Will. "Would you mind coming back tomorrow?"

"No," said Will. "It's no problem for me. I like the drive."

"Then that's settled," Gaither said. He stood up and reached for Will's hand. "It was lovely meeting you. Tomorrow you must stay for lunch or supper, depending on when you arrive. My regards to the calf and its mother."

Again, Will left them alone.

"You're sure this isn't an imposition?" Burke asked Gaither.

"I have no relatives," Gaither answered. "My friends are scattered around the globe. Believe me when I say that I'm happy to have the company. Now, I believe you wanted to talk about Amos and Tess Hague."

"Yes," Burke said.

"You said that your interest has something to do with a project about the Civil War," Gaither continued.

Burke cleared his throat. "I'm afraid I wasn't entirely forthcoming in that regard," Burke admitted. "I'm a photographer, and I've been working on a project of a sort that began with a book about the Civil War."

Gaither regarded him without expression. "And now we come to the part where you have not been entirely forthcoming, I take it?"

"I didn't intend to be," said Burke. "It's just that things have taken a sort of . . . peculiar turn."

Gaither sat back and crossed one leg over the other at the knee. "Peculiar? In what way?"

Burke was apprehensive about proceeding. He realized now that he'd been hoping that Sam would handle this part of the conversation. Now that the responsibility had fallen on him, he wasn't at all sure he could ask the questions to which he was seeking answers. He had brought with him some of the photos he'd taken at the Hague farm, and they sat in a portfolio beside him. But now he couldn't imagine showing them to Gaither Lucas.

"Mr. Crenshaw, I assure you that I have experienced many peculiar things in my lifetime. I believe there is nothing you might want to know—or say—about my family that would upset me."

I wouldn't be so sure, Burke thought. He took a breath to calm himself. "I'm curious about Amos and Tess Hague," he began before he could talk himself out of it.

"That's hardly peculiar," Gaither assured him.

"We haven't gotten to that part," said Burke.

Gaither took a drink of tea. "I assume what you really want to know about is how the Hague farm came to be the Wrathmore farm," he said. He didn't wait for Burke's answer before continuing. "It's a sad story, and one very few people know."

"All I know is that in 1911 Calvin Wrathmore claimed ownership of the Hague farm. What I haven't been able to find out is *how* he claimed ownership."

"Calvin Wrathmore—my grandfather—claimed ownership due to the right of inheritance," said Gaither.

Burke shook his head. "I don't understand."

"Before I continue, do I have your promise that you will publish none of what I tell you?" asked Gaither.

"Of course," said Burke. "I'm simply curious."

"For reasons you in turn promise to share with me," Gaither added.

"Yes."

"Very well," said Gaither after a moment. "I may be a foolish old man, but I believe you. The answer to your question is that Calvin Wrathmore was not my grandfather's given name."

"What was it?"

"Cain Hague," said Gaither.

Burke heard himself inhale sharply. "Amos and Tess's grandson?"

Gaither shook his head. "No," he said. "Their son. Born in 1869."

"Now I'm really confused," Burke said. "I didn't know they had children."

"My grandfather ran away from home in 1884," said Gaither. "Shortly after the marriage of Tess Hague to Peter Woode."

Wait until I ask him about Peter Woode, Burke thought. *He might find that peculiar.* But for the moment he kept that secret to himself.

"I was told that my grandfather did not approve of his mother remarrying," Gaither continued. "At any rate, he left home at the age of fifteen and apprenticed himself to a carpenter. He also changed his name, to Calvin Wrathmore. Poetic, isn't it?"

"And he never spoke to his mother again?" asked Burke.

"Not to my knowledge," said Gaither. "She died around the turn of the century, I believe."

"In 1903," Burke said. "So why wait until 1911, after Peter Woode's death, to make a claim on the farm?"

"I can't answer that," Gaither replied. "My mother never knew. As you've obviously done some research on the matter, you know that my grandparents were killed in a fire set by Peter Blackburne in 1920. Only my mother survived."

"But I understand that Blackburne was acquitted."

Gaither nodded. "He was. Nonetheless, he was guilty. My mother saw him running from the house."

Burke didn't contradict the statement. He was hardly going to suggest that Gaither's mother might have lied, or at the least been mistaken. Anyway, there was no point. He was more interested in the revelation that Calvin Wrathmore was actually Amos and Tess's son.

"That means that Grace Woode was Calvin's half sister," he said.

"It does," Gaither agreed.

"Which means that Tanya is your"—Burke tried to picture the family tree Caroline Ayres had made—"second cousin thrice removed," he concluded. "Or something."

"Tanya?" Gaither said.

"Tanya Redmond," said Burke. "Tess and Peter Woode's great-great-great-great-granddaughter. Her mother had a picture of Tess and Peter Woode."

"I'm afraid I'm not acquainted with that branch of the family tree," Gaither said. "After Peter Blackburne killed my grandparents, relations understandably cooled a bit. There were no annual reunions or holiday get-togethers."

Burke smiled at the joke despite the grimness of it. "But Blackburne didn't know he was related to Calvin Wrathmore, anyway, did he? I mean, how could he if he didn't know Calvin was really Cain Hague?"

"But he did know," said Gaither. "That's how Calvin claimed ownership of the farm. He revealed his identity to the court. There was a record of Cain Hague's birth, of course, and he also had supporting evidence."

"What was that?"

Calvin smiled. "The wedding rings of Amos and Tess Hague," he said. "Would you like to see them?"

CHAPTER 23

The rings were gold. Gaither kept them in a blue velvet box in the top drawer of his bureau. Rather than bring them down to Burke, he had brought Burke up to his bedroom on the second floor. Like the rest of the house, it was beautifully appointed with antiques and thick rugs on the floor. The windows were closed, and the air held the smell of lavender.

"Very ordinary, aren't they?" Gaither said as he took one of the rings out and laid it on Burke's palm. "That one was Amos's."

Burke held the ring between his fingers. It was indeed a plain gold band, unremarkable except that it had once been worn on the finger of a Civil War soldier.

"Now look inside," said Gaither.

Burke brought the ring closer to his eye. On the inside of the ring he could just make out words engraved in the metal. He tried to read them, but they were too faint.

"It says, 'And the beautiful day passed well,'" Gaither told him. "And inside the other is written, 'And the next came with equal joy.' Both have the initials AH and TB in them as well."

"That's unusual for that time, isn't it?" Burke asked. "They didn't generally engrave rings, I don't think."

Gaither nodded. "It is a bit odd," he said. He took the ring back from Burke and returned it to the box. "Which is precisely why Calvin's possession of them was taken as proof of his parentage. Also, he looked exactly like his father." He looked at the rings a moment before shutting the box. "My mother told me that my grandfather pressed these into her hand and told her to run from the house the night it was on fire. They're the only things she took with her."

"You said earlier that Calvin—Cain—ran away after his mother married Peter Woode."

"I suppose he thought Tess was somehow betraying Amos by re-marrying," Gaither said.

Burke hesitated before continuing. Did he really want to tell Gaither Sam's theory regarding Peter Woode? Although Gaither seemed like an open-minded person, would he really want to know that Peter Woode might really have been Elizabeth Frances Walsh? *Then again, it's not as if he comes from that side of the family,* he argued. *Still, finding out your step-great-grandfather was a woman might be a little bit of a stretch.* It was a difficult call, and again he wished Sam were there to help.

"Have you ever heard of a Thomas Beattie?" he asked instead.

"Tess's brother," Gaither said. "He worked on the farm, I believe. My mother mentioned him several times. It was a bit odd, actually. She said her father spoke about Thomas only when he was drunk, which I gather was not an infrequent occurrence. In fact, the fire that killed my grandparents was eventually blamed on Calvin knocking over an oil lamp in a drunken stupor, although my mother swears he was as sober as a stone that night."

"Have you been to the farm?" Burke asked.

"No," said Gaither as he put the box back into the drawer. "Well, once or twice as a child, but only with my father. My mother refused to go back."

"But you still own it?"

"I do," Gaither confirmed. "After the fire my mother went to live with her mother's sister in Maine. She grew up there, and when she was eighteen, she was told that there was a great deal of money com-ing to her from her father, as well as the land where the farm was lo-cated. A year later she married my father, Bertram Lucas, and told him that she wanted to return to Vermont. They bought this house in nineteen thirty-two. As my mother wouldn't live on the land she owned, my father wanted to sell it, but my mother wouldn't allow it." He paused. "It annoyed my father greatly," he added, chuckling. "He thought he could get a great deal of money for it. I remember stand-ing with him in the grass, looking at the ruins of the farm, and him muttering about what a damn fool my mother was."

"And yet you haven't sold it, either," Burke remarked.

Gaither smiled. "No," he said. "I haven't. I suppose I keep it because I know it meant something to her. Silly, I know, but I've always been a sentimental sort. Derek used to say I would keep the snow from every Christmas if I could find a way to save it."

"Derek?" said Burke. "Your brother?"

"No, no," Gaither said. "I have no brother. Derek was my lover." He looked at Burke. "I believe they call them domestic partners now," he said. "Or is it husbands, now that we can marry?"

"I'm sorry," Burke said. "I didn't mean to pry."

Gaither waved away the apology. "I wouldn't have told you if I wanted to keep it a secret," he said. "I'm too old to care what anybody thinks of me. And, anyway, if I'm not mistaken, there's something between you and that handsome young man who brought you today."

"Well, yes, there is," said Burke.

Gaither clapped his hands. "The old gaydar isn't on the fritz, then, after all," he said. He looked at Burke with a smile. "I love that word. Gaydar. So clever."

"I'm afraid mine is broken," Burke said. "It never occurred to me that you were gay."

"It's because I'm teeming with masculinity," Gaither joked. He walked to the nightstand beside his bed and picked up a framed photo. "Derek said my mother made me a sissy and the army made me a man. Not very enlightened of him, but not entirely untrue."

Burke looked at the photo, which Gaither had handed him. It showed Gaither standing beside a shorter, heavier man in front of a Nash Rambler. Both had crew cuts and wore dark suits.

"That was taken in 1955," Gaither said. "I was twenty-two, and Derek was thirty-six. We'd been together about a year."

"Where did you meet?"

"At a weekend party," Gaither answered. "In those days we didn't have so many options for socializing. Very few bars and so on, particularly in this part of the country. Every weekend someone with a house in the country would host a party for ten or twenty of us. Sometimes we would drive for hours to get there."

"It was all gay men?" asked Burke.

"Some lesbians," Gaither said. "Half would dress in suits, and the other half would wear girly things. They'd pretend to be married couples for the weekend. The boys were less dramatic, although there were a handful of queens who put on the make-up and camped it up."

"It actually sounds kind of fun," said Burke.

Gaither nodded. "It was *enormously* fun," he said. "You know, everyone now talks about how dreadful it was for us in those days, as if we were Anne Frank and family hiding in an attic in fear for our lives. But really we had some wonderful times. Some terrible ones, too, some of us, but mostly I have fond memories of those weekends. As I said, I met Derek at one of those parties. It was hosted by an old army buddy of his. The Major, we called him, although I don't know that he really was one."

"It sounds like you were all in the army," Burke commented.

"Most of us were. Derek was in the Second World War, and of course, I was in Korea. It never occurred to us that we couldn't—or shouldn't—be there. Not like today."

"In some ways we seem to be going backward," said Burke, handing the picture back to Gaither. "Derek is very handsome, by the way."

"Isn't he?" said Gaither. "The first time I saw him, I nearly dropped my gin and tonic." He stroked the glass on the photo. "I miss him every day."

"How long were you together?"

"Fifty-three years. He died two years ago this December. We went to bed one night, and in the morning he was gone. He hadn't even stirred."

"I'm sorry," said Burke.

"As am I," Gaither said, setting the photo down. "But fifty-three years is a long time. My parents had barely twenty when my father died of a heart attack, and of course, you know what happened to my grandparents."

"I can't even imagine fifty-three years," said Burke.

Gaither cocked his head. "Why not?" he asked. "In fifty-three years you'll be ninety-three, and Will won't be more than seventy or so."

Burke shook his head. "I don't think we'll get that far," he said. He could feel Gaither waiting for more details, but he didn't want to discuss his romantic failings. Instead he said, "Now I have something I want to show you."

They returned to the parlor, where Burke opened his portfolio and brought out several of the photographs he'd taken at the farm. He spread them out on the coffee table for Gaither to look at. "At first I thought there was something wrong with the cameras or the film," he began to explain.

"Ghosts," Gaither said, picking up one of the shots and examining it more closely.

"Well, that's one theory," Burke said cautiously.

"My mother used to talk about ghosts," said Gaither. "In the last years of her life she developed Alzheimer's. She regressed to the point where she couldn't remember what she'd eaten for breakfast that morning but could describe in minute detail things that had occurred in her youth. The night of the fire, for instance. Many times she would wake up screaming, convinced she was back in that house. She thought I was her father, and while I tried to comfort her, she told me how she'd seen Peter Blackburne running away. It's why I believe so strongly in his guilt."

"And she talked about ghosts?" Burke prodded.

"Yes. She remembered seeing them on the farm when she was a girl. Sometimes in the fields. Sometimes at the pond. Sometimes even in the house. She told her parents about them, but they didn't believe her. Eventually, she stopped speaking about them. She never mentioned them to me until her mind began to go backward in time."

"Did she ever say who they were?"

"Amos Hague and Thomas Beattie," Gaither answered.

"Why would they haunt the farm?"

"Well, Amos drowned there, in the pond. I suppose if you believe in such things, it would make sense that he would want to stay around."

"I didn't know he drowned there," Burke said. "Do you know how Thomas died?"

Gaither shook his head.

"Then I assume you don't know that they died on the same day a year apart and are buried next to one another."

"No," Gaither said. "I didn't know that. How very odd."

"There's more," Burke told him. "Sam has reason to believe that Peter Woode was a woman."

Gaither raised an eyebrow. "It would be very difficult for her to be the father of Grace, then, wouldn't it?"

"I've been thinking about that. Tess and Peter married not long after Amos's death, which has always seemed a little strange to me. It's possible Tess was pregnant by Amos."

Gaither thought about this. "If that's true, then Grace and Cain were fully brother and sister," he said. "That makes the squabbling over the farm even more tragic, doesn't it?"

"It does," Burke agreed. "And if Cain knew Peter Woode's secret, it might explain why he ran, and why the wedding rings were of such importance to him."

Gaither leaned back. "It's all terribly gothic," he remarked. "Like a Faulkner novel. Have we any proof of any of this?"

"Not really," Burke admitted. "Sam is the one who pieced it together."

"I look forward to meeting this Sam Guffrey," said Gaither. "He has an interesting mind."

"That he does," Burke said. "And I know he'll love talking to you."

"This is a lot to digest," said Gaither. He looked at the clock on the mantel. "And as it is now a quarter past noon, I believe we are entitled to a drink to aid us in this endeavor. Shall we?"

Burke followed him into the kitchen. Burke sat at the table there, drinking from a glass of excellent merlot Gaither had poured for him, while Gaither prepared a light lunch.

"If Peter Woode really was . . . What did you say her name was?"

"Elizabeth Frances Walsh," Burke said.

"Elizabeth Frances Walsh. If he were really she, does that mean Tess was a lesbian?"

"Don't ask me," said Burke. "It took me a couple of years to get the whole transgender thing straight in my head, and now the kids are saying that we should get rid of labels and be whatever we want to be."

"It's a brave new world," Gaither remarked as he tossed a salad. "I fear it's leaving me further and further behind. It was so much easier when all we had to know was whether we were tops or bottoms."

"Believe me, that one is still a problem," Burke assured him.

Gaither set the salad on the table. "Are tops still scarce?" he asked. "In my day they were all bottoms. Fortunately, both Derek and I were ambidextrous."

Burke laughed at the openness of the question. "They're still pretty hard to find," he said. "But I think that's changing." He thought of Will, and how he had been surprised at Burke's suggestion that a man had to be one thing or the other. He had to admit, too, that being on the bottom hadn't been all that unpleasant. In fact, thinking about it now caused a familiar stirring in his groin.

And maybe you're changing, too, he thought. Was it so ridiculous, the idea of him and Will as a couple? Earlier it had seemed so, but now he wasn't sure. Yes, there was the age difference, and Will was immature in a lot of ways. Also, he seemed afraid of breaking out of Wellston. But perhaps all he needed was some encouragement.

Burke thought back to Gaither's comment about how he and Will might someday be celebrating fifty years together. He tried to imagine it. Will certainly seemed to enjoy being with him now. At least in bed. But what about when he was fifty and Burke was seventy? What then? Or would it matter? Maybe by then sex wouldn't be so important.

"Can I ask you something personal?" he heard himself say to Gaither.

"By all means," Gaither answered. "The more personal the better."

"Did you and Derek still make love? You know, after all those years."

Gaither grinned. "If you're asking me if we were still hot for each other, we were," he said. "Of course, it wasn't like it was those first years, but that was also part of the joy of it."

"And now?" asked Burke.

Gaither looked at him over his glass of wine. "If you're asking me whether you'll be sleeping in the guest room or in *my* room tonight, I should warn you that I snore quite loudly."

For a moment Burke wasn't sure how to respond.

Then Gaither grinned. "Relax," he said. "I'll be a good boy. Besides, you can always lock the door from the inside if you fear being violated in the night."

CHAPTER 24

"How's the cow?"

"What?" said Will. "Oh, she's good. Calf's good. Everyone's good."

Burke refrained from asking him if they were also *well*. "You look tired. It must have been a long night."

"Yeah, it was," Will answered. "I didn't get much sleep."

Burke sat back, looking out the window. His evening with Gaither had been a welcome break from staying with his father and Lucy. They'd talked well into the night, about everything from relationships to photography. Gaither reminded Burke a little of Sam. Both had wide-ranging interests and ideas, and conversing with them left him feeling energized rather than exhausted, as he sometimes felt after spending several hours with his friends in Boston.

Will had phoned a little past ten to say he was coming and had arrived in time for lunch. He'd said little during the meal, which Burke attributed to his being so tired. After promising to return soon for another visit, they'd left for the journey home.

"Gaither's an interesting guy, isn't he?" Burke said.

Will shrugged. "I guess," he said.

"He told me some great stories about when he and his lover were our ages. Well, closer to your age than mine. They were fourteen years apart." Burke watched Will's face for a reaction but got none. "He asked if we were a couple," he added.

Will turned and looked at him. "Really? He thought I was gay? Why?"

"I don't know why," Burke replied. "Does it matter?"

Will didn't answer. Instead, he turned on the radio to a country music station, filling the silence between them with Waylon Jennings and Jessi Colter singing "Storms Never Last."

"You weren't even born when this song was a hit," Burke remarked. He was immediately sorry for saying it, realizing that in some way he was trying to irritate Will into saying something.

"I like the older stuff," Will said.

Burke wondered if this was meant to apply to whatever it was that was going on between them. Was he older stuff, too? *He could at least say* classic, he thought.

"Songs now don't really say anything," Will continued. "Most of them don't even make sense. But these," he said, nodding at the radio, "they're about something. You ever listen to George Jones? Tammy Wynette? Their songs are amazing."

"Where'd you ever hear them?" asked Burke. "As I recall, your father was more into Bruce Springsteen and Metallica than he was country."

"My grandfather," said Will.

"Doc Janks?" Burke said, surprised. "I thought he was only into classical and jazz. Every time I was over there, he was playing Bach or Coltrane or something brainy."

"Yeah, well, he wanted everyone to think he was all sophisticated. But when he took me with him on his rounds, he always played Merle Haggard, Johnny Cash, Loretta Lynn. He said it was music that told a story."

"But your father doesn't like that, does he?"

Will shook his head. "I don't think he ever knew Granddad liked it. The two of them—they didn't really talk too much. Kind of like me and my dad."

"And me and mine," said Burke. "I wonder what makes it easier to talk to our grandfathers than our fathers."

"I don't know," Will said. "But it is. I don't think my father knows one thing about me, really."

"Have you tried talking to him?"

Will laughed. "Tried? Sure. About how to cure hoof rot and bloat. Anything else and he acts like I've asked him what position he and my mother like to do it in."

"I'm sorry to hear that," said Burke. "I wish I could tell you how to change that. The truth is, I don't know myself. The older we get, the less I think my father and I know about one another."

"But if you had a kid, I bet he'd know," Will remarked. "Then maybe he could explain it to you."

"Like those diseases that skip a generation," Burke suggested. "Only every other generation understands each other."

They rode in silence for a long time. Burke wanted to ask Will several things, chief among them whether he thought of Burke as his father's friend or as a man with whom he was becoming involved. But although he tried several times, he couldn't bring himself to say the words.

"I've been thinking about what you said about coming to Boston," he said eventually.

"What about it?"

"I think you should," said Burke. "Maybe you'll like it enough to stay for a while." *Maybe even with me,* he thought.

Will nodded. "Maybe," he said. "You never know."

There was a decided lack of enthusiasm in his response, and Burke wondered what had changed since their afternoon in Will's room, when he'd seemed so excited about the possibility of coming to the city. He almost asked but found that he didn't want to know.

"Would you mind dropping me at the library?" he asked. "I want to talk to Sam about some of the things Gaither told me."

"No problem," Will said. "I've got to do some things with Dad this afternoon. Can Lucy pick you up?"

"Probably. Or Sam can give me a ride home. Don't worry about it."

"Maybe we can get together tomorrow?" Will said.

Burke felt his spirits lift. "Definitely," he said. "I'd like that."

They continued without talking, but now Burke felt more relaxed. Will wanted to see him again. He was surprised at how that made him feel. Maybe there was more to his feelings for Will than he'd realized. Maybe the fear that Will didn't return them was more frightening than he'd imagined it could be. But now that fear was gone.

At the library he considered giving Will a kiss good-bye. But they were parked right outside, and anyone coming out would see them. He settled for patting Will's shoulder as he helped him out of the truck and saying, "Let's talk tomorrow."

"Will do. Say hi to Sam."

Burke walked into the library to find Sam seated at a table with Freddie Redmond. Freddie was reading from a book, working through the sentences slowly and methodically. Sam, seeing Burke, held a finger to his lips. Burke stood silently, listening as the boy read.

"'Perhaps he would never have dared to raise his eyes, but that, though the piping was now hushed, the call and the summons seemed still dominant and im . . . im . . .'"

"Sound it out," Sam said. "Im."

"Im. Per."

"It's actually *peer,*" Sam said. "It's one of those weird words."

"Im-peer-ee-us," Freddie tried. "Imperious."

Sam nodded. "Perfect," he said. "Keep going."

"'Dominant and imperious. He might not refuse, were Death himself waiting to strike him instantly, once he had looked with mortal eye on things rightly kept hidden. Trembling he obeyed, and raised his humble head; and then, in that utter clearness of the i-*min*-int—'"

"*I*-min-int," Sam corrected him.

Freddie nodded and repeated the word correctly. "'Imminent dawn, while Nature, flushed with fulness of incredible colour, seemed to hold her breath for the event, he looked in the very eyes of the Friend and Helper; saw the backward sweep of the curved horns, gleaming in the growing daylight; saw the stern, hooked nose between the kindly eyes that were looking down on them humourously, while the bearded mouth broke into a half-smile at the corners; saw the rippling muscles on the arm that lay across the broad chest, the long soup-el—'"

"*Su*-pull," said Sam.

"Supple," Freddie repeated. "Supple. What's that mean?"

"Soft," Sam explained. "Something that can bend."

"Oh," said Freddie, beginning again to read. "'The long supple hand still holding the pan-pipes . . .' What are those?"

"Something like a flute," said Sam. "I'll show you a picture later."

"'The pan-pipes only just fallen away from the parted lips; saw the splendid curves of the shaggy limbs disposed in majestic ease on the sard—'"

"Hold on," Sam interrupted. "What's that word?"

"Sard?" said Freddie.

"Why do you think that?"

"Well, it looks like *sword,*" Freddie explained. "And you don't say the *w* in *sword.*"

"That's right," said Sam. "But that's an exception. This time you do say the w sound."

"So it's swu-ard?" Freddie said.

"Close," said Sam. "Make it one syllable. Sward."

"Sward," Freddie repeated. He sighed. "Why's English have to be so weird?"

Sam chuckled. "I know. It can be, can't it? But you're doing really well."

"What's a sward, anyway?"

"It's a patch of grass," Sam told him. "This part of the sentence means the person is lying on the grass."

"Then why can't he just say 'lying on the grass'?"

"The author is using poetic language," said Sam. "It fits the scene."

"If you say so," Freddie said, sighing. "Should I keep going?"

"There's just a little left," Sam said. "Let's finish up."

Freddie returned to the book. "'On the sward; saw, last of all, nestling between his very hooves, sleeping soundly in entire peace and contentment, the little, round, podgy . . .' Podgy?"

"It means chubby."

"'Podgy, childish form of the baby otter. All this he saw, for one moment breathless and intense, vivid on the morning sky; and still, as he looked, he lived; and still, as he lived, he wondered.'"

"Great job," said Sam as Freddie shut the book.

"What does it mean?"

"What does what mean?"

"*All* of it," said Freddie. "It's all one gigantic sentence that doesn't make any sense. I get the parts about Mr. Toad and the cars and the weasels and all that, but this is just weird."

"It is a little weird," Sam agreed. "I'll explain it more tomorrow. Your mom will be here any minute now, and I don't want to keep her waiting."

"But I want to know!" Freddie objected.

"Tell you what," said Sam. "Why don't you tell *me* what you think it means?"

"But I don't know," said Freddie. "That's why I asked."

"What's going on in the story?"

"Rat and Mole are looking for the missing baby otter," Freddie said. "They're in a boat, and they find an island."

"Right," Sam said. "And on the island they see something."

"The thing with horns," said Freddie. "And hairy legs. And it's playing the flute thing."

"See?" said Sam. "You got it all along."

"Yeah, but who *is* it?"

"That's what we'll talk about tomorrow," Sam assured him as the front door opened and Tanya came in.

"How'd it go?" she asked her son.

"Okay," Freddie answered.

"Better than okay," said Sam. "He did a fantastic job."

"I did *okay,*" Freddie repeated. "I didn't understand it all."

"Tomorrow," Sam promised him. "And tonight look up any other words you don't know, okay?"

Freddie nodded as he ran for the door.

"Did he really do okay?" Tanya asked Sam when Freddie was out of earshot.

"He really did," Sam confirmed. "I don't think he'll have any trouble passing the literacy test I got the school to agree to."

Tanya closed her eyes and sighed. When she opened her eyes, they were wet with tears. "Thank you again," she said.

"It's my pleasure," Sam told her. "I'll see him tomorrow at one."

Tanya followed her boy out of the library, and Burke sat down across the table from Sam. "That was pretty heavy stuff," he said.

"No kidding," Sam agreed. "I almost skipped that chapter. A lot of people do. It's kind of out of place with the rest of the book. But he's a bright kid. Even if he doesn't understand all of it, he gets the basic idea. And he learned a bunch of new words."

"I don't think *I* understood most of it," Burke told him.

"Rat and Mole are looking for the baby otter," said Sam. "They meet the Piper at the Gates of Dawn—their version of God. He's the Horned God who watches over the creatures of the woods. They can't believe they're seeing him in person. It's a kind of religious experience."

"Isn't that a little serious for a children's book?"

"*The Wind in the Willows* is a serious book," said Sam. "As Freddie said, it's easier to follow Mr. Toad's adventures, but there's a lot more to it. It's really about the connection the animals have to the woods and the river. Toad tries to get away from those things and act like a human, and that's what gets him into trouble."

"I get it," said Burke, grinning. "This is more of your 'cities are evil' philosophy."

Sam held up his hand. "You caught me," he said. "I'm trying to turn the kid into a pagan. Don't tell Tanya."

"One of these days you'll have to explain the whole pagan thing to me," Burke said. "But right now I have some things to tell you."

For the next half hour he told Sam everything he'd learned from Gaither Lucas. At each new revelation Sam's eyes grew wider, and when Burke was finished, Sam just shook his head.

"Wow," he said. "Just wow."

"I know," said Burke. "It's completely wild, isn't it?"

"I don't even know where to start," Sam said.

"Oh, I forgot one more thing," said Burke. "The engravings inside the rings. I knew I wouldn't remember what they said, so I wrote them down." He took a piece of paper from his pocket and handed it to Sam.

"'And the beautiful day passed well,'" Sam read. "'And the next came with equal joy.' That's from Whitman."

"Whitman?"

"Walt Whitman," Sam said. "Hang on."

He got up and disappeared into the stacks. A minute later he returned with a book. "*Leaves of Grass,*" he said as he sat down and started leafing through the pages. "The most well-known version was published in eighteen sixty, so Amos and Tess would have known it."

Several times he stopped and ran his finger down a page, only to keep looking. Finally he stopped. "Here it is."

*'When I heard at the close of the day how my name had
    been receiv'd with plaudits in the capitol, still it was
    not a happy night for me that follow'd,
And else when I carous'd, or when my plans were
    accomplish'd, still I was not happy,
But the day when I rose at dawn from the bed of perfect
    health, refresh'd, singing, inhaling the ripe breath of
    autumn,
When I saw the full moon in the west grow pale and dis-
    appear in the morning light,
When I wander'd alone over the beach, and undressing
    bathed, laughing with the cool waters, and saw the
    sun rise,*

*And when I thought how my dear friend my lover was
    on his way coming, O then I was happy,
O then each breath tasted sweeter, and all that day my
    food nourish'd me more, and the beautiful day pass'd
    well,
And the next came with equal joy, and with the next at
    evening came my friend,
And that night while all was still I heard the waters roll
    slowly continually up the shores,
I heard the hissing rustle of the liquid and sands as di-
    rected to me whispering to congratulate me,
For the one I love most lay sleeping by me under the
    same cover in the cool night,
In the stillness in the autumn moonbeams his face was
    inclined toward me,
And his arm lay lightly around my breast—and that
    night I was happy.*

Sam shut the book. "It's from the 'Calamus' section of *Leaves of Grass*," he said.

"'Calamus'?" Burke repeated.

"Another name for sweet flag," said Sam.

"As in the plant Amos Hague wrote to Tess about? The one he said he crushed because its smell reminded him of her?"

"Yes," Sam said. "But it's odd that they would have these lines engraved in their rings."

"I think they're really lovely," Burke countered.

Sam shook his head. "That's not what I mean," he said. "You know Whitman was gay, right?"

"I've heard," Burke said. "I admit I haven't really read much of him."

"Many of his poems are homoerotic," Sam continued. "But the 'Calamus' poems are considered the most overtly so of all his work. And this poem in particular talks about how he longs for his lover and is only happy when they're together. Even the calamus is symbolic. If you haven't seen one, it looks like an erect cock."

"I've seen one," Burke told him. "And yes, it does. But maybe Tess and Amos liked the *idea* of the poem. Really, did anyone then know this was about two men? It's not as if they sat around in graduate school, dissecting every line."

"Perhaps not most people," Sam admitted. "But to anyone who felt the way Whitman felt, I think it would mean a great deal." He ran his fingertips over his beard as he thought for a minute. "You said the rings also had initials in them, right?"

"AH and TB," said Burke.

"And the letter you read was addressed to TB as well," Sam continued.

"Yes. TB. Tess Beattie."

"Or maybe Thomas Beattie," Sam said softly.

CHAPTER 25

"It's so white," Burke said.

He looked at his forearm. Where the cast had been, the skin was pale and raw looking. When he scratched it, skin flaked away. Also, it seemed thinner than his other arm. He clenched and unclenched his fist.

"Put lotion on it," Dr. Radiceski told him. "That will clear up the dryness."

Burke, turning his arm over, noticed for the first time that there was a scar running along the underside of his arm. "What's this?"

The doctor looked at the scar. "They put two pins in," he explained. "Didn't they tell you?"

Burke shook his head. "Or maybe they did," he said. "I don't remember it, though."

"There are some in your leg as well," said the doctor.

"Great," Burke said. "More scars."

"You can always tell people you were injured running with the bulls or something," Dr. Radiceski suggested. "They'll think you're super butch."

Burke smiled. He was so relieved to have the cast off his arm that he really didn't care if he had scars or not. "Any chance of taking this one off a little early?" he asked, indicating his leg.

"I'm afraid not. But soon."

"You sound like my mother when I asked her when Christmas was coming," Burke complained. "Or my father when I asked him how much longer till we got where we were going."

"Speaking of your father, how's that situation?" the doctor asked him. "As I recall, you were having a bit of a time."

"Actually, it's been okay," Burke told him. "Mostly because we almost never see each other. How about you and your dad?"

Dr. Radiceski shook his head. "Crabbier than ever," he said. "And now he and Dale are best buddies, so when I get home, both of them start in on me. Last night I told them *they* should be lovers."

Burke laughed. "I bet your father loved that."

"He said if he were thirty years younger, he'd give it a go."

"Nice. Maybe he could have a talk with my father," said Burke.

"I see your friend isn't with you today," Dr. Radiceski remarked.

"No," Burke said, a hint of irritation in his voice.

Will was supposed to have brought him, but that morning he'd called and said he couldn't. No explanation, just, "I have something I have to do." Burke hadn't pressed him for more information. He'd simply asked Lucy if she could take him to his appointment. Now she sat in the outer room, waiting for him.

"I'm sorry," said the doctor.

"Don't be," Burke told him. "Like I said, we aren't really a thing, anyway."

The doctor was looking at Burke's most recent X-rays. "Well, I think we can take the leg cast off a week earlier than I expected. That should cheer you up."

Burke leaned his head back and let out a sigh. "Finally," he said.

"It will still take some work to get you back to normal," Dr. Radiceski said. "The muscles have atrophied a bit, and your knee in particular will be stiff."

"But I can do that back in Boston, right?"

"If you want to. I can recommend a great PT here, though. If you decide to stay."

"I don't think so," Burke said. "I might be doing a show here in Montpelier, though."

"Oh yeah? Where?"

"Actually, now that I think about it, I don't know the name of the gallery. The owner's name is Colton Beresford."

"I know Colton," said the doctor. "Dale and I had dinner with him and Luke last week."

"Why am I not surprised?" Burke said. "Does every gay person in Vermont know all the others?"

"Yes," said Dr. Radiceski. "And if we don't know someone, we can always look him up in the directory they give you when you move here. Oh, and his gallery is called the Colton Beresford Gallery. Do you want me to write it down?"

"I think I can remember," Burke teased.

"I look forward to seeing the show."

"And I look forward to seeing you in three weeks," Burke said, standing up.

He collected Lucy from the waiting room, and they returned to the car. Burke didn't suggest getting lunch. Although he was loath to admit it, part of him wanted Will to have called while he was gone, and he was anxious to get home and see if there were any messages.

"Three weeks," Lucy said as she started the car. "We'll be sorry to have you leave."

"You might be," said Burke. "I think Dad will be relieved."

"I don't know why you say that," Lucy replied.

"Come on, Lucy. How long have I been here? Six weeks? He and I haven't talked about anything except weather, the horses, and my accident."

"He's just not a talker," said Lucy. "You should know that."

"He talks to you, doesn't he?"

"Well, yes," Lucy admitted.

"Then he must have said *something* about how he feels about me being here," Burke insisted.

"He'll be sorry to have you leave," said Lucy firmly.

"That good, huh?"

Lucy sighed. "He doesn't know what to say to you," she said. "The last time you lived with him, you were a boy."

"He didn't say much then, either," Burke told her. "It's not as if anything's changed. I just thought maybe we'd gotten to the point where we could at least try."

Lucy was quiet as they drove through town. Burke was afraid he might have offended her, and was about to apologize when she started speaking again.

"Have I told you about my daughter?" she asked.

"You have a daughter? I thought you said you lost your baby."

"I did," Lucy said. "But I had another. Her name is Theresa, although now she calls herself Chloe. She's thirty-nine, or will be on the twenty-eighth."

"Does she live here?" asked Burke.

"Phoenix," Lucy told him. "With her husband and two children."

"Why don't you see them more often?"

"When Theresa—Chloe—told us that she was engaged to David, Jerry and I told her we thought she was making a mistake. She was in college, a junior, and he was her art professor. I told her it would never last and that he would leave her for another student."

"But he didn't?"

"No," said Lucy. "They've been together almost twenty years. The twins are eighteen. They just graduated from high school. Chloe sent me pictures."

"It sounds like she's gotten over it," Burke remarked.

"I wouldn't go that far," said Lucy. "For the first five years she wouldn't speak to us at all. She returned birthday and holiday cards, moved without telling us where they were going. Then David convinced her to make contact. He'd started to go to AA, and it was part of the whole 'asking for forgiveness' thing, I guess. Anyway, that's when Jerry and I found out we had three-year-old grandsons. Things got better after that, but it's really only been since Jerry died that she's made any real effort." Her face had a hard look to it, which Burke had never seen before. "I'll never forgive her for that," she said.

"I can't imagine what it must have been like," Burke said, not knowing what else to say to her.

"One of the great lies we tell ourselves is that just because we're related to people, we have to like them," said Lucy. "This will sound terrible, but I don't like my daughter. I love her. I love her very much. But I don't like who she is, and I don't like what she did to us." She glanced at Burke. "It's a horrible thing to not like your child. Even harder than knowing that your child doesn't like *you*."

"I don't dislike Dad," Burke said.

"I'm not saying you do," Lucy replied. "And I'm not saying he doesn't like you. I'm saying that there's nothing more complicated—or fragile—than the relationship between parents and their children. It's like no other relationship there is. And no one tells you how to make it work. Either you find your way or you don't."

"So what's my way?"

"I just told you, you have to figure it out for yourself."

"How can I when he won't talk about anything?"

Lucy sighed. "All you can do is try," she said.

"That's a shitty answer," said Burke.

Lucy nodded. "It sure is," she said. "But it's the only one I've got.

If they had a pill that would fix every dysfunctional family in the world, don't you think they'd be selling it?"

"I don't think the world is ready for that kind of happiness."

"Probably not," Lucy agreed. "So since we're being all huggy bunny, how about you tell me what's going on with you and Will Janks?"

"Nothing," Burke said instantly. "Why?"

"I thought so," said Lucy, obviously disbelieving him. "Don't worry. I'm not going to say anything to your father. Or Mars. I'm just being nosy."

Burke groaned. "I don't know," he said. "It's all a little weird. I mean, he's Mars's kid, and he's really young, and he has a girlfriend. It just sort of happened."

"At least you have good taste," Lucy said. "You have *that* in common with your father, anyway."

"He started it," said Burke. "Not that I didn't think he was attractive. But I never would have . . . if he hadn't . . . if . . ."

"No need to explain," Lucy assured him. "We'll just call it a summer fling, how about that?"

"I guess that's what it is," said Burke.

"Do you want it to be more than that?"

"No," Burke answered. "Yes. Maybe. There are a whole lot of ifs in that answer."

"I don't like what Theresa did," said Lucy, "but I will say this for her—she didn't let what Jerry and I thought about her relationship with David stop her from listening to her heart."

"She could just as easily have been wrong about him," Burke argued.

"That's not important. What's important is that she took the chance," said Lucy. "It's something I wish I'd done more of when I was younger."

"You don't regret marrying Jerry, do you?"

"Oh, no. Not for a minute. But there were other men—and a woman or two—I said no to because I thought it would be too complicated. Jerry was an easy choice. Not a bad one, but an easy one. Your father was slightly more risky."

Burke laughed. "I have to admit, I've sometimes wondered about that. The two of you are so different."

"That's what I like about it," said Lucy. "But it's also something I had to get over. Jerry and I were very similar. I always knew what he was thinking, what he wanted, even if he didn't say it directly. With Ed I never quite know. That's why it's interesting."

"Are you saying I should take a chance with Will?"

"I'm not saying you *should* do anything. But don't *not* do it just because it might be hard."

Burke made a vague noise. He wasn't sure he agreed with his father's girlfriend. Taking chances was a romantic idea, but there were practical considerations, and with Will there were a whole lot of them. On the one hand, he was sweet and funny, and his enthusiasm both in and out of bed was electrifying. On the other, he seemed to be unwilling to change his life in ways that would make it possible for them to be together. Unless he changed his stance about that, it rendered all the positive points moot. But there was always a chance, wasn't there?

"We'll see," he said. "One thing at a time. Dad might be an easier thing to cross off the list first."

"List?" Lucy said. "Your life isn't a list."

Burke scratched at his arm. It was itching ferociously. He watched flakes of dead skin fall away like snow. His wrist ached. He wondered what Will would say when he saw him looking like he had a pterodactyl limb.

"Don't shut down on me," Lucy said. "Let's talk this out."

Burke fixed her with a look. "You first," he said. "Let's talk about these 'one or two' women you passed up."

Lucy grinned. "Touché," she said.

CHAPTER 26

"It makes sense," Sam insisted. "Amos and Thomas were lovers. Tess was their cover. Nobody would have thought it was odd that Thomas lived on the farm, too. It was the perfect situation."

"Then how do you explain Peter Woode?" asked Burke. "And the fact that Tess had at least two children?"

"The children are easy," said Sam. "Amos fathered both of them. Tess was pregnant when he died, which is why she married Peter Woode so quickly. That way everyone would think Grace was his daughter."

"But *how* did she get pregnant? You know, if Amos and Thomas were gay?"

"Maybe they used a ladle," Sam said, grinning. "I don't know. Maybe Amos wasn't the father of either of them."

"Which brings us back to Peter Woode. Explain him."

"Okay," Sam replied. "Now just go with this. Amos befriended William Holburne during the war. Maybe William saw something in him, or the other way around. It doesn't matter. Then Amos found out William was really Elizabeth Frances Walsh. He's gay, right? So he understands not being like everyone else. He also knows the infantry is no place for a young woman. They stage William's death. That wouldn't be difficult. Then Amos sends William to live with Tess and Thomas. Only, he can't be William anymore, in case someone recognizes the name. That's when Peter Woode is born."

It took Burke a moment to work through the twists and turns of Sam's story. When he got to the end, he said, "I still don't get why Tess married Peter."

"Maybe she was a dyke," said Sam. "Maybe she just wanted other men to leave her alone. Maybe she loved him and didn't care what was between his legs. It doesn't really matter."

Burke rolled the window next to him down farther, letting in warm summer air. It smelled of hay. In the field that ran along the road, clover grew high, the purple heads bobbing in the breeze.

"Well?" Sam said after several minutes had passed.

"It makes sense," said Burke.

"You don't sound totally convinced."

Burke shrugged. "It's just that we can't *prove* any of it."

"Why do we need to prove it?" Sam asked.

"It's a mystery," said Burke. "Mysteries need to be solved."

"Not always," Sam rebutted. "Isn't it enough that we've figured it out? It's an amazing story."

"I guess," Burke admitted.

"You like things you can see," said Sam. "Things that are solid, right? You don't like unknowns."

"Who does?"

"I do," Sam told him. "I don't care if I can prove any of this. I just care that it might have happened—that it probably did."

"But don't you want to know that you're right?"

"It would be nice," Sam admitted. "But only because then we could tell the story to other people. And we can do that, anyway. Think about it. The story would make a great book."

"There's one thing I still don't understand," Burke said. "Why did Cain Hague run away? And why would he take his parents' wedding rings?"

"Why do teenagers do anything?" said Sam. "Maybe he was mad that his mother was remarrying. Maybe he loved his dads and didn't like Tess. We don't know how much of a mother she was to him. It's just another part of the puzzle."

"This means Peter Blackburne killed his uncle," Burke realized. "You know, if Grace and Calvin were sister and brother."

"But they never knew it," said Sam. "More tragedy. Practically Shakespearean." He pulled the car to a stop in a small parking lot beside a row of shops. "Here we are."

The Colton Beresford Gallery had a large plate-glass front window. In it hung a very large painting—about five feet on each side—of a German shorthaired pointer dressed in a black antebellum gown and holding in her paw three long ribbons that were attached like leashes to the necks of three identical red-haired little girls.

"It's called *Mrs. Humphries and Her Grand Champion Old-World Children,*" Sam told Burke.

"It's brilliant," proclaimed Burke. "Who did it?"

"An artist named Sarah Higdon," Sam said. "She specializes in anthropomorphized animals. It could easily be too cute, but what she does is comment on human society by turning us into animals. Wait till you see her other stuff."

As they entered the gallery, Colton appeared from somewhere in the back, dressed in black jeans and a black V-neck cashmere sweater with a white T-shirt beneath it.

Eyeing him, Burke couldn't help but remark, "It certainly *looks* like a New York gallery in here."

Colton laughed. "You can take the boy out of New York," he said.

Burke was already looking around the space. First, he headed toward more paintings by the artist whose work hung in the window. As Sam predicted, it was unlike anything he'd ever seen. Most of the canvases were large, and most featured cows, rabbits, or pigs.

"They're oddly moving, aren't they?" Colton asked, coming to stand beside Burke. "See how the cow is naked and the pigs are waving Bibles at her? Sarah says she's the cow and the pigs are the people who told her she was evil for not conforming to what they thought a good girl should be. It's titled *Judging Venus.*"

"You see more in them the longer you look at them," Burke said.

"That's what good art does. Come take a look at these." Colton led him to another wall, which featured a dozen intricately constructed religious icons. They were made of pieces cut from food packaging—mostly candy wrappers and breakfast cereal boxes. Although the pieces were small enough to resemble mosaic tiles, there was enough of the original lettering and design visible to make identifying the brands fairly easy.

"Religion as a consumer product," said Burke, looking at a particularly beautiful Madonna and Child made from Froot Loops boxes, bubble-gum wrappers, and the silver foil from a Hershey bar. "Clever."

"Pop art, Vermont style," Colton joked.

The rest of the art in the gallery was equally interesting. In addition to paintings, Colton was showing pottery, glass art, and even several large sculptures built out of old machine parts. Although Burke couldn't picture a lot of the things in a New York gallery setting, it wasn't because they weren't good enough. It was because they were in some ways too good. They didn't try too hard, and they didn't make the *viewer* have to try too hard.

"So?" Colton asked after Burke had wandered through the gallery's four large rooms. "Shall we do a show of Burke Crenshaw photographs?"

"I still don't know," said Burke. "Not that I don't like the gallery," he added quickly. "It's great. The work you have here is fantastic. I just don't know that I have anything to say."

"Just keep thinking about it," Colton told him. "If you get inspired, you know you have a home for your work."

"The images from the farm are interesting," Burke said, thinking out loud. "But they're not enough. Something is missing from them."

Colton patted Burke on the back encouragingly and turned to Sam. "Are you going up to Destiny this weekend?"

"I think so," Sam answered. "I haven't been in a while, and they're doing a full-moon circle."

"And just maybe you'll have a repeat with Pussy Willow?" Colton said.

"It's Dandelion, and for your information, he happens to be a very nice guy. He's a social worker in New Hampshire." Sam looked at Burke and quickly looked away. "But no, I'm not expecting him to be there."

"Sam dragged me to one of these things," Colton told Burke. "You have to see it to believe it. All of these fairies singing and dancing to drums around a bonfire. Half of them naked. It's crazy."

"Fairies?" Burke said. "Isn't that kind of anti-PC?"

"Radical Faeries," said Sam. "It's what they call themselves. Basically they're pagan men. Some women, too. Some trans. They don't really define themselves in any particular way, so it's hard to explain."

"Like I said, you have to see it for yourself," Colton said. His face brightened. "You should go," he said to Burke.

"I don't know," Burke said. "I'm not sure I'd fit in."

"If *I* can fit in, you sure can," said Colton. "I'm a nice Presbyterian boy, and nobody tried to sacrifice me to the Horned God or anything."

Sam rolled his eyes. "Nobody sacrifices *anything,*" he said. "Stop giving him the wrong impression."

"Not true!" Colton objected. "There was that guy who threw the doll thingy into the bonfire."

"It's called a poppet," said Sam. He looked at Burke. "It's a figure made out of branches and leaves and flowers and whatever else you want to use. You put your intention into it and burn it to release your charge."

"Of course," Colton said. "How silly of me for thinking it was a doll."

"You don't have to come if you don't want to," Sam said to Burke.

Burke was about to thank Sam for giving him an out, but suddenly he heard himself say, "Actually, it might be nice. If nothing else, it gets me out of the house."

"It's pretty rustic," Sam said. "Cabins. Outdoor showers. A lot of walking. It might be bad for your leg."

He doesn't want me to go, Burke thought. *He doesn't think I can handle it. Or maybe he's embarrassed.* Whatever the reason, the usually unflappable Sam seemed nervous. Again, Burke was surprised to find that this made him more determined to go.

"I think I can manage," he said. "That is, if you don't mind."

"No," Sam said a little too quickly. "I don't mind at all. Okay, then. We'll go. It will be fun." He smiled brightly.

"Take your camera," Colton told Burke. "You might find that inspiration you're looking for."

On the car ride home Sam said, "You don't have to come to Destiny this weekend if you don't want to."

"No, I do," said Burke. "It sounds . . . interesting."

Sam scratched his beard. "About the camera," he said. "It's considered bad form to take pictures of people without their permission."

"Don't worry. I'm not going to play *National Geographic* photographer."

"I didn't mean it that way," Sam replied. "I know you wouldn't do that. It's just that sometimes people treat these gatherings like they're freak shows. Not often, but enough that it can be a problem. The Faeries are pretty much anything goes, and if you're not used to it, it can be a little bit much. But everyone respects everyone else's boundaries."

"Got it," said Burke. "So, are you a Faerie?"

Sam took a moment to answer. "Sort of," he said. "I'm more of a garden-variety pagan. But I like the Faerie energy, and they put on really good gatherings."

"Explain the pagan part. I mean, I have a basic idea, but what exactly does it mean?"

"To me?" said Sam. "Because again, every pagan can have a different idea of what it means."

"To you, then," Burke said.

"To me, it means living my life in a way that allows me to be everything I can be."

"Didn't the army use that line?" Burke joked.

"We had it first," said Sam, smiling. "To me, it also means helping others become the people they're meant to be."

"Like Freddie Redmond."

"Like Freddie Redmond," Sam agreed. "It's really a way of approaching your life more than anything else, or being connected to the world and the other creatures in it. There can be other things, depending on your particular approach. Magic. Deities. Rituals."

"Magic?" Burke said, thinking that Sam was joking.

"We're not talking Harry Potter," said Sam. "It's more a way of working with energy to effect change."

"So there are gods and rituals. Unless I'm missing something, it sounds a lot like all the other religions."

"No," Sam said. "Not really. There's no one deity—some pagans don't follow any deity at all—and nothing about having to be saved from sin. Most religions are concerned about what happens when you die, about going somewhere better than here as a reward for faithful service or whatever you want to call it. Paganism teaches that being here *is* the reward, and that we need to make the most of it and leave the world a better place."

"That makes more sense than believing a virgin had a baby who died for our sins, and that if we don't believe that he did, we'll go to hell," Burke said.

"There are pagan stories about dying gods as well," said Sam. "But nothing about hell. You never know, though. Maybe the Christians are right."

"I hope not."

"There's no way to really know," Sam said. "That's why they call it faith. Maybe we're all right. Maybe whatever you believe is right. This works for me."

"I have to say, I haven't thought about it a whole lot," Burke told him. "I mean, we went to church when I was a kid, at least at Christmas and Easter. But we never talked about it. I pretty much let go of it all when I went to college."

"So, what's your life about?"

"I don't know," Burke said. "Me, I guess. That sounds selfish, doesn't it?" He didn't wait for Sam's answer. "I guess it is. But it's true. My life is all about me. What I want. What makes *my* life better."

He waited for Sam to say that there was nothing wrong with that. After all, hadn't he said that paganism was about enjoying life now? *You know that's not what he meant,* he told himself.

"I think most people embrace religion because it gives them a set of rules," Sam said. "They tell themselves that as long as they follow those rules, they'll be happy. But how often do those same people hurt others, or themselves? How often are they still miserable? That's what I find so interesting. They follow the rules, and they still aren't happy."

"Are you happy?"

"Mostly," said Sam. "You?"

Burke thought about his life back in Boston, the one he'd thought he couldn't wait to get back to. He thought about his work, and how instead of doing his own projects, he'd accepted commercial work because of the good money. And he thought about the failed relationships.

"No," he said, his voice catching in his throat. "I really don't think I am."

CHAPTER 27

"Sam!"

Before Sam could reply, he was caught up in a hug by a large, burly man wearing only white boxer shorts and a leather harness to which was attached a pair of small, delicate wings made out of gauzy purple material and decorated with glitter and rhinestones. The man's substantial belly hung over the waistband of his shorts, and there was more glitter scattered throughout the reddish hair on his chest and in his bushy beard. He was accompanied by two other men of similar build and similarly attired.

"Hey, Ginger," Sam said when he was put down and could breathe. He gave the other two men hugs as well. "Burke, this is Ginger, Thadeus, and Jonas."

"Nice to meet you," said Burke, eyeing the trio with some amusement.

"Let me guess," Sam said. "You're supposed to be—"

"Radical Bearies!" the three shouted.

"Naturally," said Sam, grinning. "You're adorable."

"You should see Thad's magic wand," Jonas said. "He's made some alterations."

"Not tattoos," said Sam, grimacing.

"Just a Prince Albert," said Jonas.

"I'm sure you'll see it soon enough," said Ginger. "These two can't manage to keep their clothes on. Speaking of which, shouldn't you two get out of your civvies?"

"This is Burke's first gathering," Sam told him. "I think we'll ease him into it."

Ginger looked at Burke. "A virgin! Let us know if you need any help breaking him in. Where are you guys bunking?"

"Cabin," Sam said. "I thought camping would be too much, what with Burke's leg."

"We're tenting it," Jonas told them. He pointed in the direction of a field where several dozen tents were set up. "The one with the bear flag. Stop by later."

"We will," Sam promised. "Once we get settled in."

The men wandered off, and Sam and Burke continued down a path worn into the grass.

"That was . . . different," said Burke.

"We call them the three bears," Sam said. "They're a trio. Ginger and Thadeus have been together about fifteen years. Jonas joined the family four or five years ago."

"They're lovers? All three of them?"

Sam nodded. "And three of the nicest guys you'll ever meet. Just watch out if they ask you to play Goldilocks."

"How does that work?" Burke asked. "Being a trio, I mean."

Sam shrugged. "Like any other relationship, I imagine. Probably just with a bigger bed."

"I have enough trouble with *one* other person. I can't imagine two."

"It wouldn't be my thing, either," Sam agreed. "But it works for them. And look at it this way—if one of you doesn't want to do something, you always have another option."

They arrived at a group of six small cabins that backed up against the woods on the far side of the field. Sam opened the door to one of them and looked inside. "It's free," he said. "Let's claim it."

Inside the cabin were four bunk beds and not much else. The bare floor was swept clean, and wire screens covered the two large windows. A battery-powered camp light sat on a small table, which was the cabin's only other furnishing.

Sam opened the rucksack he'd brought with him from the car and took out two air mattresses and two sleeping bags. Unrolling the first mattress, he blew it up and placed it on one of the bottom bunks. A sleeping bag went on top of it. He repeated the routine with the second mattress.

"I assume you want to be on the bottom," he said to Burke as he placed the mattress on the bunk above.

"It will be just like summer camp," Burke remarked. "Except I suspect we won't be making key chains in arts and crafts."

"Don't laugh," said Sam as he unrolled the second sleeping bag. "They do have an arts and crafts cabin. Actually, it's more of a dress-up cabin. People bring all kinds of things you can use for costumes. We can get you kitted up as anything you want. Maybe a satyr?"

"I think I'll just be me. But thanks." Burke hesitated before asking, "Are you going to do anything?"

"I don't know," Sam said. "I kind of like the bears' outfits. How do you think I'd look in wings?"

Burke had a mental image of Sam in boxers. He'd never seen him shirtless, but he could tell from what he'd seen of his chest in the V of his shirts that he was hairy. It was actually an appealing visual.

"Go for it," he said, feeling oddly embarrassed.

Sam laughed. "We'll see. For the moment I'm sticking with this." He pulled a kilt out of the rucksack. It was a tartan in several shades of green with thin red stripes. "It's the Guthrie tartan," Sam said. "We became Guffreys when Great-granddad passed through Ellis Island and they couldn't make out his accent."

Sam sat on the lower bunk and removed his shoes and socks. Then he stood up and dropped his pants. Burke turned away when he saw that the boxers were going next. He pretended to look at something out the window, and when he turned around, Sam was wearing the kilt. He had taken off his shirt, however, and was bare-chested. As Burke had suspected, his torso was heavily furred. He was surprised, however, by the gold rings that pierced Sam's nipples.

Sam was lacing up a pair of black, thick-soled Doc Martens shoes. When he was done, he stood up. "Well?"

"Very not librarian," Burke answered.

"I'm not a librarian this weekend," Sam told him. "I'm just me. That's what Destiny is all about. You okay to walk around some?"

"Can I bring my camera?"

Sam nodded. "Just ask before you take anyone's picture. Most people won't care, but you get the one or two who don't want anyone knowing they do this kind of thing."

They left the cabin and walked into the field, moving between the tents. Voices—and lots of laughter—filled the air, and the smells of incense and occasionally pot drifted over them. The people Burke saw were of all different types. Some were dressed casually in shorts, others were elaborately costumed, and some were just plain nude. Several people waved to Sam or called out greetings. Sam introduced Burke to a number of them, and Burke tried to remember the sometimes peculiar names: Bluebell, Orion, Pixie Moondrip, Endora.

Several times Burke asked permission to take someone's picture, and each time he was received enthusiastically. It wasn't difficult to get his subjects to pose for him, and he went through his first roll of film quickly. He was halfway through his second when they came to the tent of the three bears. Ginger was seated in a camp chair outside, and Jonas was painting his face with blue make-up. Concentric circles ringed Ginger's eyes, and spirals decorated each cheek.

"You look like a raccoon," Sam teased.

Ginger reached out and tugged on one of Sam's nipple rings. "Behave yourself," he said.

"There," Jonas said, drawing the last line of a star on Ginger's forehead. "Who's next?" He looked at Burke. "How about you?"

"Oh, I don't—"

"Sit!" Ginger ordered, standing up and taking Burke by the shoulders.

Burke sat, still objecting. Before he knew what was happening, Ginger was pulling his T-shirt up and off.

Ginger looked down at him, a smile playing at the corners of his mouth. "Not bad," he said. "Not much fur, but nice, anyway."

Burke wasn't sure how to respond. Fortunately, he didn't have to. Jonas was already painting him. He had swapped the blue color for a silvery gray and proceeded to mark Burke's chest with a series of what looked like comets racing every which way, some of them falling down toward his crotch.

"If you want, he can paint your cock silver, too," said Ginger. "That would look good."

"I think this will be enough," Burke said. "But thanks."

"Suit yourself." Ginger turned to Sam. "It would look great in the moonlight, though, don't you think?"

Sam nodded. "It would be very dramatic," he agreed. He looked at Burke and winked. Burke frowned at him, but he knew Sam was just playing along.

"There you go," Jonas said a minute later. "All done."

"Here," Ginger said, taking Burke's camera. "Let me get a picture."

"Be careful!" Burke said. "That's a—"

"Hasselblad," said Ginger. "I know. Now, shut up and pose with Sam."

Burke stood up with Jonas's help. Sam came over to him and put his arm around his waist.

"Say, 'Sodomy,'" Ginger ordered.

"Sodomy!" Sam shouted as Burke tried to manage a smile.

"Now you do us," said Ginger, handing the camera back to Burke. "Thadeus! Get your hairy ass out here."

Thadeus emerged from the tent. He was naked, and Burke couldn't help gasping when he saw the size of the dick that swung between his legs. A thick Prince Albert ring pierced the tip.

"I told you you'd see it soon enough," said Ginger as he dropped his own boxers and stepped out of them. Jonas was following suit. "You remember the story of the three bears," Ginger continued. "Well, Thad's too big, and I'm just right. That leaves the cub here as too small, but as you can see, it's all relative."

He stood in the middle, and Thadeus and Jonas flanked him. Burke framed them in the camera's viewfinder. The three men looked totally at ease, both with one another and with the camera. Burke took several frames of them before putting the camera down.

After promising to meet up with the bears later, Sam continued with the tour. There wasn't a whole lot else to see: the outdoor showers, the garden, the big main house. "Three Faeries live here year-round," Sam explained. "They take care of the place. I thought about doing it myself, but I think I'd get bored."

"I can't imagine you ever being bored," Burke said. "Your mind is always going in twelve directions at once."

"I think that's the nicest thing you've ever said to me."

"Sometimes I transcend my asshole-ishness," said Burke. "Asshole-ity. Whatever."

"You're too hard on yourself," Sam told him. "You need to let go of that. Toss it in the fire tonight."

"About that," said Burke. "What exactly are we doing?"

"It's a full-moon circle," Sam said. "Part of it is the whole wild-man thing. You know, like wolves howling and celebrating and whatnot. The other part is about manifesting change in your life. The full moon is a good time to start new things. Basically, you pledge to work on whatever it is you want to work on from one full moon to the next. During the first half of the cycle, while the moon is waning, you get rid of whatever is standing in your way. Then you spend the waxing half working to reach your goal."

"The howling part sounds easier."

"You'd be surprised at how well it works," said Sam. "If you put energy into it, that is. It's not like you just decide you're going to get your novel written or stop smoking or whatever and it magically happens without you doing anything."

"There's always a catch," Burke joked.

For the rest of the afternoon they walked around and Burke took pictures. He went through five rolls of film before it was time for dinner, which was a kind of communal affair where people shared food they'd brought, as well as some delicious food prepared by volunteers in the camp kitchen. As he'd been throughout the day, Burke was struck by the spirit of cooperation that pervaded the meal. He was feeling less and less uncomfortable, and when several men complimented him on his body decoration, he actually started to enjoy it.

As twilight settled over the camp, people began to gather in the field. A large portion of it was empty of tents, and now Burke understood why. A bonfire was waiting to be lit in the center of a bare patch of earth from which all the grass had been cleared to prevent it from catching on fire. The campers arranged themselves in a loosely formed circle around it. Some talked, while others played drums and other instruments, improvising melodies.

Sam had brought a camp chair for Burke to sit on because of his leg. Burke felt a little conspicuous, but no one seemed to notice. Sam himself sat cross-legged on the ground.

"How do you know when it starts?" Burke asked.

"It already has," said Sam. "It's an organic thing. Just watch."

For a while nothing much happened beyond the drumming and music continuing. Darkness came, and the moon rose huge and silver above the field. But still the only light came from the fireflies that flickered in the grass and from the occasional flashlight carried by newcomers to the circle. Burke, seated in the darkness, had no idea how many people were there.

Then, unexpectedly, there was a flash of flame as someone lit the tinder beneath the bonfire. As it caught hold and started to burn, the circle emerged from the darkness. Burke caught his breath when he saw that there was now a solid ring of people gathered around the fire. The flames lit up their faces and reflected off their bare skin.

The drumming became more rhythmic, now coming from all directions, and the various other instruments began playing together. Someone stood up, walked into the circle, and began to dance. His movements were unrehearsed; he simply moved to the music. A moment later he was joined by several people, all of them dancing alone but somehow together. Watching them, Burke felt himself slipping into a comfortable place as the fire, the music, and the night drew him into a cocoon of warmth.

As Sam had predicted, the night unfolded without design. More and more people got up to dance. Then someone let loose a joyous howl, which was followed by more howls and the raising of arms to the sky. Laughter rose up with the smoke. Burke smelled the pungent scent of burning sage.

"Do you mind if I dance for a little bit?"

Sam's request momentarily startled Burke. "No," he said. "Go on. I'll be fine."

Sam got up, slipped his shoes off, and made his way into the circle. For a few minutes Burke could see him, but then he was lost in the swirling sea of bodies, swept to the other side of the fire. He reappeared minutes later, only to melt again into the crowd.

Then he was in front of Burke again, this time accompanied by Thadeus, Ginger, and Jonas.

"Come on," Thadeus said. "You're dancing with us."

Burke had no time to object as he was drawn to his feet by several strong arms. They led him into the circle. There the five of them formed their own little circle, their arms around each other's shoulders or waists. Burke was held up by Ginger on one side and Thadeus on the other. Their flesh was warm against his, and their sweat-slicked skin gave off a musky scent.

They moved to the music, first in one direction and then in the other. Burke, buoyed up by the other men's bodies, felt as if he were being lifted up by them. He looked across their little circle and saw Sam watching him, smiling. He smiled back, unable to help himself. He was filled with an unfamiliar feeling, of friendship and happiness that had nothing to do with anything other than being with people who accepted him the way he was.

He didn't know how long they danced. Eventually, their circle broke apart, and Jonas and Sam led him back to the chair. He didn't want to sit, but his tired leg demanded it. Sam stood beside him, a hand on his shoulder.

"Not bad for a crippled guy," Sam teased.

"Not bad for a guy in a kilt," Burke countered.

"It's the bears," said Sam. "You can't not have a good time around them. They won't let you."

Burke laughed. "I kind of got that," he said. He looked out at the bonfire. "So, how does this manifesting thing work?"

"Just think of something you want to accomplish, and promise yourself to do it for the next moon cycle," Sam said.

"That's it?"

"It can be. Some people perform a ritual. That's what I was doing out there."

"How do you mean?"

"The dancing," said Sam. "I thought about what I want to do. As I danced, I imagined energy building up inside of me—energy to fuel what I need to do. I imagined drawing it from the fire, from the ground, from everyone around me. When I imagined myself full of it, I released it into the universe as a way of signaling the beginning of my process."

"You make it sound like you had a cosmic orgasm," Burke said.

"It sort of is," Sam agreed. "And some people do use orgasm to do the same thing—release their energy. I expect there will be quite a bit of that going on tonight, actually." He laughed.

"What is it you want to work on?" Burke asked him.

"That's a secret," Sam told him. "I'll tell you at the next full moon."

"How will I know you're not lying? You could just *say* it worked. I wouldn't know the difference."

"You'll just have to trust me," Sam said.

"I've heard that before."

"Not from me," said Sam. "I mean it." He gave Burke's shoulder another squeeze.

I believe you do, Burke thought, closing his eyes and feeling the pressure of Sam's hand.

CHAPTER 28

"Who doesn't like funnel cake?"

"Me," Burke said, batting away the piece of powder sugar–covered dough Sam was waving around. "It's a heart attack on a plate."

"'What is food to one, is to others bitter poison,'" Sam countered.

"Let me guess. Julia Child?"

"Lucretius. But I'm fairly certain they were contemporaries." Sam popped another piece of funnel cake into his mouth.

The Newton County Summer Daze was in full swing. The annual celebration occupied the whole of the county fairgrounds. There were rides of dubious safety, an arcade of games, at which most players were guaranteed to lose, and vendors offering everything from the funnel cakes Burke refused to eat to egg rolls on a stick. Sam had already sampled one of those as well.

"We should try everything on a stick," he suggested, eyeing a booth offering the ubiquitous skewered hot dog, a hallmark of fairs everywhere.

"You already have," said Burke. "I don't know why you haven't gotten sick yet."

"I can eat anything," Sam told him.

Burke sniffed the air. It smelled of animals—cows and horses and pigs. "We're getting near the livestock," he said.

"Great," Sam said. "I want to see the chickens. Come on."

Burke didn't argue. He figured that in the livestock barn he was at least safe from the horrible rides and awful food, not to mention the shockingly haggard-looking band currently playing on the grandstand. Their most recent hit had been a quarter century ago, and they were clearly tired of playing it. But the middle-aged fairgoers dancing and singing along about working for the weekend seemed not to notice.

The inside of the livestock barn was hot. Electric fans placed around the space did little to cool it and succeeded mostly in just pushing the smells from one corner to another. Weary 4-H members stood near their animals' pens, looking wilted and bored. Even the animals appeared to have had it with the fair. Instead of looking over the gates of their pens in search of food or pats, they sat in the corners with their backs to their admirers.

"Chickens!" Sam said excitedly, heading for the rows of cages containing the birds.

Burke followed without enthusiasm. He looked for a place to sit down, but every chair was occupied, so he trailed Sam as he walked down the line of fowl in cages.

"Aren't they beautiful?"

"They're chickens," Burke said. "If they were fried, they'd be beautiful."

"Chicken hater. How can you not appreciate that?" Sam pointed to a large black chicken whose head was crowned by a ridiculous explosion of feathers.

"I can appreciate it," said Burke. "On a plate. With potatoes. I suppose now you're going to hit me with a quote about chickens."

"I know only one," Sam said. "It's from E. B. White."

"The *Charlotte's Web* guy?"

"Right. He said, 'I don't know which is more discouraging, literature or chickens.'"

"That doesn't make any sense," said Burke.

"Not really," Sam agreed. "But you asked. Oh, look at those Buff Orpingtons."

Burke looked at the little girl whose chickens these seemed to be. Maybe eight or nine, she wore overalls and a 4-H shirt. Her hair was tied in pigtails, which lay limply against her damp neck. A spray of freckles blanketed her nose. A blue ribbon was attached to one of the cages next to her.

"First place," Burke said. "Congratulations."

The girl smiled wanly. "Thanks," she said. "But all I did was feed them. As soon as this stupid fair is over, they're going in the freezer. And next year I'm going to be a cheerleader. Four-H sucks."

"Good luck with that," Burke said, walking away to see what Sam had found now.

"Burke!"

Burke turned to see Mars Janks coming toward him. Will was with him, along with a young woman Burke didn't recognize.

"Hey," Mars said when he reached Burke.

"Hey," said Burke. He nodded at Will. "Hi, Will."

Will smiled nervously. "This is Donna," he said.

Of course, Burke thought as he said hello to Donna. *Who else would she be?*

Donna was pretty. She had a thin, boyish body with small breasts and narrow hips. Her hair was cut short, and if she wore make-up, Burke couldn't detect it. *This explains a lot,* Burke thought. *She might as well be a teenage boy.*

"Are you here with your dad and Lucy?" Mars asked.

"Um, no," Burke said. "With a friend."

As if he'd been called, Sam approached. "You've got to see these Lakenvelders," he began. Then he saw the others. "Oh, I'm sorry. Hey, Will."

Will nodded but said nothing.

Burke introduced the others to Sam. "This is Mars, Will's father. And this is Donna, his girlfriend. Will's girlfriend, not Mars's," he added, speaking too quickly.

"Nice to meet you," Sam said. "When are you going to come around the library again?" he asked Will. "Haven't seen you in a while."

"Yeah," said Will. "I've been busy. You know how it is."

"Will's been helping me a lot this summer," Mars said proudly.

"Right," said Burke. "How's the calf?"

"Calf?" Mars said. "What calf?"

"The one Will helped you birth," Burke elaborated.

Mars looked at Will, who was suddenly very red. "We haven't birthed any calves," he said.

"But Will said that—," Burke began. "No. Wait. It wasn't Will. It was my father who was talking about a calf. Never mind." Burke looked at Will, who didn't meet his gaze.

"Mostly it's been sheep and horses this summer," Mars said, oblivious to the exchange. "Some pigs. That's why we're here. I fixed up one of the sows. I hear she picked up a ribbon."

"That's some pig," said Sam.

"You've seen her?" Mars asked.

"No," Sam answered. "It's from *Charlotte's Web*. Charlotte writes it in the web over Wilbur's pen. Burke and I were talking about the book earlier, and it made me think of it."

Mars looked at Sam for a moment. "Oh," he said. "Okay." He turned back to Burke. "Did you hear the good news?"

"Dad—," Will said.

Mars waved him away. "We can tell Burke," he said. "He's practically family."

"But we haven't even—"

"Will and Donna are engaged," Mars announced.

Burke felt his stomach sink. He looked at Will, who was biting his lip. Donna, though, was beaming. She held out her left hand, displaying the diamond on her ring finger. Burke just stared at it, saying nothing.

"It's beautiful," Sam said loudly, startling Burke back to the moment.

"Yes," Burke agreed. "Really beautiful. Congratulations to you both. When's the wedding?"

"We're thinking Octo—," Donna began.

"We don't know," Will interrupted.

"But you'll definitely be getting an invitation," Mars assured Burke. "Doesn't it make you feel old?" he added. "I can't believe my son is getting married."

"It certainly does," said Burke.

Mars clapped him on the back. "Well, we should go take a look at that sow. You fellows have a good time."

"You too," Sam said.

Will hurried past them, his arm around Donna. When he was out of earshot, Sam said, "That was unexpected."

Burke sighed. "Not entirely."

"You okay?"

"Oh, yeah," Burke answered. "It wasn't like he and I were going anywhere."

"Mmm," Sam murmured. "Hey, I saw a kid eating a fried Snickers bars on a stick. How about we find us one of those?"

"Why not?" said Burke. "And maybe a fried banana on a stick and some of that calamari on a stick. Then we can go on the Scrambler and see what happens."

"Now you're talking," Sam said. "Let's get out of here."

* * *

"Thanks for letting me come over. I didn't know if you would want to see me."

Will stood on the porch. Burke was in the doorway, his arms folded over his chest. In the twenty minutes since Will's phone call, he had managed to work his anger up.

"I don't know that I want to," he said.

Will ran his hands through his hair. "I didn't mean for you to find out that way. I don't even want . . . Dad's the one who . . ." He paced a few steps up and down the porch. "Are you alone?"

"My father and Lucy went to a movie," Burke said. "I didn't want to go."

"Because of—"

"Because it's a Clint Eastwood movie, and I hate Clint Eastwood."

"Can I come in?" asked Will.

Burke hesitated. Letting Will in the house probably wasn't a good idea. Then again, he didn't want to have this conversation standing on the porch. He stepped aside and motioned Will inside. He closed the door behind him.

Will sat down on the couch. His hands hung between his legs, and he threw his head back, letting out a loud groan. "This is so fucked up," he said.

"Nobody's making you get married," Burke reminded him. "You're a big boy. You can do what you want to."

Will shook his head. "You don't get it."

"Get what?" Burke said, getting angry. "Get that it's hard? Get that it's terrifying? Get that we shouldn't have to do it at all? Yeah, Will, I do get that, because I went through it."

"It's different for you," Will argued. "You don't want to be married. You don't want kids."

"How do you know what I want?"

"Well, do you want kids?"

"No," Burke said. "But that's not the point. You *can* get married. You *can* have kids. You can do anything you want to."

"It's not the same," said Will. "People don't treat you the same. They're all like, 'There's those gay boys with their Chinese baby.' And no matter how many states let homos get married, it doesn't change what people think. And calling some guy your husband just sounds freaky."

"Let's assume you're right," said Burke. "Which you aren't, by the way. But let's assume you are. Are you saying you're not gay?"

Will tapped his fingers together. "I'm not *gay* gay," he said.

"That sounds like being *kind of* black," said Burke. "What do you mean?"

"I mean, I like making it with guys," Will said. "But that's just sex. I don't think I could ever be with another guy. Not forever."

"Do you like sex with Donna?"

"I told you, she's a virgin, remember?"

Burke had forgotten about the purity ring. "Right," he said. "I forgot. And when you've done it with other girls, you've thought about guys the whole time." He fixed Will with a look. "I hate to be the one to break it to you, my friend, but you're gay. *Gay* gay. With a capital *G*. And I'm not sure, but I think your fiancée might have a little secret of her own."

"Donna? What about her?"

"In case you hadn't noticed, she looks like she stepped out of a boy band. But come to think of it, that might be perfect. If she's a dyke, you can be each other's cover." *Like Tess Beattie,* he thought.

Will stood up and walked over to Burke. He put his hands on Burke's waist. "Don't be mad," he said. "It doesn't have to change anything. You know, with us."

He looked into Burke's eyes. When he smiled, Burke felt his anger melt away. *He's just a kid,* he told himself. *He's just scared. You can help him.*

Will leaned forward, his lips parting. Burke allowed himself to be kissed. He closed his eyes and pulled Will tighter. Their tongues met, and Burke felt Will's hard-on pressing against him. One of Will's hands found its way to Burke's cock and squeezed.

"Let's go upstairs," Will whispered. "You can fuck me in your bed."

Burke started to agree, then stopped. He pulled his mouth away from Will's. "No," he said, breaking their embrace.

Will looked at him, his eyes troubled. "Why?" he said. "I told you, it's okay."

"That's just it," said Burke. "It's not okay. What you're doing is not okay, and what I'd be doing if I went upstairs with you would not be okay."

Will shook his head. "I don't understand. We're just going to fuck around. It doesn't hurt anybody."

"Maybe not," said Burke. "At least not now."

"But that's all we're talking about," Will said. "Now. And right now I know you want to get naked and let me blow you."

"You're right," Burke told him. "I do want to do that. But I'm not going to. Listen, I know how you feel. I really do. But it's not how *I* feel. I'm not going to tell you you're making a mistake, because it's your choice. But I won't be part of it. Not anymore."

Will looked as if Burke had slapped him. "You think you're better than me?" he asked.

"No," Burke said. "I just think we've made different choices. That's all."

Will grunted. "You mean I'm making the wrong one. Well, it hasn't worked out so well for you, has it? Where's your *husband?* Where's your perfect life?"

Anger flashed through Burke. "You want to spend your life chasing cock behind your wife's back, go ahead. Let guys fuck you in rest-stop stalls. Hook up with guys online. Maybe you'll even find a fuck buddy—some other guy who says he just likes to get it on with guys sometimes. That sounds like a *great* life."

Will glared at him, the muscles in his neck tensing. "You know, the other night my dad said he thinks you might be queer. My mother asked why you weren't married, and that's what he said. And you should have heard him. He sounded like he was telling her you had *cancer.*"

Burke felt as if he'd been punched in the stomach. "He said that?"

Will nodded. "Now, imagine what he'd say if it was *me* he thought was queer."

Burke didn't speak for a moment as thoughts raced through his head. "People change," he said finally.

"Not fast enough," said Will.

He started to walk past Burke, but Burke grabbed his arm. "Don't hide who you are," he said. "Please, Will."

Will looked into his eyes. The anger in them was gone. Now he just looked like a sad boy who'd had a fight with his best friend. Burke wanted to take him in his arms, not to make love to him, but to comfort him.

"I'm not like you," Will said softly. "I can't be."

CHAPTER 29

"Need any help?"

Burke looked into the room his father used as an office. Ed was seated at a desk. In front of him was a pile of plastic parts for a model. The air smelled like glue.

"These directions don't make any sense," said Ed, peering at a piece of paper over his glasses. "I don't see any part A thirteen."

Burke walked over and looked over his father's shoulder. "What is this supposed to be when it's done?"

"SPAD Thirteen," his father said. "A French airplane," he added when Burke didn't respond. "World War I."

"Oh," said Burke. "Sounds interesting."

His father grunted as he rummaged through the pile of parts. Burke knew this was his way of not so subtly letting his son know that he was busy and wanted to be left alone.

"When did you start building models?" Burke asked, not giving in to the temptation to leave.

"Couple of years ago."

He's not going to make this easy, Burke thought. *Fine. If that's how he wants to play, we'll do it his way.*

"Dad, when did you first think I might be gay?"

Ed dropped the piece he was holding. "Damn it!" He retrieved the piece, took up the bottle of glue, and went back to work. "I don't know."

"Was it before I was out of college?" Burke asked, pressing. "When I was a kid? You must have thought about it."

"Why?"

"Because isn't that what parents do? Don't you wonder what your kids are going to be like? What kind of lives they'll have? Didn't you wonder why I never had any girlfriends?"

"No," said Ed. "Just figured you were a little slow getting started, is all."

Burke didn't give up. "Then when *did* you figure it out? Because I never told you, and I'm assuming that you didn't hear it for the first time just now."

Ed set down the parts he'd just glued together. "What's this about?" he asked.

"I'm just curious," said Burke. "Are you saying you and Mom never discussed it? Not once?"

"We might have," Ed replied. "What does it matter? You are what you are, and that's that. Nothing to be done about it now."

"You make it sound like I have a sickness," said Burke. He couldn't help but think of Will's comment from the night before. *He sounded like he was telling her you had* cancer.

"That's not what I meant."

"Do you wish there was something I could do about it?"

"All I said was it's over and done with," his father said, an edge to his voice. "There's no point in discussing it further."

"Yes, there is," said Burke. "I want to know what my parents thought about who I am."

"You never told us what you are. Why do it now?"

"*Who* I am, Dad. Not *what*. And you're right. I should have told you, instead of letting you figure it out. But why pretend you and Mom never talked about it? There had to have been a moment when one of you said, 'You know, I think Burke might be gay.' Who said it first, you or Mom?"

"I don't remember," Ed snapped.

"I think you do," said Burke. "You just don't want to talk about it, just like you won't talk about anything to do with Mom or me or how you feel. Jesus Christ, I don't know how Lucy puts up with you."

"That's enough!" his father shouted. He stood up. Burke could see that his hands were shaking.

"Dad, I didn't mean to—"

"You want to know when we knew?" his father interrupted. "When you stopped coming home for Christmas. Your mother said the only reason you wouldn't come home is because you had something to hide. At first she thought maybe you were embarrassed by us, by this place. She thought maybe we weren't fancy enough for you, now that you were living in the city."

"I was never embarrassed," said Burke.

His father ignored him. "Then one night she was watching some program on the television. I don't know what it was. It doesn't matter. There was some gay fellow in it, and he was talking to his friends about how his sister didn't want him to bring his boyfriend to her wedding, because it would upset their parents. And your mother turned to me and she said, 'Do you think that's why Burke doesn't come home anymore?' She was about to call you right then and ask you, but I told her not to. I said even if you were, it was none of our business."

He stopped talking. Burke looked at his face, which suddenly looked very old. "You didn't want to find out it was true," Burke said. "Did you?"

Ed cleared his throat. "It was none of our business."

"I should have told you," said Burke. "I shouldn't have made you guess."

"It was a long time ago."

"It wasn't that long ago," Burke retorted. "And if I'd said something, maybe we wouldn't have spent the last twenty years not talking about it."

"People do too much talking," Ed said.

"But we could have—"

"It broke her heart," his father said angrily. He lowered his voice. "It's what killed her."

Burke stared at him, stunned. "You think I killed her?"

"I think it hurt her more than anything else could. You were her baby, but she didn't know what you were, and you wouldn't tell her." Ed sat down. "You were like one of those changelings left behind by something that stole her real boy."

Burke couldn't believe what he was hearing. Did his father really believe what he was saying? Did he really think Burke was somehow responsible for his mother's death?

"What would you have had me do?" Burke asked finally, his voice shaking.

His father shook his head, then looked up at his son. "I'd rather you'd been normal," he said.

Burke felt his face flush. He tried to speak, but all the air had been sucked from his lungs, and his mouth refused to work. He felt his heart pounding, and for a moment he thought he might not be able to move. He watched as his father turned back to his model, picking up a piece and applying glue to one end.

Then the air came rushing back in, and Burke found his voice. "You bastard," he said. "You fucking bastard."

"Don't speak to me like that!" his father said. "Not in my own house."

"You and your house can go to hell!" Burke roared. "How dare you accuse me of killing her? How do you know what she felt? You never fucking talked to her! How do you know she didn't die just to get away from *you?*"

Ed leapt up, pieces of the model scattering on the floor. He looked down helplessly at them, then at Burke. His mouth twitched. Burke turned his back and walked out, leaving his father standing there.

Sam answered the phone on the second ring. He said he would be there to pick Burke up in half an hour. Burke used the time to pack his bags and put his photography equipment back into the boxes in which they'd been shipped. His father had shut the door to his office.

Burke was glad that Lucy wasn't there. She was playing cards with some of her friends. If she'd been at the house, she would undoubtedly have tried to stop Burke from leaving, maybe even attempted to broker a peace deal between him and his father. But Burke wasn't interested in that. He just wanted to be as far away from his father as possible.

Sam arrived with five minutes to spare. He carried Burke's things to his car while Burke sat in the front seat, anxious to be on their way.

"You're sure you want to take *everything?*" Sam asked as he loaded the box of developing chemicals into the trunk.

"I'm sure," Burke answered. "I don't want to have to come back."

As they drove back to Sam's house, Burke looked out into the night. The moon was still close to full, and the countryside was gilded in silver. For a moment he almost thought he might be dreaming everything that had happened in the last hour. Then he remembered his father's face—how he'd looked at Burke as if he were looking at the face of a murderer. Burke shut his eyes, blocking out the image.

"Thanks for coming," he said.

"No problem," Sam answered. "Do you want to talk about it?"

"No," said Burke. "I really don't. Not now, anyway."

"Anytime you're ready," Sam said.

"I won't be there forever," said Burke. "I promise. As soon as I can, I'll go back to Boston. I can get around by myself now, anyway. There's really no reason to wait until the cast comes off. I'm sure I can bribe Gregg into coming up to get me."

"You can stay as long as you want to," Sam assured him. "The guest room hasn't seen much use. It will be nice to have company."

"I won't cramp your style, will I?"

"What style?" asked Sam.

"You know, with the menfolk," Burke teased.

"Oh, right," said Sam. "Well, if you come home and there's a sock on the doorknob, just stay away from the room where all the shouting and pounding are coming from."

Burke leaned back in his seat, trying to stretch his leg. "What a great couple of days this has been. First Will, now this."

"What happened with Will?" Sam asked. "I mean, anything besides the weirdness at the fair the other day?"

Burke told him about his meeting with Will. "It was like the last temptation of Burke or something," he said when he was done. "I should have just fucked him. Not fucking him hasn't worked out so great."

"You know that's not true," Sam said.

"No?" said Burke. "Maybe he's right. Maybe we wouldn't be hurting anyone. Maybe marrying Donna and letting everyone think he's *normal* really is the right thing to do. Maybe *I'm* the one who's got it all wrong. After all, I killed my mother."

"You didn't kill your mother."

"Well, I sure didn't make her life any easier," Burke countered.

"Lying about who you are wouldn't have made it any easier, either," Sam reminded him.

"Easy for you to say," said Burke. "Your father didn't accuse you of killing your mother."

"No, he didn't," Sam agreed. "But that's probably because *he* killed her."

Burke thought at first that he was joking. Then he saw Sam's face. Illuminated by the moonlight, it looked like it was carved out of stone. His eyes looked straight ahead, not blinking.

"I was eight," Sam said. "My sister was nine. We came home from school one afternoon, and there were four police cars and an ambulance parked in front of our house. My aunt Cilla, my father's sister, was there. She wouldn't let us go inside. She said something bad had happened and that we would be spending the night at her house. Of course, we asked her where our parents were. I don't remember what she said. Something about them needing to help the police, I think."

"When did you find out?"

"The next morning," said Sam. "I woke up early. It was a Saturday. Everyone else was asleep, so I turned on the television to watch cartoons. Only it was too early and the news was on, and there were pictures of my mother and father. I don't know how they got them. At first I thought maybe they'd won something. Then I heard the woman on the TV say that they were both dead. Murder-suicide is what she said."

"Holy shit," Burke said.

"I woke up my sister and told her, and we both woke up my aunt. At first she didn't want to tell us anything, but since I'd seen it already, she didn't have much choice."

"Why'd he do it?"

Sam sighed deeply and exhaled loudly. "He thought she was having an affair," he said. "And maybe she was. We never found out for sure. My father was depressed most of his life. He refused to take medication. He said it was only for weak people, and that all you had to do to stop being depressed was try harder. Only, when that didn't work, he tried drinking himself out of it. That afternoon he drank himself and my mother out of it for good."

"Where did you and your sister go?"

"We stayed with our aunt and uncle. My mother's parents were dead, and her brother already had six kids of his own. At first the court didn't want us living with any of my father's relatives. The social worker assigned to us thought it would be too traumatic and suggested we be put into foster care. But my aunt Cilla pitched a fit and said they would take us over her dead body. Probably not the best choice of words given the circumstances, but the judge apparently got the message."

"Still, that must have been weird, living with them after what your father did."

"At first," Sam agreed. "Kids at school said stupid shit. Some people gave my aunt a hard time. But she and my uncle loved us like we were their own. From the first day we moved in with them, we knew that. And after a while that was all that mattered."

"How did you not hate him?" Burke asked.

"I did hate him," said Sam. "For a long time. I hated him for being mentally ill. I hated him for drinking. I hated him for killing my mother and destroying our family. But at some point I realized that hating him wasn't changing anything. It wasn't making me feel better, and it wasn't bringing my parents back from the dead. So I stopped."

"How do you feel about him now?"

"I'm sad that he didn't get the help he needed," Sam answered. "I'm sorry he thought his mental illness was something to be ashamed of."

"And your sister?"

"Angie? She's still angry. Can't let go. She blames what happened for everything that's gone wrong in her life, when really the only thing wrong is that she inherited some of our father's faulty wiring and his stubbornness to accept it."

"She's . . ."

"Bipolar," said Sam. "We both are. Only, Angie won't treat hers."

"Wow," Burke said. "And you seem so well adjusted."

Sam laughed. "I've learned how to live with it," he said. "Meds help. And mine doesn't manifest itself in physical mania. It's all in my head. You know how I can think of twelve different things at one time? That's how. My mind is always going. I used to think it was weird when people would say they weren't thinking about anything. I couldn't imagine *not* thinking about things every single moment."

"Is your sister the same way?"

"Poor Angie has it tough," said Sam. "She gets the physical mania *and* the emotional ups and downs. Still, she could control it if she'd do what the doctors tell her to. She just doesn't want to."

"Why wouldn't you want to?"

"It's like a drug," Sam said. "The manic episodes are really exciting. The crash afterward is fucking hell, but when you're caught up in that rush, you don't think about anything else. A lot of people don't want to take meds, because they don't want to lose that."

"This is making what my father said seem like nothing," Burke remarked.

"We each get our own shit," said Sam. "And it's all hard in one way or another. All you can do is deal with your particular shit the best you can."

They turned onto the road that led to Sam's house, pulling into his driveway a few minutes later.

Turning off the car, Sam turned to Burke. "Do you like Douglas Adams?"

"Of course," Burke said. "What sane person doesn't?"

"Do you remember in *Hitchhiker's* when Ford and Arthur are first picked up by the *Heart of Gold,* and Zaphod is freaking out about it, and Trillian is doing something to achieve normality?"

"Vaguely," Burke told him. "Apparently, I've been out-nerded."

"Trillian has a great line in that scene," Sam continued. "She gets everything under control, and then she says, 'We have normality. I repeat we have normality. Everything you still can't cope with is therefore your own problem.' I love that, because it's true. We all have our own problems. We can help each other out, but ultimately we have to deal with our problems ourselves."

"Where are you going with this?" Burke asked, slightly confused.

"Welcome to your *Heart of Gold,*" said Sam, gesturing at his house.

CHAPTER 30

"These came for you today," Lucy said. She handed Burke two large, thick envelopes.

"The pictures," said Burke. "I forgot all about them. Thanks."

He'd been at Sam's house for two days. He'd made no attempt to contact his father or Lucy, and was surprised that Lucy had known where to find him.

"I went to the library first," Lucy said. "I figured Sam would know where you were."

"I should have called you. I'm sorry I didn't. It's been a little . . . weird."

"Your father didn't tell me everything that was said, but I think I've got the gist of it," said Lucy.

"I don't know that you do," Burke told her. "He basically accused me of killing my mother."

"He was angry," said Lucy. "He didn't mean it."

Burke smiled tightly. "I don't know much about my father," he said. "Clearly. But I do know one thing—he never says anything he doesn't mean."

"He was *upset*," Lucy said, trying again. "Don't just walk away."

Burke looked at her face. He could tell she was near tears. They pushed at the corners of her eyes, threatening to spill down her cheeks.

"I know you want to make this okay," he said gently. "I know you're thinking about your daughter."

"Don't make the mistake I made," Lucy begged him. "Please don't make that mistake."

"Have you told Dad that?"

Lucy nodded. "You know how stubborn he is," she said, sniffing. "That's why I think it's up to you."

Burke nodded. "That's what I thought," he said. He sighed. "I can't do it, Lucy. Not right now. Honestly, I don't know if I ever can. He said some terrible things."

"Just think about it, Burke," she said. "Please?"

"Sure. And thanks for bringing these over."

Lucy opened her arms. Burke allowed her to hug him. He felt her thin frame beneath his hands. She was shaking. Burke wanted to tell her that everything would be all right. But he couldn't lie to her. He couldn't make that promise.

Lucy let go. She didn't say anything, just reached out and touched his arm. Then she turned and walked back to her car, leaving Burke to shut the door before he started crying.

When he'd calmed himself, he took the envelopes to the living room and sat down with them. He opened the first one and pulled the photos out. They were some of the shots he'd taken at Destiny. The one on top was of the three bears.

And it was good. It was *very* good. Somehow it captured the energy of the trio, the love that existed between them. Burke saw it in the way they stood, the way they looked unflinchingly into the camera. The image radiated happiness, friendship, even lust, in a way that made it more than just a portrait. Burke was amazed.

He looked at the next picture, and the next. Each was a portrait, and each moved him as much as the one of Ginger, Thadeus, and Jonas did. He opened the second envelope and looked through the rest of the images. As he did, an idea formed in his mind. He didn't just have a bunch of portraits; he had a potential *show*. And it wasn't something he'd set out to do. It had just happened, because he'd allowed the camera to see what he saw.

He wanted to call Colton and tell him he had something for him. He wanted to call Sam. He wanted to share his excitement with *someone*. But then he saw his father's face and heard his words, and the fire of his excitement was extinguished.

He slumped back against the couch, the stack of photos in his lap. Suddenly they didn't excite him. They were dull, pedestrian, nothing more than snapshots. He tossed them on the coffee table.

The photos on top slid aside, revealing one he hadn't yet seen. It was the photo of him and Sam, the one Ginger had taken. He picked it up and looked at it more closely. He was leaning against Sam. Their hips were touching, and Sam's hand was tucked around Burke's waist, one finger hooked through the belt loop of Burke's pants. The paint on Burke's chest, caught in black and white, shimmered.

But what struck him most was the expression on his face. He looked happy. Usually in photos he was tense, pained. In this photo he was relaxed. His smile was natural, not forced. Yet as he remembered it, he'd been anxious. He hadn't wanted Ginger to take his picture.

It's Sam, he realized. Sam had changed him, helped take away the tension that normally gripped Burke in unfamiliar situations. And he'd done it without Burke even knowing it. Was *he* aware of it? Had he done it on purpose?

True, there had been that moment between them at the dinner party. But it had passed, and since then Burke hadn't thought about Sam in a romantic way. He wasn't Burke's type. And they were so different.

It's a bad idea, he told himself. *You've finally found a friend—a real friend. Don't fuck it up doing something stupid just because you feel like shit and need something to pick you up.*

He set the picture down. He was right; it was a stupid idea. Besides, Sam wouldn't want someone like him. He should be with someone more free spirited, someone more like himself. *I'm too uptight for him,* he thought.

But he could still tell Sam about his idea for a show. He knew his feelings about the photographs were temporary, caused by his anger at his father. But in a day or two, maybe a week, he would be able to look at the pictures more objectively. Then he would decide if he could make a cohesive collection. And he would ask Sam his opinion, too.

That left the question of what to do with the rest of his day. He didn't want to just sit around. Nor did he want to go take pictures. He wanted to do something for Sam, something to thank him for his kindness. He knew it couldn't be easy for someone used to being alone to suddenly have a houseguest.

He decided to make dinner. Although he hadn't cooked in a long time, he liked to do it and was good at it. But as he couldn't very well get to a grocery store, he was going to have to make do with whatever Sam had in the house. He got up and went to investigate the kitchen.

The results were not encouraging. The refrigerator held the left-over Chinese from their take-out dinner the night before, along with numerous half-empty condiment bottles, a large container of plain yogurt, three eggs, and in the vegetable crisper, three desiccated apples. But there were also some nice tomatoes, and behind a jar of blue cheese dressing, he found some garlic. Sam had a small garden behind the house, and Burke was fairly certain he'd seen basil there, as well as the ingredients for a presentable salad.

In one of the cupboards he discovered several boxes of pasta, and he knew he would be okay. All he had to do was make sauce and throw together the salad. And that he could easily do in the two hours before Sam got home from the library.

The garden yielded everything he needed, and soon enough he'd chopped and diced and tossed everything into a saucepan. Adding a good quantity of a bottle of red wine he found in another cupboard, he waited until the sauce was simmering nicely, then turned the flame down and left it to cook.

He still had an hour. To pass the time, he decided to read. He'd left his books at his father's house, not wanting to take anything that belonged in the house with him. But Sam had books everywhere. Shelves filled with books. Books in stacks beside the couch and arm-chairs in the living room. Books lying facedown on tables and the floor. Everywhere you looked, there was a book.

Burke went to the nearest bookcase and scanned the rows of ti-tles. Most of the books he'd never heard of. Then one caught his eye. *In the Wood of the Holly King.* He saw Sam's name on the spine, and he remembered.

He took the book out and carried it to the couch. The cover was a black-and-white drawing, beautifully rendered, of a forest in winter. Walking between the bare trees was a man wearing a crown of holly. He held a candle in his hands, and on his shoulder was perched an owl.

Burke opened the book and flipped through the pages. He didn't know if he should start at the beginning or just pick something at random. He decided to close his eyes, fan the pages, and put his fin-ger down when he felt ready.

When he opened his eyes, he saw that he had selected a story simply titled "Midsummer."

As twilight fell on the longest day of the year, the Green Man found himself wandering far from home. He had risen early that morning with a desire to walk to a part of the valley he had yet to visit, and by afternoon he had lost himself among the hills and vales. Yet even though darkness would soon cover the land, he was not afraid. He knew that the way home would appear when he needed it, and he had spent more than one night asleep under the stars. He had food in his pack and water in the stream he walked beside, and the whole of the world was his waiting bed.

It happened that as the sun and the moon passed one another in the sky, the Green Man came to a wood. Deciding to take his rest beneath one of the trees casting shade over the mossy ground, he made his way among them until he came to a clearing. The circle was filled with the scent of bluebells, and the Green Man was made drowsy by their smell. While he knew it was foolish for any mortal to spend even half an hour within a faerie circle, he found himself unable to keep his eyes open. He lay among the flowers and soon was dreaming of wild things.

He awoke with a start to the tinkling of bells. When he opened his heavy lids, he saw that it was dark. Moonlight flooded the circle and gilded the leaves with silver, and for a moment he saw only the shadows flitting against the pale backdrop like figures in a pantomime.

Then a light sparked before his eyes, followed by another, and still others. Fireflies floated in the air around him, moving lazily in the warm night like tiny boats on the sea. They danced away from him and stopped, as if waiting for him to follow. Somewhere beyond the edge of the clearing, he heard laughter.

The Green Man stood, rubbing the sleep from his eyes. The fireflies rose and encircled him, casting a pale ring of light. They flew forward, gently urging him on, and he found himself walking out of the clearing and onto a narrow path he couldn't remember seeing during the day.

The path led deep into the woods, and the Green Man was glad for the light of the fireflies as he found himself walking between towering trees whose branches hid the moon from view. As he walked, he heard the merry sound of the bells from time to time, and every now and again a laugh would reach his ears.

Suddenly, the path took a turn and opened upon another clearing. Here the moonlight was bright, and the Green Man had to shield his eyes. As he did, the fireflies around him rose up and exploded in bursts of gold. When the Green Man was able to see again, he found that he was surrounded by a host of faeries. They darted around him, and he knew then where the laughter he had heard came from. Their voices were rich and merry, and they all talked at once so that the sound was like that of moth wings in his ears.

He stood, watching, as the faerie hosts filled the clearing with their beauty. They swooped and twirled in interlocking circles, some with wings like those of dragonflies, some with butterfly wings, and some with no wings at all. He had heard the tales of these creatures and had even believed them. But to see them before him was to be enchanted beyond words or movement.

"They were right in saying that you were fair," said a voice from within the swirling lights.

The golden, whirling cloud of faeries parted like curtains being drawn aside, and the Green Man saw standing before him a woman of unearthly beauty. Her skin was the color of lilies, and her eyes the green of deep water. Her hair was black like a winter night and fell about her shoulders in curls that trailed to the ground. On her head was a crown of roses and lavender, and her dress was of the palest silver, as though woven from cobwebs and moonlight.

"It is not every mortal who is invited to my midsummer gathering," said the woman. "How came you to lie in the circle where my servants found you?"

"I am sorry," said the Green Man, afraid of having offended the lady. "I was tired and wanted only to rest."

She smiled cooly. "Those who sleep on my doorstep often find more than rest," she said. "Answer me this— Would you be my king?"

The Green Man lowered his head. "I am no king," he said. "I am but an ordinary man."

Laughter filled the clearing as the faeries flew like gusts of summer wind. The Green Man looked up and saw that the lady was laughing with them.

"No one is ordinary who is brought to the court of Maeve," she said. "Come and join us."

The faeries once more darted around the clearing, filling it with blinding light. When the light died, the Green Man saw that the place was decorated as if for a grand feast. A table made of a fallen tree was spread with leaves and mounded high with good things to eat. The branches were hung with lights, and music came from somewhere in the treetops as unseen players piped and fiddled.

The Green Man saw, too, that they were no longer alone in the clearing. Guests filled the spaces between the trees and circled the edge of the place. Each wore a mask, and it was impossible for the Green Man to tell if behind the faces they were human or something more. A great owl-headed woman stood beside a man with the ears of a hare, while elsewhere a trio of goat-legged boys played on silver flutes. As the Green Man looked upon them, he saw that each was more fantastic than the next, and all gazed back at him where he stood beside the faerie queen.

Maeve took the Green Man by the hand and led him to the table crowded with revelers. He seated himself beside a man with the laughing face of a bear, and the attending faeries set before him a cup filled with sweet wine. He drank it as he reclined in the soft moss and waited to see what would happen next.

Maeve returned to the center of the circle and clapped her hands together once. "Enter the Oak King," she commanded.

There was a rustling in the trees and then a man stepped into the clearing. He was dressed in clothes of deepest gold, and on his head was a crown of oak leaves,

*heavy with acorns. His face was covered by a mask show-
ing the brilliant face of a shining sun, so that the Green
Man could not see his features. He carried in his hand a
staff of gnarled wood, and he walked slowly toward the
faerie queen, as though coming to the end of a long journey.*

*"Merry meet," she said when he reached her, holding
out her hands to him. "It is long since you began your
reign. Now it is time for rest."*

*She clapped her hands in the air once more, and the
musicians began to play a slow but steady rhythm. The
Green Man watched as Maeve took the hand of the Oak
King and the two danced. Their movements were gentle,
like the slow ripple of the wind through the ripening
fields. Hand in hand, they traveled the edge of the circle,
moving in the direction of the sun through the sky.*

*After they had made one tour of the clearing, the music
began to increase in time and the guests joined their queen.
They danced around the Oak King, still masked, who was
spun from hand to waiting hand as he was guided in his
steps. Many times he was passed around the circle by the
faerie queen's guests, until finally he was brought,
breathless, back to the center, to the waiting queen. She
took him in her arms and placed a kiss on his mouth,
after which he collapsed to the ground.*

*"The Oak King is dead," cried the queen, and the crowd
was silent.*

*Again, there was a rustling in the trees, and in came
six men dressed all in gold. They carried on their shoulders a litter made of birch branches and decorated with
summer flowers that filled the air with their scent. They
came to the place where the fallen king lay and lowered
the litter to the ground. Then they gathered the king into
their arms and laid him on the litter.*

*Maeve bent over the Oak King's face and removed the
golden mask. As she did, the Green Man gasped, for he
saw his own familiar features, stilled in death. Maeve
motioned to him and smiled.*

"Come," she said. "It is time for you to take his place."

The Green Man rose to his feet and stepped forward, not believing what he saw before him. He approached the Oak King and stood beside his body.

"How can this be?" he asked.

Maeve looked into his eyes. "Remember," she said, "you are in my kingdom now. This is the night when the wild magic runs strong, the time when the waxing year and the waning year meet. You will see much here that you would not see in your world. But fear nothing."

"What am I to do?" the Green Man said.

"You are to take your place as Holly King," Maeve told him. "The king of the waning year. Until now you have learned much about who you are. You have followed the year as it grew to fullness. Now it is time to use that knowledge, to come into the fullness of your self and celebrate all that you have learned. But first you must make your own mask like that of the Oak King."

She gestured to the table at which the Green Man had been sitting, and he saw that the food and drink had been replaced by piles of flowers, leaves, stones, and feathers. He walked over to it as Maeve spoke.

"Create the face you wish to show to the world," she said. "Make manifest your own vision of who you are, for this is the night of giving birth to our true selves. Show us who you are beneath your skin."

The Green Man knelt and began to make his mask. He formed a covering of holly leaves, dark and shining. To this he affixed different items as he was drawn to them, building one on the other until he had before him the face he saw when he dreamed. His hands did the work of his heart, and soon he was finished. Then he picked up his mask and carried it to where Maeve stood waiting.

"It is beautiful," she said as he held it up for all to see. She took the ends of the ribbons attached to the mask and secured them around the Green Man's head.

"Now," she said, "we will make the magic real."

At the queen's signal, the faeries fluttered around the

Green Man. They stripped him of his traveling clothes and placed on him robes of green and red. On his head they placed a crown of holly and evergreens.

"Dance with me, Holly King," said Maeve when they were finished, and the music began.

The Green Man took her hand and followed as she led him around the circle. The sound of the faerie drums and bells filled his ears, and he stepped lightly with his queen. The faerie court sang and laughed, watching their new king dancing in the moonlight, and the Green Man laughed with them. In their midst, he felt filled with the possibilities of magic. He looked at the Oak King where he lay on his deathbed in the center of the ring, and he knew that it had taken much to become that part of himself. Now it was time to take on the mantle of the Holly King and step into the darkening year.

The music played and the Green Man danced on, faster and faster. He saw those around him through new eyes and felt the magic coursing in his veins. His head swam with the sound of voices and music, and he closed his eyes and lost himself in the whirling magic of midsummer night until he no longer knew if he was sleeping or awake.

When finally the music ceased, the Green Man opened his eyes and found himself alone in the woods. The night was gone, and the first faint stirrings of sunlight crept across the dewy grass where he stood. Gone were Maeve and her curious faerie court. Gone were the red and green robes. And gone, too, were the Oak King and his attendants. Only the Green Man remained, still wearing the mask of his creation and feeling the magic spinning within him.

The shortest night of the year was ended, and the drawing in of the days had begun. The faerie queen and her court had seen in another king and carried an old one away with them for renewal. Now was the time of the Holly King. As the Green Man walked into the morning, he carried his mask in his hands and the memories of his night in Maeve's woods in his heart.

Burke shut the book. The story was peculiar, but he liked it. He wasn't sure he actually understood all of it, but it had left him with a sense of peace.

"What did you think?"

Sam's voice startled Burke, who jumped. "I didn't hear you come in."

"Is that because you were so engrossed in my deathless prose?"

"Actually, yes," said Burke. "I read only one story, though."

"Which one?"

"The one about the Green Man," Burke answered.

Sam laughed. "They're *all* about the Green Man," he said. "The book is a story cycle about an Everyman—the Green Man—celebrating the eight seasonal festivals of the pagan year. You started right in the middle."

"Then I guess I'll have to start over from the beginning."

"Please do," said Sam. He sniffed the air. "Do I smell pasta sauce?"

"Shit!" Burke exclaimed. "I forgot about dinner."

He scrambled up as quickly as he could and hobbled into the kitchen. Fortunately, the sauce was all right. He breathed a sigh of relief.

"And here I thought we'd be having warmed-over General Tso's Chicken," Sam said, coming over and looking into the saucepan. "This is a nice surprise."

"Reserve your review until you actually taste it," Burke said. "Now, go wash up while I get the pasta started."

"Yes, dear," Sam said, laughing. "And then you can tell me all about your day."

"Smart-ass," Burke replied. But as Sam went off to get ready for dinner, he couldn't help but think, *I will tell you all about it. And then I want you to tell me all about yours.*

CHAPTER 31

The noise of the saw made Burke grit his teeth. Then Dr. Radiceski was pulling apart the two sides of his cast, and when Burke looked down, he had two legs again. True, one of them looked as if it belonged to a cave-dwelling creature with a skin condition, but it was still a leg. He tried to stretch it and yelped in pain.

"Careful," the doctor said. "Remember, you haven't moved that knee in a long time. The muscles have tightened up." He placed one hand beneath Burke's lower right leg and the other beneath his knee. Slowly, he stretched Burke's leg out, then back, making sure his knee was tracking correctly. "How's that feel?"

"Better than having a cast on," said Burke. "Can I stand up?"

"Let's give it a try," the doctor answered.

Burke swung his legs over the edge of the table and slid off, putting most of his weight on his left leg. He set his right foot on the floor and gently shifted his weight to it. It felt strange after so many weeks of being one-footed, but it didn't hurt too terribly badly. He took a tentative step, wobbled, and grabbed at Dr. Radiceski's offered arm, then tried again. This time he managed three more or less normal steps across the room.

"Good," the doctor said. "It will take a while until you're a hundred percent, but this is a great start, considering they had to pin you."

Burke turned and walked back to the examination table. "It feels so weird," he remarked. "I got used to having just one usable leg."

"It's amazing how we adapt," Dr. Radiceski said. "One of our dogs had to have a rear leg amputated. Cancer. I swear he came running out of the operating room as if he'd always had three legs."

"Are you comparing me to a dog?" asked Burke.

The doctor nodded. "I am," he said. He was writing something in Burke's file and pointed his pen at him. "The difference is that my dog never complained about having only three legs."

Burke laughed. "So, now what? Do I come back?"

Dr. Radiceski nodded. "In a couple weeks I want to do another set of X-rays, just to make sure everything is where it's supposed to be. Unless you're heading back to Boston, in which case I'll transfer you back to Dr. Liu."

"I'll stick with you," Burke told him. "You have a better bedside manner."

"Then you're good to go," the doctor said. "Just don't overdo it. No playing rugby or swing dancing for a while yet."

"Spoilsport," Burke teased.

He went to put his shoes on and realized that he'd forgotten to bring along the right one. He'd become so used to wearing only one that it hadn't occurred to him that he would need both for the trip home.

"Here you go." Dr. Radiceski handed him a single flip-flop. "Nobody ever remembers to bring the other shoe. We keep a couple of pairs of these around."

"Stylish," said Burke as he slipped the flip-flop onto his foot.

"You're lucky. That's the only right one I have left. Unless you want a pink Hello Kitty one, but I doubt it would fit."

"This will be fine," Burke assured him as he stood up. "Thanks."

He walked down the hallway, still a little unsteady, and into the waiting room. Sam looked at his leg, then down at the single flip-flop. "This is a good look for you," he remarked.

"I refuse to conform to fashion," Burke said.

"What do you want to do to celebrate?" Sam asked as they walked to the car.

"Actually," Burke said, "I want to go to the Hague farm."

"More pictures?"

Burke shook his head. "Something else. Do you mind?"

"Not at all," Sam said. "Let's go."

An hour later they pulled to the side of the road near the farm. Sam surveyed the ruins. "Hard to believe something so awful happened here," he said. "It's so beautiful."

"You haven't seen the best part," said Burke as he walked into the grass.

Sam followed him as he made his way toward the trees and the pond beyond. He hadn't come to see the house. An idea had planted itself in his head, and rather than question it, he had decided to see where it led.

They passed through the trees, Sam exclaiming at the beauty of the place, and emerged into the clearing where the pond awaited them.

"Here we are," Burke said. "What do you think?"

Sam surveyed the area. "This is where Amos drowned, isn't it?"

Burke nodded. "Yeah," he said. "Like you said, it's hard to imagine something so awful happened here."

"And what are we doing here?" Sam grinned.

"Taking a bath," Burke said, pulling his T-shirt over his head. His shorts were next, and then he was naked.

Feeling a rush of excitement, he walked quickly to the pond and stepped into the water. The shock of the cold raised gooseflesh on his skin, but he continued going in until he was up to his waist in the water. Then he turned and fell, resting on his back and looking up at the sky. The water held him up, caressing his body. Where it touched his right leg, it seemed to soothe away the remaining pain.

"Coming in?" he called to Sam.

In answer Sam shucked his clothes off. Burke caught only a glimpse of his naked body before Sam was running to the edge of the water and jumping. He seemed to fly for a moment, suspended in the air with a lopsided grin on his face before he landed on his stomach a few feet away from Burke. He disappeared under the water for a moment, then came back up. He shook his head, water flying from his hair and beard.

"It's *cold!*" he said.

"Not for long," Burke assured him.

Sam turned onto his back and floated next to Burke. He kicked his feet a little to stay up, and the resulting wake made Burke rock slightly. It was like being in a cradle, he thought. He closed his eyes and sank into the water, letting it close over his chest so that only his face was exposed.

He couldn't help but think about Amos Hague. What had Amos

been doing in the pond when he drowned? If he couldn't swim, why would he go in? Will had said that the water closer to the bottom was really cold. What must it have been like, sinking down into that water, unable to breathe? The idea made Burke shudder.

Suddenly he was overcome by the urge to find out. He turned and dived, even as his mind told him to stop. He pulled with his arms and kicked, forcing himself down. The sunlit surface disappeared, and he headed for darkness. Then the water turned icy, and he recoiled from it. He turned, looking up toward the surface, and knew he had made a mistake.

He tried to swim up but couldn't. It was as if something was holding on to his legs, dragging him deeper. He clawed at the water, unable to move. Then his mouth opened, and he called out for help. He could see light shining through the bubbles that escaped from his lips, taking the remaining air in his lungs with them.

And then something was coming toward him. For a moment it blocked out the light. Then strong arms were around him, and he was rising. His eyes were open, and through the rushing water he saw a face looking at him. It was the face of Amos Hague.

His head broke the surface into the bright sunlight. He gasped, taking in air and choking. Then he remembered Amos Hague, and he struggled, trying to get free from the arms that gripped him.

"Relax. It's me." Sam's voice calmed him, and he stopped thrashing and just floated, his breathing returning to normal. Sam's body beneath his was solid and reassuring. He was okay. He wasn't going to drown.

"What happened?" Sam asked.

"I don't know," said Burke. "It felt like someone was pulling me under. And that's not the weirdest part." He told Sam about seeing Amos Hague's face. "It wasn't really scary, though," he said when he was done. "I mean, it freaked me out, but it was almost as if he'd come to save me."

"It's the pond," said Sam. "Do you want to get out?"

Oddly, Burke didn't. Now that the panic was past, he was strangely happy. Sam had yet to release him, and the feeling of their bodies pressed together was one he didn't want to end right now. Instead, he placed his hands on top of Sam's own where they held him around the chest.

"No," he said. "I like this."

Sam's fingers moved apart, allowing Burke's to slip between them. Neither said anything. Burke's head was on Sam's shoulder, their cheeks touching. He could feel Sam's heart beating beneath him.

He let go of Sam's hands and turned so that they were facing one another. His arms slipped round Sam's waist and drew him in. Then their mouths met in a gentle kiss.

"This would be easier on dry land," Sam said when they parted.

They swam to the edge of the pond, and Sam pulled himself onto the large, flat rock where Burke had once seen turtles sunning themselves. He sat with his feet in the water and extended his hand to Burke, pulling him up beside him. The rock was warm beneath Burke's bare skin, cutting through the cold of the water.

"That's better," Sam said, turning and taking Burke's face in his hands.

This time their kiss was longer and more passionate. Burke's hands roamed across Sam's back, then onto his furry belly. When he wrapped his hand around Sam's hard cock, Sam groaned.

"Lie back," Burke ordered.

Sam did, stretching out on the rock and putting his hands beneath his head. His dick stuck up, and Burke had only to lean down and take the head in his mouth. Sam's skin was cool beneath his lips but warmed up quickly as Burke moved up and down the length of him.

He wanted Sam to come. He wanted to taste him and feel the salty spray against his throat. But after a few minutes Sam reached down and lifted his head away.

"Come up here," he said.

Burke stretched alongside him, their legs touching. Sam reached over and gripped Burke's cock, sliding his hand up and down it, squeezing the head. Burke did the same, matching Sam's strokes. Their forearms brushed against one another as they jacked each other off.

Burke came hard, covering his chest and stomach in sticky heat. Before he was done, Sam joined him. His cum shot up, geyserlike, and fell back again, dewing the hair on his torso as Burke milked the last drops from him. Then Burke was straddling him and leaning down, pressing their bodies together, and once more kissing Sam's mouth, his neck, his chest. His tongue flicked against the small bead at the center of Sam's nipple ring, and he took the nipple into his mouth, biting gently. Sam lifted his hips.

Burke took Sam by the wrist and moved his arm back, pinning it to the rock. His mouth moved into the thicket of hair beneath Sam's arm, and he buried his nose there, smelling water and sun and sweat. Sam's hand slid down Burke's back, coming to rest on his ass, his fingertips grazing the space between. He kissed Burke's neck, then nuzzled more aggressively.

"That's going to leave a mark," Burke whispered, returning his attention to Sam's nipple.

Sam grinned. "That's the idea," he said.

Again their mouths met. Sam's beard was rough against Burke's lips, but he liked the feeling of it. He put his hand against the side of Sam's face, stroking it.

"Tell the truth," Sam said in between kisses. "You faked that whole drowning thing just to get into my pants."

"You weren't wearing pants," Burke reminded him. "And no, I didn't." He kissed the tip of Sam's nose.

"We should rinse off," Sam suggested.

"I don't know," said Burke. "I kind of like having you all over me."

"If you stay on top of me much longer, we'll be glued together."

Burke laughed. "Okay," he said. "Come on."

He stood up and turned around. When Sam was up as well, Burke took his hand and jumped, pulling him into the pond. For some reason the water felt warmer than it had earlier, even as far down as his feet.

"Something's different," Sam said. "Can you feel it?"

Burke nodded. "It's nice," he said.

"Maybe we warmed it up," Sam joked, taking Burke's hands and pulling him closer. "Shall we go all the way and see if we can turn it into a steam bath?"

They swam to shore, where they sat in the sun for a few minutes to dry off, then got dressed. As they walked back through first the trees and then the grass, Burke thought again of the face in the water, and suddenly a thought came to him. Something that Gaither had said.

"I think I know what happened," he said. "To Amos and Thomas. They died a year apart, right?"

"To the day," Sam said.

"I think Thomas drowned in that pond first," Burke said. "And I think Amos went after him. I don't think it was an accident."

"You think he killed himself?"

"To be with Thomas," said Burke. "I don't know. It's just a feeling."

"So you're saying what? That Thomas's ghost tried to drown you and Amos helped me save you?"

"I don't think anyone tried to drown me," Burke said. "But maybe they were trying to tell us what really happened here."

"I thought I was the one who was supposed to believe in stuff like that," said Sam.

"Maybe you're rubbing off on me."

Sam took his hand. "You could be right," he said. "Stranger things have happened. Let's see if we can find out anything concrete about Thomas's death."

"And if we can't?"

"I have some other ideas," said Sam.

"Care to share them with me?"

"Later," Sam replied. "Right now I want to get home and start your physical therapy."

"Physical therapy?"

"Didn't the doctor say you should work on stretching your leg muscles?" Sam said, squeezing Burke's hand.

CHAPTER 32

"He seems to be walking just fine."

Burke stood at the fence, looking over it at Old Jack. His father was leading the horse around the paddock, watching his feet as he moved.

"Seems he isn't the only one," his father said.

Burke opened the gate and went inside. Going over to Old Jack, he rubbed the horse's nose. Jack immediately butted Burke with his head.

"You're right," Burke said. "I brought you an apple."

He brought the apple out from behind his back and held it out to the horse, who took it and started chewing. Bits of apple fell from his lips.

"It doesn't take much to make him happy," Burke remarked, scratching Old Jack's ears.

"Not much, no," said his father.

"Not like people," Burke said.

"I suspect you want to talk some more," Ed said.

"I do," said Burke. "But not now."

His father looked at him, a puzzled expression on his face.

"I don't think either of us is really ready to talk," Burke continued. "Not in the way we need to. So I'm just going to say I'm sorry if anything I said hurt you."

His father ran his hand along Old Jack's back. "I guess we both said a lot of things," he said.

Burke nodded. "We did," he agreed.

His father continued to pet Old Jack. After a minute he said, "They say that when a woman has a boy child, the first time she holds him in her arms, he replaces the husband in her heart. Doesn't shove him aside as such, but maybe fills up the space the husband used to occupy a little more than he did. Your mother loved you more than anything in this world."

"I know she did," said Burke.

Ed spoke again. "It's different for the father. I don't think there's ever anything a man loves more than his wife. I've heard women say they couldn't bear to lose a child. That's how I felt about your mother. But I did bear it. Sometimes I didn't think I would, but I did." He finally looked up at Burke. "I don't want to find out if I could bear losing my child, too."

Burke reached across Old Jack's back and touched his father's hand. "You won't," he said. He pulled his hand back. "I've got to go," he said, "but we'll talk soon."

His father waved, saying nothing. But he didn't have to. Burke knew that something had changed between them, just as something had changed between him and Sam. Where this change would lead him in his relationship with his father, he didn't know. But the door had been opened, and that was a start.

He got into Sam's car. Driving himself to his father's house had been a bit of an adventure. The car wasn't an automatic, and adjusting to pressing the clutch with his left foot was almost like learning to drive all over again. Several times he had forgotten to push it in and had ground the gears, making him glad that Sam wasn't in the car to hear him mistreat it.

He'd wanted to see his father before the evening's activities. Somehow he knew that it was important for him to clear those feelings out of his head as much as possible. They weren't gone completely, and might never be, but he did feel better.

When he arrived at the Hague farm, there was another car already parked by the side of the road. A sticker on the bumper showed a brown-striped flag with a black bear paw where the field of stars would normally be. Seeing it, Burke couldn't help but laugh.

He got out and walked through the grass. The late afternoon sun was warm but not hot, and shadows were already creeping across the field. Soon it would be twilight. Burke looked at the ruins of the farmhouse as he walked by. The stones were touched with gold as the sunlight moved across them, and the flowers sprouting from the cracks were motionless in the still air.

He made his way down the low rise to the trees and passed through them. When he reached the pond, he saw the others there. Ginger, Jonas, Thad, Sam, and Gaither stood on the far side, near the large rock. Sam, seeing Burke, waved. Burke waved back and made his way along the shoreline, skirting the edge of the pond.

"How'd it go?" Sam asked.

"Okay," said Burke. "We'll see what happens."

Gaither came over and gave Burke a hug. "Hello, love," he said. "It's good to see you again."

"Thank you for coming," Burke said. "I hope the drive down wasn't too awful."

"Much easier than when we had to use the horse and buggy," said Gaither, feigning seriousness.

"You'll stay the night with us, won't you?" Sam asked.

"Of course he will, and so will we." Ginger hugged Burke. "It'll be a slumber party, only some of us won't be wearing pj's."

"Saints preserve us," Gaither said, looking heavenward.

"So, what exactly are we doing?" Burke asked.

"Ask Jonas," Ginger said. "He's the one who came up with the ritual."

They gathered around Jonas, who smiled at them shyly through his beard. "Well, Sam told me that Thomas Beattie drowned here while swimming with Amos Hague."

"Right," said Sam. "I was able to track down a newspaper article about it through the archives of the Vermont Historical Society. Apparently, the two of them were swimming here, and something happened to Thomas. Amos tried to save him, but Thomas drowned."

"And a year to the day later—on this date, as it happens—Amos drowned here as well," Jonas said. "We think on purpose. All right, what I'd like to do is a ritual to send these boys on their way. It sounds as if they've been hanging around this farm long enough."

"And just how do we do that?" Gaither inquired.

"We're going to let them know that we know their story," Jonas said. "That we remember them. My guess is that they've been waiting for someone to figure it all out, which it sounds like Sam and Burke have."

"By accident," Burke said.

"Nothing is an accident," said Thadeus. "You're just the first ones who listened to them."

"This is pretty straightforward," Jonas said. "We're going to raise some energy, then disperse it by jumping into the pond. All you have to do is follow my lead. Oh, and it works best if we do it skyclad."

"Skyclad?" Gaither said.

"Naked," said Ginger, already stripping off his clothes.

Burke looked at Sam. "Why am I not surprised?"

Sam chuckled. "Actually, it's pretty traditional to do it this way."

Burke turned to Gaither. "You don't have to do this if you're—"

"Do what?" Gaither asked, folding his socks and putting them on top of the neatly folded pile of clothes he'd already removed.

"Never mind," said Burke, suppressing a laugh. I should have known he'd have no problem with it, he thought. It had been Sam's idea to invite Gaither, and at first Burke had resisted. But given Gaither's connection to Amos, having him there seemed fitting, and so Burke had asked him to come.

When they were all undressed, Jonas had them sit in a circle on the rock. Burke sat between Gaither and Sam, close enough that their knees were just touching. Jonas, who was across from Burke, closed his eyes and began to speak.

"Close your eyes," he said. "Now feel the rock beneath you. Feel its connection to the earth from which it's made."

Burke focused on the warmth soaking into his skin out of the rock. He pictured the rock cradled in hands of earth.

"Now imagine that there are roots descending from your body into the rock," Jonas said. "The roots go through the rock and into the earth below it. They go down, down, down until they reach a pool of golden light. Draw this light up through the roots, up through the earth, and into your body. Let the light fill your body."

Burke tried and was surprised to find that doing what Jonas asked wasn't as difficult as he'd worried it would be. Instead of feeling silly or embarrassed, he felt as if he really was filling up with light. He pictured the light as liquid gold, pulsing with energy. He imagined it entering through the roots and flowing through his veins.

"Join hands with the brothers on either side of you," said Jonas, his voice soft yet commanding.

Burke reached for Sam and Gaither, felt their hands in his.

"Let the light inside of you pass through your hands and into your brothers' hands. Picture it flowing from one body to the next. Feel it flow like water out through your left-hand fingertips and in through the right as it moves clockwise around the circle."

In his mind Burke saw Gaither to his left, drawing the light out of Burke's body and into his own. At the same time, Burke drew light from Sam. The light mixed inside of him, becoming brighter and warmer before flowing on until all six of them were glowing.

"The circle is cast," Jonas said. "Open your eyes."

Burke half expected to see the others actually glowing. But they looked the same. Still, the atmosphere around them had changed. It was more electric, and his skin tingled.

They were still holding hands and continued to do so as Jonas called out, "Amos and Thomas. We, your brothers, invite you into our circle. Come, be with us and rest."

The air was still. Even the crickets had stopped chirping.

"Amos Hague and Thomas Beattie," Jonas cried, "we celebrate your love here tonight, we who are also lovers of men. Come, be with us and rest."

A breeze blew across the water. In the dusk a bird, startled, flew up from the grass.

"Welcome, brothers," said Jonas. "Rest here in our circle. The time for wandering is over. We release you from this place, carrying your names in our hearts." A moment later he began to chant. "Out of earth and into water, love and light will be reborn."

He repeated the words again, several voices joining with his. On the third repetition, Burke joined in, followed by Gaither. Now all six of them were chanting the words, their voices combining to form one.

"Out of earth and into water, love and light will be reborn," Burke intoned.

They kept chanting, and time stood still. Burke didn't know how many minutes went by as he concentrated on the words he spoke. They were so simple, yet they held so much meaning.

Then the chant changed. As Burke finished saying the first part of the chant, Jonas began it again, so that they were now singing it as a round.

"Out of earth and into water," Jonas chanted as Burke said, "Love and light will be reborn."

By unspoken agreement they formed two groups, every other man singing the same line. Their voices rose and fell like waves. "Out of earth and into water," Burke sang as on either side of him Sam and Gaither chanted, "Love and light will be reborn." Burke looked at

Thadeus, Jonas, and Ginger, sitting across from him. Their eyes sparkled, and on their faces were expressions of joy.

At some point they stood. Still linked hand to hand, they swayed slightly as they continued to chant. After some time the chanting slowed, and one by one the men stopped singing, until only Jonas sang the last line. When the sound of his voice faded into the night, he looked around the circle.

"Feel the energy," he said. "Feel the power we've raised in this circle. Amos and Thomas, we give this energy to you, and we send you on your way!"

He dropped Ginger's hand and, still holding Thadeus's, ran to the edge of the rock and jumped. Like a chain, the other men followed, one after the other, still holding hands. As they leaped into the pond, they shouted joyously.

Burke, pulled by Sam, in turn pulled Gaither toward the water. There was a momentary rush of air as he jumped, and then he was in the water. It closed over his head, but then he surfaced, laughing, in time to see Ginger jump last into the pond with a happy shout.

The water was alive with bodies as they splashed one another. Slowly, they calmed down and floated, looking up at the stars, which were just beginning to come out. Burke felt hands touching his body, and he in turn touched others, bumping into one and floating away again.

Gaither was the first to speak. "Farewell, Great-grandfather," he said. "Safe journey."

Arms went around Burke, and Sam whispered in his ear. "That was pretty neat, huh?"

Burke laughed. "Neat? The man who has a quote for every occasion can only come up with *neat?*"

"How about this? 'Love must be as much a light, as it is a flame.'"

"I'll take that," Burke said. "Who said it?"

"Thoreau," said Sam.

"How appropriate," Burke remarked. "You know, the whole pond theme and all that."

"I do my best," said Sam.

Burke leaned against him. "Do you think we really did anything?"

"Do you?"

Burke thought for a moment. He listened to the splashing of the other men, to their voices talking and laughing. He felt a lightness inside of him. Maybe it was all in his head, but did it matter? Had the spirits of Amos Hague and Thomas Beattie really visited them, and had they really helped put them to rest? It was something that could never be proved. But did he believe it?

"Yes," he said. "I do."

CHAPTER 33

Burke picked up a piece of cheese, put it in his mouth, took it out again. "I can't eat," he said, wrapping the cheese in a cocktail napkin and stuffing it into his pocket.

"Relax," Sam told him. "Everything is going really well."

This was true. The photographs—all thirty-six of them—were hanging exactly where he wanted them. They were big, twenty-four by twenty-four inches framed. Each was a portrait of a man or men. Many of them came from the film he'd shot at Destiny. Others were new.

His favorite photo was one he'd taken of his father only a week before the opening. It had taken some persuasion, and a lot of help from Lucy, to get Ed to pose for him, but in the end he had done it. It was taken in his father's bedroom. Ed was sitting on the edge of the bed, his hands in his lap. Behind him, on the dresser, were two photos. One was of him and Burke's mother on their wedding day, and the other was of him and Lucy standing in front of a field of yellow flowers, with their arms around one another's waists.

He'd hung it in a place of prominence so that it was the first piece people saw when they entered the gallery. So far everyone who passed through the door had stopped to look at it. But the only person whose reaction he wanted to see was his father's. He hadn't shown Ed the photo beforehand, partly because he wanted to surprise him, but also because he was afraid that his father wouldn't like the air of vulnerability the photograph revealed. The camera's eye had captured the face of a man who had been brought low by the death of one love and then revived by the unexpected arrival of a second chance. It was, Burke thought, both touching and inspiring, a portrait of the face of love, which could be both beautiful and cruel.

And Ed *did* like it, or at least Burke thought he did. His father's reaction was typically muted, but Burke had several times looked toward the door to see Ed standing in front of his own portrait, an almost childlike expression on his face, as if he were seeing himself for the first time.

Another favorite almost never made it into the show. It was the photograph of Will among the ruins of the farm, with the ghostly figures of Amos and Thomas behind him. He'd asked Will for his permission to use it, and at first Will had said no. But just one day before the opening he'd called and relented. He'd given Burke no explanation. Nor had he come to the show.

Burke couldn't believe how many people *had* come to see his work. Most of them he didn't know, but there were some familiar faces: Colton and Luke, of course, and Nan and Sophie. Dr. Radiceski was there with his lover and his father, who seemed particularly fascinated by the nude photos of the three bears, who were also there in person. In one corner Gaither was talking to Tanya Redmond, who had brought Freddie and was fighting a losing battle trying to keep him away from the food table.

"Do you think they're reliving the family drama?" Sam mused.

"I don't know," said Burke. "As nice as Gaither is, somehow I don't see him inviting her to Thanksgiving dinner."

"Personally, I think we should hook Gaither up with Dr. Radiceski's father. If he isn't a queen, I'll shave my beard."

"Please don't," Burke said. "I've gotten to be quite fond of that beard."

"Only because it tickles your balls," Sam teased.

"That's just an added bonus," said Burke. He looked around the room, trying to see who was looking at what. The photographs were, of course, for sale, but for once he wasn't thinking about the money. He wanted people to *like* what he'd done. If they wanted to pay him for it, that was great, but it was more important to him that they understood what he was saying with his art.

As he scanned the faces in the gallery, he realized that sometime during the past three months he had made friends. And not just casual friends. *Good* friends. *Real* friends. Friends he liked talking with. Friends who made him feel alive.

And then there was Sam. After their first kiss at the pond, Burke had moved into the bed in Sam's room and had yet to leave. His clothes hung in the closet, next to Sam's; his toothbrush stood beside Sam's in the bathroom glass. Over the weeks the references to him returning to Boston had gradually grown less and less frequent.

"Penny for your thoughts," Gaither said.

Burke smiled. "I was just thinking about things," he said.

"How very specific," said Gaither. "Hardly worth the penny. But I think what I paid for that photograph of our three ursine friends more than makes up for it."

"You bought the bears?" Burke said. "You didn't have to do that."

"Actually, I did," Gaither replied. "Ginger made me a wager. If I could correctly identify the four obscure sexual practices, young Jonas would clean my house once a week for a month. In the nude. If I lost, I would buy the photograph."

"Dare I ask what you missed?"

"I correctly defined shrimping, teabagging, and felching," Gaither informed him. "I was done in by figging."

Burke made a face. "I don't know what that is, either."

"Well," Gaither began, "it's when you take a piece of peeled ginger and stick it—"

"There he is!" interrupted a loud voice.

Burke looked up to see Gregg walking toward him. He ran to his old friend and gave him a big hug. "You came!"

"Of course I did," Gregg said. "Did you really think I'd miss your big night?"

"But you had to leave the city," said Burke. "How did you survive?"

"Montpelier has a Starbucks," Gregg answered. "And a gay B and B. As long as I don't leave the city limits, I'll be fine. Besides, I'm leaving on Sunday. And you're coming with me."

"What?"

Gregg took his hand. "It's *time*," he said. "Your leg is better. You've had some fresh air. You've taken some pictures. Now you need to come back to Boston. Fall is coming, and you know that's the only tolerable season there. You don't want to miss it. Besides, look what they've done to you. Is that flannel?"

Burke didn't say anything. He looked at Gregg's face. He'd almost forgotten that they'd once been lovers. That seemed a lifetime ago. He was no longer the man he'd been then, nor even the man he'd been the day he'd stepped out of Gregg's car and walked into his father's house. At some point that man had died and a new one had been born.

"Seriously," Gregg said. "You need to come home."

Burke looked across the room to where Sam was now standing, talking to Nan. Sam, as if sensing him, turned. He smiled, and Burke felt his stomach flutter. He looked at Gregg.

"I am home," he said.